Critical Praise for *Anna In-Between* by Elizabeth Nunez

- Winner of the 2010 PEN Oakland Josephine Miles Award
- Longlisted for the IMPAC Dublin Literary Award

"A psychologically and emotionally astute family portrait, with dark themes like racism, cancer, and the bittersweet longing of the immigrant."
— *New York Times Book Review* (Editors' Choice)

"Nunez has created a moving and insightful character study while delving into the complexities of identity politics. Highly recommended."
— *Library Journal* (*starred review*)

"Nunez deftly explores family strife and immigrant identity in her vivid latest . . . with expressive prose and convincing characters that immediately hook the reader."
— *Publishers Weekly* (*starred review*)

"A new book by Elizabeth Nunez is always excellent news. Probing and lyrical, this fantastic novel is one of her best yet. Fall into her prose. Immerse yourself in her world. You will not be disappointed."
— Edwidge Danticat, author of *Brother, I'm Dying*

"Nunez offers an intimate portrait of the unknowable secrets and indelible ties that bind husbands and wives, mothers and daughters."
— *Booklist*

"Nunez's fiction, with its lush, lyric cadences and whirlwind narrative, casts a seductive spell."
— *O, the Oprah Magazine*

BOUNDARIES

by *Elizabeth Nunez*

Published by Akashic Books
©2011 Elizabeth Nunez

ISBN-13: 978-1-61775-033-5
Library of Congress Control Number: 2011922901

Akashic Books
PO Box 1456
New York, NY 10009
info@akashicbooks.com
www.akashicbooks.com

For my sisters

ACKNOWLEDGMENTS

My thanks to Johnny Temple, the brilliant and courageous publisher of Akashic Books, and to Ibrahim Ahmad, an attentive and perceptive senior editor, for their gentle encouragement and sound advice. Thanks too to my dear friend Pat Ramdeen Anderson, my first reader, whose editorial advice always points me in the right direction. I remain grateful for the support and love of my sister Mary Nunez. My son, Jason Harrell, continues to brighten my life.

I know quite a bit about expatriation.
You always hit a glass ceiling.
—Michael Ignatieff

ONE

Seventeen years after Anna Sinclair chose to move permanently to New York and the pain that constricts the heart of every immigrant who has left behind family—a mother, a father, sisters, brothers, cousins, aunts, uncles, grandparents—the land she loved as a child, the land that nurtured her as a child, has finally become unbearable. She decides to return to her island in the Caribbean, this time not for the week or two she goes every other year, but for a whole month, because her parents are old, her father in his mideighties, her mother fifteen years his junior; because she fears there is not much time left to be with them; because she wants to imprint on her mind's eye the color and texture of the earth once familiar to her as the markings on the palm of her hand; because she wants to savor the scent and taste of the sea she loved, trade winds that suffuse the air in every corner of the island so that even in the swamp-filled land of the prosperous enclave where her parents built their house more than twenty years ago, salt from the sea corrodes metal within weeks and houses bleed orange where nails are hammered into wood slats.

Anna's plan was all this: to spend time with her parents, to gather memories to sustain her through winter days and the suffocating heat of summers on a continent dense with people and the things people make that threaten to choke off forests, rivers, lakes, denuding mountains. It was about closure too. Paula, her friend, an immigrant like herself living in New York, has forced her to admit there are quarrels yet unresolved with her mother, resentments she still bears though she is an adult, a woman one year shy of forty.

Then everything changed.

She is three days on the island when her mother, Beatrice Sinclair, shows her the lump on her breast and the one under her arm lodged in her lymph nodes. The one on her breast bleeds. Neil Lee Pak, the family doctor and their friend, sends her mother to Dr. Ramdoolal, the best oncologist on the island. Dr. Ramdoolal does not need a biopsy to confirm what is plainly evident. Beatrice Sinclair has breast cancer. He tells Anna her mother has allowed the cancer to fester and bloom. *Allowed*, he says, making it clear that her mother is responsible. Because there is no way Beatrice Sinclair could not have seen, could not have felt the tumors rising inexorably under her skin. No way John Sinclair, her husband, could not have known. The doctor implies this with an accusing glance at John Sinclair, who is in his office, sitting in a chair, on the other side of his desk, next to Beatrice and Anna.

Anna is in shock, stunned by her parents' silence, their complicity in a shared secret that may cost her mother her life. There are four stages, she is told. Surely her mother's cancer is in the fourth stage, surely it is terminal. It has ulcerated, bled.

No, Dr. Ramdoolal says. Her mother has her age on her side and a cancer that is slow growing. She could live to be ninety, he says.

Hope swells her father's despairing heart.

She will need chemo to reduce the tumors, Dr. Ramdoolal advises, before a mastectomy is possible. Her tumors are too large. "Bleeding, you know," he says. "We may not be able to stop it."

Color drains from her father's face; Anna's fingers turn cold.

"But not to worry; we'll reduce the tumors," Dr. Ramdoolal assures them. He has one caveat. The surgery must be done in the States. The island has good doctors—he is a good doctor, he says, studied at Cambridge—but the island does not have adequate hospitals. Gurneys in corridors serve as beds for overcrowded wards, and newspapers, not sheets, cover thin mattresses. "Go to the States, Mrs. Sinclair," Dr. Ramdoolal urges.

Beatrice Sinclair refuses. She is a patriot. She will not have surgery in the States. She will have surgery on her island home. She has faith in her country, in her doctors, she insists.

"Then stay here," Dr. Ramdoolal says. "Stay here if you want to die."

His bluntness angers Anna, but terrifies her too.

Prosperity has come to the island on the second wave of an oil boom and the government has built a new hospital, stocked it with the latest newfangled medical instruments and equipment, but no one, it seems, had given thought to beds and linens. Surgery was the thing. Every man for himself afterward. Yet it is not the scarcity of beds and linens that scares Anna; it is the inability of the government to solve the problem of electrical outages that occur with frightening frequency on the island, shutting down traffic lights and turning roadways into a nightmare of cars and trucks snarled for miles around tight bends on the narrow roads. When lights go out and air conditioners no longer operate, work ceases at offices plunged into the sweltering heat. In hospitals, surgery has to be abandoned. There is an article in the newspaper about a patient who died when the machines shut down. And there is another story Anna overheard, whispered to her mother by a friend who does not yet know of her mother's tumors. Bribes have to be paid to customs officers if you want your goods cleared from the shipping docks on time. The woman's cousin, suffering from brain cancer, is forced to wait weeks for chemo. The drugs have arrived on the island, but the doctor has refused to pay the bribe. This is what happens when the government controls the hospitals, say the detractors of the system of socialized medicine the island has inherited from the British colonizers. We forget we are flawed creatures, the sons and daughters of Adam and Eve. We crave the incentives and rewards of capitalism.

"Go to the States," Dr. Ramdoolal implores her mother. "You get service for your money."

There are other considerations. Anna's mother gives another reason for her intransigence. For it is deliberate intransigence, Anna is convinced, that allows Beatrice Sinclair to remain defensive in spite of a death sentence that looms if she refuses surgery in the States, going so far as to accuse the good doctor of maligning his own country, of betraying his own people. She could die, Dr. Ramdoolal has said. But Beatrice Sinclair explains to her husband, John, and her daughter, Anna, that she fears having surgery in a country that has doctors and equipment for Americans and doctors and equipment for African Americans. She has seen the protest marches on cable TV; she knows about the statistics: American jails are crowded with black men.

Anna wants her mother to live. She wants her to go to the States for surgery, but her motives are not entirely altruistic. If her mother has surgery on the island, she, as the daughter, her mother's only child, would be expected to stay by her side. This is the natural duty of a daughter whose mother who is ill. The daughter abandons her work, she abandons her life. This is what Dr. Ramdoolal assumes that she will do, that she will stay on the island until her mother recovers from the rounds of chemo she must undergo to reduce the size of her tumors.

Naturally, she responds. *Naturally.*

Her father makes the same assumption. When Anna hesitates, he practically begs her to stay. There's no changing your mind? A question asked with all the tenderness and hope of a father pleading with his daughter to remember the days and nights he has loved her unconditionally.

Anna promises to stay, but she cannot stay as long as her father would like her to. She will remain there until her mother has her last round of chemo, but not for the weeks afterward while she recovers. If her mother insists on surgery on the island, she will come back, but in the meanwhile, she needs to be in New York. It has taken her years to climb up the ladder at Windsor, an internationally renowned publishing company where she is head of Equiano, Windsor's imprint for writers of color. Tanya Foster, her boss, has given her four weeks. Anna is afraid if she is away from her office much longer she might jeopardize her position. There are writers who need her, one writer in particular, Bess Milford, whose manuscript she has finished editing and has e-mailed to Tanya. Bess Milford is a true artist, her novel exquisitely written, but it is a literary novel and might not bring much profit to Equiano. Tanya Foster warned her of that probability when she reluctantly approved its acquisition simply on Anna's recommendation. Anna knows Tanya has not read the novel, so she includes a synopsis when she e-mails the edited manuscript, hoping that if Tanya is still too busy to give attention to a book she does not think will be worthwhile commercially, the synopsis will do the trick to persuade her to at least commit to a reasonable marketing budget. For Anna wants to try. She is determined to prove to Windsor that Equiano can still be successful if the company publishes literary fiction by black writers. She needs to be in New York to set the wheels in motion so that the novel will get the promotion it deserves.

Then a stroke of good luck. Paul Bishop, an oncologist who was born and raised on the island but now lives and works in New Jersey, is home for the celebration of his parents' fiftieth wedding anniversary. He drops by to visit the Sinclairs, who are happy to see him. Paul Bishop is the son of Henry Bishop, a union organizer whom Anna's father came to admire and respect when, as personnel manager of the major oil company on the island, he negotiated the end of the oil field workers' strike that was crippling the company. Anna suspects that Paul Bishop's visit is not accidental. She thinks Dr. Ramdoolal has sent him and she is relieved, for he arrives at a time when her mother has only one more treatment left to endure and the decision must be made soon as to where she will have surgery.

Dr. Bishop immediately allays Beatrice's fears. He tells her that what she sees on American TV beamed to the Caribbean is grossly exaggerated. America has changed, he says. There are laws now since the passage of the Civil Rights Act. In his hospital she will be treated the same as any patient, black or white. He offers to do the surgery himself. It takes him a while but eventually he convinces Beatrice to trust him. She does because Paul Bishop is a son of the soil, a compatriot. John Sinclair trusts him too because Paul Bishop's father is Henry Bishop. Anna is grateful to Paul since she can now return to her job in New York.

She does not have to choose, to risk interrupting the life she loves in New York: work that is meaningful for her. Her mother has agreed: she will go to the States for her surgery.

But there is more than gratitude Anna feels for Paul Bishop. She likes him. He is not a particularly handsome man, but he has presence, she finds. There is something about him, something comforting and reassuring, which puts her immediately at ease. Though she cannot remember that they met when she was four or five, he seems familiar to her. It helps too that, like her, Paul Bishop is a hyphenated American, a Caribbean-American, with a foot in both worlds. He will be patient with her mother, for he understands the culture that shapes her views, her sometimes seemingly erratic behavior. The next day he calls and invites Anna to dinner.

"I thought you two would get along," her mother says, barely hiding a triumphant smile.

Anna grimaces. She was mortified when her mother kept insisting that her father tell them whether Paul Bishop is single or not. "Does he have a wife?" her mother had asked. But later, Anna must admit, she was glad her mother forced her father to answer. Paul Bishop is divorced; he does not have a wife.

"It's only dinner," Anna says to her mother. "He leaves the next day."

"And soon you'll be in New York."

"He lives in New Jersey."

"My surgery will be in New Jersey where he practices," her mother says.

They are in her mother's bedroom. Her father is in the garden, feeding his fish in the pond that faces her mother's prize orchids. At seventy-two, Beatrice Sinclair is still beautiful. Her husband reassures her almost daily that her head, almost totally bald now from the disastrous effects of chemo, makes her profile even more distinctive. He tells her she looks regal, like the image of an Egyptian queen on an ancient coin. He says he can see her beautiful brown eyes more clearly now, that he loves the way her high cheekbones contrast with the soft slope of her cheeks. He says he always thought her lips were perfect, and that without the distraction of hair, he can see how perfectly her fuller top lip balances the thinner lower lip. He says she has kissable lips. He says all of this within Anna's hearing, for everything has changed now that John Sinclair has breached the code of privacy they share. Her secret is out. She will need a mastectomy. It is the only way to save her life. When Paul Bishop confirms that Beatrice Sinclair has no other option, her husband reaches for her hand. "We'll take showers together, Beatrice." Anna and Paul Bishop were sitting close to them in the veranda when her father said this, but he didn't seem to notice or care. Now he speaks openly of his wife's kissable lips. John Sinclair loves his wife. Anna has no doubt of that.

"You can never tell," her mother says. "You may get lucky like I am."

And her mother *is* lucky. For over forty years she has been married to a man who adores her, a man who has provided her with luxuries she could not have imagined when she lived in a tiny one-bedroom house in an impoverished part of the city, with a mother who was forced to work in the kitchen of the governor's house because her husband, an inveterate gambler, had debts so huge there was little left to buy food or pay the rent. By contrast, at the end of his career with the oil company that had hired him when he was barely out of his thirties, John Sinclair was in charge of the company's assets in the Lesser Antilles. Until he was eighty, he was given substantial retainers by the government and private companies for his skills as an arbitrator in labor disputes. He has not needed a pension. Only recently has he made use of the considerable interests his shares in the oil company have accumulated.

Beatrice Sinclair is indeed fortunate. Not only does her husband adore her, he can also afford to indulge her whims, which, to be fair, are not many. She likes to keep an attractive home, she enjoys entertaining friends, her garden is a source of pride for her, she loves beautiful clothes (her secret obsession is shoes), she expects, and is given, domestic help: a gardener, Singh, who has worked for her it seems forever; a housekeeper and cook, Lydia, who has been with her for fifteen years; the weekly laundress who comes to her home to wash and iron the linens and clothes; the boys who mow the lawn and trim the hedges and trees. John Sinclair wants his wife to have a comfortable life. He does not deny her the help she requires.

And they resemble each other. Perhaps they did not when they were young, but now their expressions, molded from years of seeing in each other's faces a mirror of their thoughts, have chiseled places where the skin was soft and softened places where bone hardened their features, so that the nose on her mother no longer seems as short as it once was, her eyes no wider than her husband's, and both their smiles curve upward the same way, the furrows on their foreheads gather in the same tiny waves between their eyebrows when they are angry. It helps that they have the same skin color, a rich butterscotch brown that tells the tale of the island's history, the peaceful Arawaks almost decimated by the war-loving Carib Indians who in turn were almost decimated by smallpox and other diseases the Spanish conquistadors brought with them. Then came

the Africans in chains to plant sugarcane and cocoa under
the lash of French planters who had already established
slave holdings in Martinique and Guadeloupe. By the time
the English had won their wars with Spain and colonized
the island, the range of skin color there was already on its
way to varying from pitch black to mocha, chocolate, and
coffee—noir and au lait. Anna herself is also the color of
butterscotch brown. She looks more like her mother than
she does her father. She has her mother's high cheekbones
and her deep-set eyes, but the shape of her nose is not the
same; she has her father's long nose that bends slightly at
the tip. Her lips are neither as thin as her father's nor as
full as her mother's. No one has yet said they are kissable.
Her father has sometimes told her she is beautiful. Only
once has her mother said so. Anna thought she was dream-
ing. Now her mother wants to be her matchmaker.

"I suppose I will see Paul when you get to the States,"
Anna says to her.

"And not before?"

"Like I said, we're having dinner tonight."

"And many more dinners after that."

"Enough," Anna says and stops her. "Please." She holds
up her hand, her palm open wide.

Her mother surrenders. "But it will be nice, Anna. You,
me, and your father in your apartment in New York."

And Anna panics.

TWO

She has thought of everything else. She has given herself every reason why her mother should come to the States, why she needs to return to New York for her writers, for Bess Milford in particular, but until her mother says, *You, me, and your father in your apartment in New York*, she has not thought of them together. Now a cold liquid collects at the base of her stomach and makes its way up her throat. She swallows and the liquid spreads down her arms and thighs.

Her parents have been to New York on many occasions, each time staying at a hotel in Manhattan, never crossing the bridge to Brooklyn where Anna lives in Fort Greene, on the cusp of gentrification. Always there have been excuses. On both sides. Her mother never finding the time between the plays she wants to see on Broadway and the meetings her husband has come to attend, Anna conveniently not protesting. She works in Manhattan; it would be easier to meet in the hotel where her parents are staying. No one objects.

If this arrangement has raised suspicions, neither Anna nor her parents have voiced them. But now, after twenty years, her mother will see where her daughter lives; more than that, she will see *how* she lives. In all the permutations of her plans to convince her mother to have surgery in the States, why has she not thought of this? Why hasn't she factored in the practical reality that her mother will need a place to stay before and after her surgery, and that this place will be her apartment?

There is tacit agreement between the immigrant and those who do not emigrate. Only good news is to be sent back home. The immigrant has a duty to spare her family and friends news of failure. The immigrant must not disappoint. This is the bargain the immigrant makes for the freedom of anonymity, for the chance to remake herself, to wipe the slate clean, to begin anew and write new history in the fantasy land that is America.

Television promises there are fortunes to be made. Even in America's congested cities, the poor drive their own cars. The family and friends of the immigrant do not want this dream shattered. Their hopes, the hopes of the community, rest on the immigrant's success. Like children believing in Santa Claus, they do not want to be told the dream is a lie.

They will not pry. No one will ask the question that could lead to the answer that the price may be too high for this exchange of the familiar for life in a strange land among people whose culture the immigrant does not understand. All want to believe in the lie beamed through the television into their living rooms: in America the streets are paved with gold. Suffering and deprivation happen in other lands, in drought-stricken Ethiopia, in war-ravaged Bosnia. Not in America.

They are enablers, all of them, the immigrant and the ones who remain at home. In Brooklyn, Anna passes stores that cater to them, shops that advertise barrels the immigrant will fill with goods and food she will ship back home, proof of her success, proof to family and friends that the fantasy exists. The immigrant holds her tongue. She does not tell of the long hours she must work. She does not say that night falls before she returns to her one-room apartment where for months the view outside her window is desolate, a concrete jungle sprouting leafless trees in patches of dirt carved out on pavements. She does not admit to loneliness. She does not say no singing birds wake her in the morning; she does not hear the soft patter of rain on a galvanized roof in the early dawn. She does not say she cannot afford to buy for herself many of the things she puts in the barrel. The illusion is to be maintained. There were celebrations back home when the U.S. embassy granted her a visa. How can you be unhappy when you have won the lottery? Impossible! they say.

Anna's situation is not as dire. She does not have to fill barrels with food and goods for her parents back home. Her parents do not need her money, her financial support. But for Anna the early days were not easy. Alice, her friend in high school who had immigrated to New York years before, invited Anna to share her apartment. She should have paid more attention to the advice Machiavelli gave to would-be princes on the loyalty of friends! *So long as you benefit them they are all yours; . . . they offer you their blood, their property, their lives, their children, when the need for such things is remote. But when need comes upon you, they turn around. So if a prince has relied wholly on their words . . .* In less than two months, Alice made it clear that Anna had worn out her welcome.

Why had she left her grassy island? There was a time she had staked her hopes in the promises of independence, the end of colonial rule, but she returned home from college in the Midwest to find nothing substantial had changed. The island was still in thrall to British dominance, though the skin color of the rulers was not the same. No longer were white men visibly in charge. The prime minister was a man of color and so were the ministers in his cabinet.

Within a mere few years, funded in part by scholarships the British gave to locals to study at the extension of the University of London that the British had established in Jamaica, there were many more dark-skinned doctors, lawyers, engineers, professors, journalists, entrepreneurs than there had been when she was in high school. Yet attitudes remained the same. And why not? They had been groomed to serve the Mother Country; they had been taught to venerate her history, her accomplishments, her beauty, her art. They judged each other by the way they spoke. The more British the accent, the more polished the person was assumed to be. At tea parties and cocktail parties they served bland hors d'oeuvres, careful not to contaminate them with spicy seasonings. The music was muted, the help required to wear the white uniforms that in colonial times had humiliated the parents of the nouveau riche. One was judged by the yardstick of British approval, every accomplishment requiring validation from the Mother Country or else deemed inferior. High school students still had to pass exams approved by the British, conflicts in law adjudicated by British courts; medical procedures needed British consultation. For Anna, the last straw was the difficulty she had finding employment.

She had received an honors degree from an established university in the Midwest and assumed she was qualified to teach high school literature and composition. Arrogantly, or so it seemed in hindsight one year later, she refused her father's offer of help. Now she knows that business gets done through an old boys' network. Her father was an important man with many influential friends. He had only to speak to one of them. But Anna had returned from a country where water jetting out firemen's hoses blasted the skin of young men and women; where snarling dogs,

straining against leashes held by officers sworn to up-
hold the law, fangs bared and dripping with phlegm, were
set loose on children. She had come back from a country
where thousands marched, risking life and imprisonment
for civil rights for those long denied them. She would not
take advantage of the privileges of her parents' social class.
She went to the Ministry of Education without references,
without the list of connections that would pave her way.

"The university of where-did-you-say?" The man who
interviewed her was patient. He explained that except for
Harvard, Yale, and Princeton, which they knew something
about, the ministry had no way of evaluating whether de-
grees from American universities measure up to the quality
of a British education. She asked him about Howard. The
prime minister of the island had graduated from that university in Washington, D.C.

"Howard is an exception," he said. He was aware of
the history of segregation in America. "You can't blame
black students if they won't let them into Harvard, Yale,
or Princeton. Howard is the Harvard for black Americans."
He handed back her diploma.

For seven months, Anna searched in vain for a job. The
response of the headmasters and headmistresses from the
schools was the same. An American degree, if it was not
from one of the universities that belonged to the Ivy League,
was not acceptable to them. In despair, Anna turned to
her father for help. In two days, he arranged an offer for
her from the headmaster of a junior secondary school, the
third tier of an educational system that determined the
fate of children by age twelve. There would be those who
would make their living with their brains and those with
their brawn. The children in the school where Anna was
assigned were the latter. They were to be prepared for oc-

cupations in trades. For the boys: construction, cabinetry, plumbing, electrical repair. For the girls: sewing, cooking, domestic affairs that would make them good housewives and mothers. For girls unlikely to marry: secretarial education, typing, and filing. But everyone had to learn to read and write English (England was the Mother Country, after all), and so there was a place in the school for Anna. Her salary could not be the same as that of someone with a degree from a British university. If Anna wanted the job, she had to accept less money.

When by chance Anna bumped into Alice, who was on holiday on the island, she was ready to leave. She had a vague plan of going to graduate school, nothing more than that, when she applied for a green card for permanent residence in the U.S. What she felt then was an emptiness, a sense of her life going nowhere, of being stuck in a rut, teaching children who had already accepted the fate decreed to them when they failed to make the passing grade on the eleven-plus exam. Already marked, they saw no purpose in reading books or learning to write beyond what was necessary to be a good cook, a good seamstress, a cabinetmaker, a construction worker. Anna wanted more for them and for herself, but there wasn't more for any of them in a system that was confident it had found the answer to the problem of children who threw spitballs in class.

Finding it difficult, if not impossible, to feel at home in America, Anna tried one more time after graduate school, baffling her mother who could not understand why she would want to come back now that she had a green card, the passport to the country where the streets were paved with gold. So seductive was the myth that many middle-class women on the island willingly humbled themselves to work in the kitchens of rich white Americans in the hopes of being sponsored. It took Anna just weeks to realize there was no place for her on the island. Her father cringed when she quoted Frantz Fanon to him, when she said that colonialism worked because the British had succeeded in colonizing minds—but the truth was, there were teaching jobs for expatriates from England and Canada, very few for local black women, and none again for her.

The standard explanation was that the island was in a transitional phase and needed foreign professionals to replace the British officials who had left. But the University College of the West Indies, an arm of the University of London, had long been established in Jamaica. By the time it gained independent status in 1962 as the University of the West Indies, not the "College of," there were many qualified locals able and ready to replace the British. But the British and Canadian expatriates had grown accustomed to spending lazy afternoons at the beach in the warmth of the tropical sun. They did not want to return to dark winter days and frigid nights.

On TV, Anna once caught a glimpse of a grim-faced brown-skinned woman in her late seventies standing quietly on the sidelines of an anti-immigration rally in England. She was holding a sign that read: We are here because you were there.

Anna chose America, land of immigrants, those willing and those ripped from their homeland in chains, a country where every living person, with few exceptions, can draw a straight line through ancestors not born here. Now, twenty years later, her mother will see where she lives in America. How she lives. And Anna panics.

THREE

D r. Paul Bishop arrives on time to take Anna to dinner. At precisely six o'clock, he rings the bell on the stone wall that encloses the house where Anna's parents live.

It is a beautiful wall made of large sand-colored stones streaked with slate and some kind of metallic material that glints even in the softening sunlight of the late afternoon. John Sinclair scoured the island for these stones. He left much of the interior design of the house to his wife, but he had insisted on this stone wall. He had said he wanted to bring the beauty of the natural world into their home. In front of the stone wall he has planted six elegant royal palm trees. Their long, slim trunks rise gracefully to the sky like the elegant ringed legs of the scarlet ibis. At the tops, fronds form an umbrella, sheltering tiny red berries clustered in the cups of spidery brown stems. Every evening when the sun is low on the horizon, John Sinclair inspects these trees for rotting berries and fronds dangling by wispy brown threads torn away from the stems. He keeps score on his long-running competition with the gardener Singh on exactly what day the berries and fronds will fall to the ground. He usually wins and collects the fallen loot in a bundle by the gate as proof of his victory, not at all reticent to gloat when Singh arrives on his bicycle early the next morning to begin working on the gardening chores Beatrice Sinclair has left for him. It is these palm trees and the stone wall that Paul Bishop admires now, marveling at how beautifully they frame the house, how the mountains that face them rise like a curtain, blue against the darkening sky.

Lydia, the Sinclairs' helper, has pressed the button on the wall in the kitchen that releases the lock on the electric gate and it grinds open. It is an imposing gate. Thick white iron rods run vertically to the top, each one ending in a sharp spike. The Sinclairs have installed this gate to protect themselves from the rash of violent murders, kidnappings, and burglaries that have overtaken the island since South American drug lords turned the quiet fishing villages in the south into way stations where they can repackage their illicit cargo bound for the U.S. in the bellies of pirogues manned by simple fishermen. Rather, what were once simple fishermen before they began sampling the cargo. Now they crave more, more to be sniffed and injected in their veins, more to wipe clean the guilt for neighbors they beheaded without remorse.

The Sinclairs once had dogs to protect them. That was before the stench of raw unseasoned cow bones that Mr. Sinclair boiled to a froth on the stove for them made Mrs. Sinclair vomit on the kitchen floor. But the dogs refused to eat the dried dog food endorsed by veterinarians who claimed to know what dogs liked. The next time John Sinclair boiled cow bones for his dogs and Beatrice vomited, he knew he had to give the dogs away. So he had iron bars installed on their windows and made plans to wire the house soon with an electric alarm system.

Anna has been anxiously awaiting Paul Bishop's arrival. Her head is swimming with scenarios that tumble one on top of the other: How will she manage? How will she explain herself to her mother when they all come together to stay in her small apartment? She tries reminding herself that she has made a good life, a decent life in America. She does not live in a sprawling house like the one her parents own; she does not have a helper or a cook, just a cleaning woman whose services she can barely afford twice a month. She does not have a garden or a gardener. She must water the house plants herself. In her neighborhood music blares from boom boxes held on the shoulders of hooded young men; sirens screech at unpredictable hours. But she has a good job, a well-paying job that has made it possible for her to purchase her apartment, small though it is. She has never had to borrow money from friends; she has never had to ask her parents for a loan. Still her fears remain. Will her mother be pleased? Will she disapprove of the way she lives her life?

She has shut herself in her room pretending she has work to do, a manuscript she has to finish editing for her boss before she leaves for New York. But she has already e-mailed the manuscript to her boss with her editorial notes; she has nothing more left to do. She picks up a magazine on the table near her bed. She cannot concentrate. She reads a page and has to reread it, forgetting in a second what she has just processed. She cannot still the throbbing behind her eyes. She tries lying down and placing a wet towel on her forehead; nothing helps. She had feigned sleep when her mother knocked on the door calling her for four o'clock tea.

When Dr. Bishop rings the bell she is already dressed, sitting on her bed, waiting for him.

"I hope I'm not too early." Paul Bishop has brought her a box of chocolates and a bouquet of white daisies with bright yellow centers. She loves chocolates. When she was a child, there was little her mother could do or say to stop her from eating too many. It occurs to her that her mother might have told Paul about her love for chocolates, orchestrating her future behind her back. Irritated by her mother's interference, she puts the chocolates on the coffee table and is about to call Lydia to take the flowers away when Paul Bishop says, "I bet you miss them. They don't seem to grow daisies here. Most of the flowers on the island are big and tall. Anthuriums, ginger lilies, birds-of-paradise. I wanted to bring you something that grows in my garden in New Jersey. A little bit of America. Our home, you know . . ."

Instantly, she is ashamed of her petty thoughts. She has accused her mother when her mother had nothing to do with the chocolates Paul has brought her. It's the daisies he wants her to notice. She takes them from him and brings them close to her nose to conceal her embarrassment. "They are beautiful," she says.

"Sorry, they don't have much of a perfume," he says.

She is glad he has stayed an extra day on the island, even if he has stayed for his own parents. He misses them, he had told her. He misses the scents of the island. But she saw the way his eyes lit up when she walked toward him and knows he has stayed for her too. Minutes ago her spirits were so low, but now she feels refreshed, energized, ready to spend a pleasant evening with him and put her worries at the back of her mind. She leads him toward the sliding glass door and out of the living room. Her parents are in their room, their absence, she is certain, conveniently staged by her mother.

In the restaurant Paul Bishop tells her how much he admired the palm trees and the stone wall at her parents' house, and how the mountains facing them seem to him like a curtain.

"I used to think if I could draw them open, I would glimpse eternity," she says.

His smile sends tiny soft waves across his cheeks. "Just what I thought, standing there waiting for someone to answer the bell." He tilts his head to one side and stares at her. "How on earth did someone let you slip out of their hands?"

Did her mother tell him that she is divorced? It does not matter; she is glad he knows.

"My ex didn't exactly let me slip out of his hands," she replies. "He left me for a pretty woman."

"He must have been blind. Any man can see how beautiful you are."

She is wearing a dress. The day before, when he came to her parents' home to persuade her mother to have surgery in the States, she was wearing slacks and a sleeveless shirt. Now she has on a white fitted cotton sheath that reveals her figure, her perky breasts, tiny waist, slim hips. She realizes now that she must have subconsciously chosen to wear this dress, with its thin spaghetti straps that expose her smooth shoulders and the rise of her firm breasts, but when she took it off the hanger she was aware only that it was a hot day and the evening could be expected to be not much cooler. But perhaps it was what Paul Bishop said to her on that first day that made her choose to wear this dress. He remembered how pretty she was when she was just four or five. Perhaps she wore this dress to recapture that moment. Paul Bishop compliments her again and a sensation of giddy happiness sweeps through her body.

"So what happened to *your* marriage?" she asks him. He is not a young man; his hair is sprinkled with gray, more so at his temples. His body is not as muscular as her ex-husband's. His stomach rises in a slight paunch and the flesh under his chin has already begun to balloon out, but he has an air about him of man secure in his skin.

"Work," he says. "Work happened to my marriage."

"Your work?"

"We married when I had just got out of medical school. The hours of a resident can be brutal. I got home late and when I did, I just wanted to curl up in bed."

"And not with her?" Anna surprises herself with this question. But the confidence he exudes is infectious.

"Are you always this direct?" Paul Bishop seems delighted with her response.

"Not always."

"I like that in a woman. I like when a woman doesn't beat around the bush and asks what she wants to know."

"So?"

"We drifted apart," he says.

Anna peers across the water. They are sitting on the deck of a restaurant that faces the sea and they have a clear view of sailboats and yachts bobbing on the shallow waves. Only one of the yachts flies the island's flag; the flags of the others are all from foreign countries. Anna has read the complaints about these foreign yachts in the letters of local boatmen published in the newspaper. Yachties, the owners of these foreign boats are called. They dump their waste in the waters around the offshore islands and then drift inland to dine at the coastal restaurants.

"If I were honest," she says, turning back to him, "I would admit that too. Tony left me for another woman, but before that, we had drifted apart."

"Was he from here?" Electric lanterns hang on the poles at either end of the deck and bathe them in a soft light, which bounces off Paul's plum-colored skin and shadows his eyes.

Anna shakes her head. "No. Not from here."

"From another Caribbean island?"

"African American," she replies.

The dinner they ordered has not yet arrived. Paul picks up the fork next to his empty plate and twirls it between his fingers. "My ex is American," he explains. "Italian."

"Foreigners," she says. "We both married foreigners."

The small band in the corner of the main dining room has begun to play a calypso. It's an old-time calypso that Anna remembers well: *Jean and Dina, Rosita and Clementina / Round the corner posing / Bet your life is something they selling.* It's a song about the American occupation of two large areas on the island. On the northwestern tip of the island the Americans had built a naval base, and an air base in the valley between the northern and central mountain ranges. The sailors and airmen wanted girls and were willing to pay for them, but now the war was over. *Yankees gone and Sparrow take over now.*

"Would you like to dance?" Paul asks. Several couples are already on the dance floor.

It has been a long time since she danced to a calypso. She fears her body will not remember the rhythms. She raises her hand to decline Paul's invitation but he is already out of his chair moving toward her.

"Come." He grasps her hand. "It's like riding a bicycle."

Paul Bishop leaves the next afternoon. He telephones in the morning to say goodbye. She is surprised how sad she feels, for she knew it was his last night on the island. But she cannot remember when she had been so happy or when she had danced so much. He was right: it all came back to her when she stepped on the dance floor. And he had been a good dance partner. He grasped her waist and held her firmly, guiding her legs. It felt good to dance again, to go out to dinner, to laugh, to talk about inconsequential matters. For after their brief exchange about spouses who had left them, they threw the past behind and allowed themselves to be swept away by the seductive beat of the music, the warm breezes wafting off a sea glistening with starlight and the rippling reflection of the rising moon, and all that existed was the present, carefree and joyous. Now he is calling to say he is leaving the island.

"I'll see you soon in the States. When do you expect to come to New York?"

Her sadness dissipates. She will see him again soon. "In three weeks," she says. But the truth is she wants to leave earlier. Needs to leave earlier.

"She's a strong woman, your mother."

"Yes, but . . ." Her voice trails.

"I mean it," he says. "Your mother's a spunky woman."

He has misunderstood her. She tells him about Bess Milford's novel. She has e-mailed the edited draft to her boss, along with a summary, but she hasn't heard from her. Now she is worried. "I really need to go back soon," she says.

"Need?" he asks. "Are you worried it won't get published?"

"Oh, no. My boss Tanya promised to publish it. I'm worried that it may not get properly marketed and promoted. No novel sells itself without lots of marketing."

"Then go," Paul says. "You can leave right after your mother has her last chemo treatment. She'll be okay. My only worry is that she could change her mind and not come to the States for surgery."

"Oh, she won't change her mind," Anna says quickly, grasping the reprieve he has given her. He has also left aging parents behind to seek his own fulfillment. He will not judge her harshly. He will not think there is something un-natural about a daughter who loves her job, who wants to get back to it as soon as she can. Her mother is ill, but she has her husband with her. She is not alone.

"Because this is not something she can put off much longer." Suddenly he's speaking to her as the surgeon he is. "Her tumors are large."

Her heart sinks. "Are you suggesting I should stay?"

"Only if you can't guarantee she'll come to the States."

She cannot make such a guarantee, but her father can. He wants her mother to live. She has promised him she will come. She will not break the promise she made to him.

"She will come for my father," Anna says.

He exhales. She hears the puff of breath released through his nostrils. She imagines his paunch flattening. "Good. Good. Then that's settled. There's no reason you can't come back to New York earlier. Your father seems very capable of taking care of your mother, and Dr. Ram-doolal will make certain she is strong enough to travel. If you have to be in New York, then go."

She does not need his permission, but his confidence eases the residue of guilt that had begun to nag her.

"And it would be good to see you again," he adds.

It has been a long time since a man told her she was pretty, brought her flowers and chocolates, and took her dancing. Yes, it would be good to see him again.

When she gets off the phone, she books her flight to New York.

FOUR

New York is in the throes of an Indian summer when she arrives two weeks later. On the sidewalks in Fort Greene, Brooklyn, old oak barrels, the slats banded together with strips of rusty iron, are overflowing with flowers in a brave show of exuberance, vines in variegated shades of green cascading down their sides. In weeks, if not days, the frost will come and the flowers will curl on themselves, wither, and die. Until then, they bloom in a defiant display of color. Impatiens, now at their peak, form hillocks of pink and red next to geraniums, their buds fully open, petals trembling in the slightest breeze. The planters are new to Fort Greene and still a surprise to old residents accustomed to rotted food and filthy scraps of paper spilling out of trash cans the garbagemen have barely emptied and then hurled onto the broken pavement in their race to jump back on the moving trucks. That was then. Now everything is different since the bubble has burst in the dot-com world of twenty- and thirty-something millionaires in Manhattan, and, like their ancestors before them, they have turned southward seeking a New World. In Brooklyn they discover treasures just waiting for the taking: century-old brownstones and limestones intricately carved, and in the interiors high ceilings, ornate woodwork, crystal chandeliers, marble-façade fireplaces. Giddy with excitement, they learn these were all once theirs, abandoned by parents many decades ago, racism fueling their flight out of the cities when the Civil Rights Act mandated the desegregation of housing that permitted blacks to live wherever they chose.

To be fair, the young millionaires offer inducements far more valuable than beads to the blacks and Latinos who had long settled in, making the neighborhood their own. The money they pay seems like a fortune to people who had to partition their homes and charge rent by the room to meet their monthly mortgage bills. It is their ticket out of the ghetto to a house without tenants, a backyard, perhaps a pool, and parks nearby. Too late they discover what realtors knew all along: the demand for housing is rising in the cities, not in the suburbs. The new owners clear the rubble and put a price five times as high on the houses that ensure the previous owners and tenants will never be able to return.

Anna was prescient enough to purchase her apartment before the onslaught from Manhattan. It is on the second floor of a six-story building, small by Manhattan standards but large in this area of elegant one-family brownstones. Her apartment is a comfortable size: two bedrooms, one she has turned into an office, along with a dining room, living room, and kitchen. When Anna first moved to the area it was not uncommon to find addicts slumped against the iron railing that bordered the building, needles and used condoms strewn on the sidewalk. She had been warned about muggings, and barely escaped being pummeled on her head with a thick wood plank one evening when two men came on either side of her as she was walking to her apartment. One grabbed her handbag and the other was about to hit her when his partner cut the straps off her handbag with a knife and took off. It was times like these she remembered when she panicked at the thought of her parents staying with her. Now she thinks she was foolish to have such fears. In the golden glow of the descending early- autumn sun, her street is a picture-perfect postcard of a gentrified neighborhood. Garbage cans are discretely placed behind iron railings, flowers bloom from window boxes and in planters mounted to the pavement on wrought-iron stands. There are no addicts swaddled in filthy clothes, nodding off against the railings, dribble coursing down their grizzly chins, no homeless indigents curled up on cardboard boxes under the shelter of garbage cans. No muggers on the street.

Inside her apartment, home at last, safe, happy to be in her own place and among her own things, she turns on the answering machine and her life, put on hold the last six weeks, returns to her in a rush of comforting waves: three calls from her friend Paula who was expecting her two weeks ago; warnings from a magazine subscription that is about to expire; the super in the building reminding her of an appointment for the exterminator to spray her apartment; the neighborhood bookstore telling her about new arrivals; the Brooklyn Academy of Music listing the fall events. Home. The final call is from Tanya Foster. She is breathless with excitement. She loves the novel Anna e-mailed to her. She has sent it to the salespeople. They think it could be a big success and have great plans for marketing it. Anna is thrilled, beside herself with joy. This is a major victory for her. She calls Paula to give her the news, but she barely manages to say hello before her friend lashes out at her.

"If the cost of the call was too much for you, don't you think you could at least have e-mailed me?" Paula's voice drips with sarcasm. Anna tries to interject, but Paula blocks her again. "I was worried that I hadn't heard from you those two weeks. I didn't know what happened. I kept imagining it had to be something terrible for you not to call. I finally broke down and dialed your parents one evening. Your father answered. You were out to dinner, he said. With a friend. And I thought, *Silly me*. Worrying about how you were dealing with your mother's cancer, and there you were having a good time with a friend."

Anna doesn't want to tell her too much about Paul Bishop. If she tells Paula too much about Paul, she will make more of her evening out with him than she's ready to admit. Paula is her age, single, but she has never been married. She had dreamed of a career in teaching—mathematics is her subject—but in the high school where she teaches, most of her time is spent keeping the children from fighting each other. There are bars on the classroom windows. At the entrance to the school, the children must pass through electronic security gates; they must be patted down for weapons. Their parents, many of them barely adults, cannot or are afraid to discipline them. Paula has talked about returning to the island, but like Anna, her working years have been in America. She fears she will not fit in again. She has given up hope, both for a husband and a meaningful career, and consoles herself with pounds of chocolate cake and ice cream by the quart. She is not obese, just ample. Very ample and very beautiful, her skin like liquid chocolate, not a blemish on it. She does not need makeup. Winter or summer, her complexion glows with a reddish undertone. She has expressive brown eyes; they dance when she is happy and turn almost black when she is angry.

Anna and Paula had the pleasure of sweets in common when Anna got divorced. But Anna returned to the gym and a diet that gave her back her former figure. Since then,

Paula has been on a campaign to have Anna remarried. It is a wish transferred from herself to her friend. If marriage is unlikely for her, she wants it to be likely for Anna. Their friendship wards off feelings of isolation among people whose history and customs remain alien to them. Yet Anna knows Paula is afraid of losing their friendship if she remarries. Anna cannot fault her for this fear. When she was married to Tony she hardly had time for Paula. Women, Paula said, drop each other like a hot potato when a man comes into their lives. Anna is determined to prove to Paula that she will not be such a woman. Never again will she allow a relationship with a man to disrupt her friendship with her best friend. So she makes light of her dinner with Paul. She does not lie, she simply gives part of the truth and withholds the rest. She does not say that Paul Bishop is a friend, could be more than a friend. She says he is a doctor, a surgeon that Dr. Ramdoolal recommended to her mother. He thinks because of her age, and because her hormones are not as active as when she was young, her mother has good chance to beat the cancer.

"It's likely Dr. Bishop will do the surgery on my mother," Anna says.

"In what hospital?" Paula asks.

Anna tells her that Dr. Bishop practices in the States. He was visiting his parents and Dr. Ramdoolal arranged for him to speak to her mother. Her mother will have surgery in his hospital in New Jersey, she explains.

"Here? Your mother will have surgery here?" Astonishment, not curiosity, raises the pitch of Paula's voice. "When?"

"She and my father will be here in a week."

"Where will they stay?"

"With me. Before and after the surgery."

For seconds that seem like minutes neither speaks. At last Paula says with tenderness that is comforting to Anna, "It'll all work out. Don't worry, Anna. Everything will be fine."

Paula does not have to be explicit. Anna can tell she is thinking as much about her as about her mother. "It's just that they have such fantasies," Anna says. "They buy into the fairy tale of the American Dream and the Land of Milk and Honey."

"They are your fantasies too," Paula says softly.

"How can you say such a thing?"

"Don't get mad with me, Anna, but I've seen how you take on their expectations. Pile them up on your shoulders."

"I don't send them barrels of stuff to impress them."

"No, but you don't let them see where you live either."

"You're not being fair, Paula. They are always busy when they come."

"Have you ever invited them?"

Anna admits she hasn't.

"The problem is that you resent your parents' expectations for you. But your mother watches TV. She knows what's going on in America. She's not naïve. I don't think she has the impressions you think she has. She'll be proud of you. You live in a beautiful apartment that you own. Fort Greene is becoming the place to live in the city . . ."

"It's not Manhattan," Anna says, but she is merely faking petulance, for little by little Paula is easing her qualms. Perhaps her mother will not disapprove of the life she has made for herself in America.

"Look how much you have achieved," Paula presses on. "Senior editor, head of Equiano Books! That's no small achievement."

"Tanya Foster left a message on my voice mail," Anna

says. "She liked Bess Milford's novel. She told me the people in sales are excited about it too."

"See, there you go! You've managed to make them take a literary novel by a black writer seriously. I see great things for you in the company, Anna. A vice presidency."

"No expectations. Okay, Paula?"

"Okay. But if or *when* that happens, your mother will be thrilled."

Tanya Foster sounds ecstatic when Anna calls the next morning. Her secretary tells Anna that Tanya has been waiting for days to hear from her. The news is all good. The woman's heels click against the tiled floor in rapid little steps as she goes to fetch Tanya.

"Anna!" Tanya is so excited she practically shouts out her name. "We've missed you here. Six weeks is a long time. I don't think we could have made it another day without you."

Hyperbole, but it is exhilarating to Anna. "Well, I'm here now," she says.

"Sorry about your mother. How is she?"

Anna tells her about the tumors, the one in her mother's left breast, the one under her arm. "She let them grow so large, she needed chemo to reduce them before she could—"

"How old is she? Seventy?"

"Seventy-two," Anna says.

"That's a long time. She's lived a long time."

A queasiness rumbles through Anna's stomach and the exhilaration she had briefly felt subsides. "Seventy-two is not that old," she says.

"She's had a good life, no?"

Her mother has indeed had a good life, but she is still

alive; she still wants more years. Anna finds herself feeling defensive of the mother she left behind. Hadn't her mother said she was no longer needed at home and urged her to go back to work? Hadn't she seemed fine after she returned home from her final chemo treatment? She wasn't nauseous; she had dinner at the usual time. Paul Bishop said her mother was strong. Even Dr. Ramdoolal approved, though he did ask if her business in New York was urgent, seeming to imply that only urgent business would take a daughter away from her mother when she was ill. But her business was indeed urgent. Tanya Foster tells her so now.

"You came back just in time. I gave the boys in the art department the summary you sent me of Bess Milford's novel and they came up with a terrific cover. They're practically buzzing with excitement."

So quickly? But Anna restrains herself; she does not give voice to the hesitation that grips her throat. She should be pleased; it has sometimes taken her weeks to get the attention of the art department for one of her books. What is it about this novel that has the boys in the art department practically buzzing?

"The salespeople are excited too. I know you'll love the cover, Anna. I can't wait for you to see it." And as if suddenly remembering how their conversation began, Tanya adds, lowering her voice, "Look, don't worry about your mother—your father is with her, right? I'm sure the doctors there will take good care of her."

Anna does not say that her mother will be coming to New York. She does not say it will be a doctor here, not a doctor there, who will be treating her. She has a week, seven days, before her parents arrive; there will be time enough to let Tanya know, if she needs to tell her. For now she does not want to lose the momentum that seems to be building in favor of Bess Milford's novel. It isn't that she thinks Tanya is insincere. She believes Tanya truly sympathizes with her, but she knows her mantra: a hundred percent to the company for a hundred percent of your salary. Tanya would think she wouldn't be able to give a hundred percent to the company if her attention is divided between work and caring for her mother. She'd think Anna would be distracted. Tanya is not married. If she has a lover, she has kept him a secret. She comes from the Midwest, Iowa. Her parents died when she was young. She has revealed nothing about siblings, if she has any, or whether she has aunts or uncles or cousins. She gives a hundred percent to Windsor Publishing Company. She expects Anna to give a hundred percent to Equiano Books.

So Anna tells her that her mother is in good hands on the island. She has the best oncologist there. She says her father is a very attentive husband. She says she isn't worried.

"Good," Tanya responds. "I knew I made the right decision when I chose you to head Equiano. When can you come in?"

Anna tells her she expects to be in the office before noon.

"Perfect," Tanya says. "I'll have the art department and salespeople come meet with you. Would one o'clock work?"

One o'clock, Anna agrees, would work well for her.

Anna spots the new man immediately. He is standing next to the Xerox machine with a stack of papers in his hand. He puts the papers in the feeder and presses the button. The machine makes a whirring sound and pages slide out to the basket below.

There is something about the man that arrests Anna's at-

tention. He is not wearing a jacket, which isn't exceptional—
only a couple of the male editors wear jackets—but his pants
look like they should be paired with a jacket, the white
cuffed shirt and striped tie part of an ensemble for a suit.
None of the men wear suits to work, especially a well-
tailored, probably designer suit like the one this man appears to be wearing. He is obviously not an office assistant
or one of the young men who are assigned the clerical tasks
of delivering the mail, ferrying manuscripts from one editor to another, filing, and copying. He could be a visitor,
but if he's a visitor, he must be a close friend of one of the
workers to have so casually taken off his jacket and be using the Xerox machine. As if this is where he works.

At the very moment this thought flits across Anna's
consciousness, she hears Tanya calling out to her: "Ah,
Anna, you're here!" Tanya comes quickly toward her and
air-kisses her on both cheeks. "How good you look! The
sun has done great things to your complexion. You pos-
itively glow. I should get some sun myself. I look like a
ghost next to you."

Tanya does not look like a ghost, but she has an ephem-
eral quality about her. She is not one of those rosy-cheeked
Midwesterners with German roots. Her background is
Scandinavian. This much she has said about her parents.
Her skin is doughy-white even in the summer, her hair
blond, straight, and lanky, falling to her shoulders, which
are slight like the rest of her body. Her arms and legs are
skinny, her hips slim, but her figure is in style these days
when anorexic models are paraded everywhere on bill-
boards, magazines, and on TV as beauties to be admired.
Tanya is quite proud of her figure and clearly has no intention of changing her size or her color. Anna has caught her
several times gazing at the models in fashion magazines on

her desk. In New York City, where the ethnic populations of Latinos, continental and diasporic Africans, olive-skinned Europeans from the Mediterranean, Middle Easterners, Indians, Chinese, and Koreans are threatening to overwhelm the majority, she stands out: an American of European ancestry with roots surely in the far northern climes. Anna thinks Tanya likes that distinction.

"Come," she says, "I want to introduce you to Tim Greene. He's our new hire."

Before Anna can ask, *For which department? Where has Tim Greene been assigned?* Tanya waves to the man at the copy machine. "Tim!"

He is flipping through the pages he has just retrieved from the basket. He pulls one from the stack and turns around.

"Come meet your boss," Tanya calls out to him.

Tim Greene walks over to Anna. He holds out his hand and a smile crosses his lips but not his eyes. "Boss, nice to meet you." Anna guesses he is in his midthirties, younger than she is by perhaps five years or so. He is tall, but not imposing. Like Tanya, he is fashionably slim. In fact, everything about Tim Greene is magazine fashionable—his clothes, his close-cropped hair, his long legs, his slim hips.

"I thought you could do with an assistant," Tanya says. "You know, with Tammy Mohun leaving so abruptly."

Tammy Mohun, an Indian from South Africa, was Anna's office assistant until their colonial pasts became an impenetrable wall neither could breach. Under apartheid in South Africa, Indians were given an advantage over blacks; in the British colonies they were given five acres or passage back to India. Before her trip to the island, Anna had briefly discussed her need for a replacement for Tammy

Mohun, but Tanya had said nothing about a new man on the phone that morning.

"Assistant editor," Tanya clarifies, beaming at Tim Greene.

"Assistant editor?" *Tammy Mohun was a secretary*, Anna thinks.

"He comes highly recommended," Tanya continues, still beaming at Tim Greene. "To tell you the truth, we poached him from one of our competitors."

"Come on, Tanya!" Tim protests unconvincingly. "I wanted to be part of the great things you're doing here. It's exciting what's going on at Equiano."

"Tim's the best," Tanya says. A faint pinkish blush climbs up her neck and stains her cheeks. But if Tim Greene's blood rose to his face with embarrassment over the praise Tanya has heaped on him, neither she nor Tanya would be able to tell. Tim Greene is dark-skinned, an African American. Of that fact, Anna is certain. There is not the slightest trace of an accent in his voice from anywhere else but America. He speaks with an Upper West Side Harlem accent: a New Yorker, but raised with relatives one generation away from that mass exodus of African Americans from the South. Anna recognizes the playful drawl, the ends of words disappearing in the back of the throat. The listener has to lean forward to hear him clearly, or must ask the speaker to repeat his words. A trick. A mask. Instinctive. It would not be easy to tell what he is really thinking.

"I plan to do my best," Tim Greene says.

"Well, I'm just glad you jumped ship."

A flicker of movement travels across Tim's lips, the muscles hardening, but in the sweetest voice he says, "Your offer was too tempting to refuse."

Tanya's eyes widen, but she does not contradict him. "I

thought what you need is an assistant editor," she explains to Anna. "Things are moving and shaking here. You've done a terrific job! The books you edited are flying off the shelves. We can hardly keep up with the demand for all that chick lit, urban lit, ghetto lit. Isn't that so, Tim?"

"Raine and B. Benton are your best sellers." The smile on Tim Greene's lips remains frozen. "I checked the figures. At last count, each of them sold more than a million copies."

Raine is the queen of black exotica. Every page of her novels sizzles with explicit sex. In B. Benton's books neighborhood gangs slaughter each other with as little remorse and as much glee as if they had crushed an army of cockroaches crawling through the crevices of their filthy apartments.

"And there are more in the pipeline," Tanya says. "See what a good job you've done, Anna? You should be proud of yourself."

These are not the books Anna wants to edit. These are the books that are necessary for Equiano to stay afloat, to remain in the black. Without them Equiano would fold, but she wants more. A better list. She has been in the publishing business too long not to know that literary fiction written by any writer, black or white, is a hard sell. But no one has questioned the intellectual capabilities of white people, no one has stereotyped them over four hundred years as intellectually inferior. One reads a strictly commercial novel by a white writer and one does not say, or secretly think: *This is to be expected. This is the best these people can do; they are incapable of doing any better. This is who these people are: the pimps, hustlers, thieves, golddiggers, abusive fathers, neglectful mothers, and oversexed lovers.* One knows one can find in almost any bookstore a rich range of styles, characters, and stories by white writers. Anna wants Equiano to publish the same. Chick lit, urban lit, ghetto lit will pay the bills, but literary fiction is essential for advancing the culture, giving us hope. What if no one had published Baldwin, Ellison, Wright, or Hurston?

But perhaps Tanya is beginning to see things her way. She seems truly excited about Bess Milford's novel. Her secretary stands patiently by the door of the conference room fluttering a stack of manuscript papers. Tanya turns toward her and nods. "Let's go," she says. "The guys are waiting for us." The secretary opens the door.

Anna has seen the guys before. They are from the art department, more new hires who arrived just as she was leaving for the island. The old team left abruptly. Fired, the rumor went. They were apparently not hip enough, not in touch with X, Y, or was it the Z generation? Anna cannot remember which letter from the alphabet she heard in reference to their departure. Their replacements, Hakim and Robert, look fresh out of college, barely in their twenties. In the six weeks since she has been away, they seem to have settled in completely, as if they've worked at the company for years. They are sprawled out on their chairs next to each other at the conference table, both dressed casually in sweaters and jeans. Hakim's hair is braided in long locks that he has gathered together in a ponytail at the nape of his neck. Robert's hair is short-cropped like Tim's, though faded toward the back of his neck. Rita from sales sits across from them. She has worked in publishing for years, though only the last two for Windsor. She is young, only in her midthirties, but compared to the guys she appears much older. She is olive-skinned, dark-haired, heavyset, a Mediterranean type, either Italian or Greek. Her close-fitting navy skirt suit hugs her wide hips and big breasts but also reveals a fairly narrow waist. She has not had children, Anna guessed correctly when they first met. Her stomach is flat like an ironing board.

When Tanya walks in, the guys sit up. The secretary puts the manuscript on the table and leaves the room. Tanya sits at the head of the table, Tim to her right. She motions Anna to take the chair adjacent to hers. No sooner does Anna settle in her chair than Rita stretches her arm over the table toward her and says in a confidential whisper that is still loud enough for the others to hear, "Loved the novel, Anna. I think we can sell this one."

Robert slides his back up on his chair. His eyes are shining, glittering almost. "Definitely," he says. "Definitely." He clamps his teeth down on his lower lip and shakes his head excitedly in rapid little movements. "It's going to be a big winner. That adultery angle is just what's happening."

"Yeah," Hakim chimes in. "Man trying to get away with keeping the wife satisfied at home and getting it on with the girlfriend. That's a seller."

The hesitation that had gripped Anna's throat when Tanya gave her the news that the boys from the art department were buzzing about Bess Milford's novel returns as alarm. She can feel her bottom lip beginning to tremble. Bess Milford's novel is not at all like that. It's not at all about a married man *getting it on* with his girlfriend. "That's not the point," she says. "It's not about a torrid affair." She presses her lips together to stop the trembling.

Tanya, who has not taken her eyes off Anna since Rita spoke, quickly interjects, "Let them finish the presentation, Anna. Hear what they have to say."

"It's about marketing, Anna," Rita says. "We like— we *love*—the novel, but in the end it's about marketing."

"Show her." Hakim inclines his head toward Robert.

There's a screen rolled up into a metal casing on the wall at the back of the room. Robert reaches for the string hanging from the center and pulls it down. The screen unfolds. "Lights!"

But Hakim has already turned off the lights and positioned himself next to the computer behind Tanya. Rita rolls her chair down and makes room for Tanya next to her. She invites Anna to sit with them.

"The cover," Tanya says, and extends her arms with a flourish.

A picture appears on the screen. A black couple, a man and a woman, are locked in a passionate embrace. The man, like Hakim, has long braided locks, but they are not pulled back. They hang loosely at the sides of his face. He is a handsome man in his midthirties, with smoldering eyes, moist full lips shadowed by a thick mustache. His shirt and pants cling to his muscular frame outlining chiseled pecs and taut buttocks. The woman in his arms is equally chiseled. Full, firm breasts strain against the buttons on her tight shirt and spill out in perfectly shaped orbs. Her hair, long and straight, flows over her smooth shoulders. Her bottom rises and arcs downward to well-defined thighs encased in a narrow tight skirt. As she reaches up, lips puckered to receive the man's kiss, the backs of her feet slip out of her red four-inch spiked heels.

"My God!" Anna gasps.

"Like it?" Robert is grinning. Like the proverbial Cheshire cat, Anna thinks with disgust.

"Well, what do you say?" Tanya asks. Hakim is smirking behind her.

Anna cannot speak.

"It's going to be a big seller," Rita says.

"That's not it, that's not it at all . . ." Anna stammers

out the words, fighting to find the right ones. "Bess Milford . . . she wouldn't—that's not the book she wrote."

Tim, who so far has been silent, swivels his body toward Anna. "It's a postcard. You know the way a postcard makes you want to travel to the place you see on it? That's all a cover is about." He is speaking to her with exaggerated patience as if she is a child. "It's just an ad to make you buy the book."

"No!" Anna stands up.

"We don't plan to change a word of the novel, Anna," Tanya says. "It will be exactly as you sent it to me, exactly the way you edited it. It'll be the same book."

"I can't believe you'd think this is right." Anna is close to tears.

"I would have thought you'd want us to get an early start on the cover," Tanya says.

"But not this one."

"I want it for the galleys. We're pushing advance production forward. You'll see. This one will bring huge advance orders from the bookstores."

"You're going to ruin the book."

Tanya places both hands on the table, the palms facedown, her fingers stretched wide. "It's business, Anna," she says. "Just business. You want us to publish this novel? I agreed, but I have to sell it. That's my job."

"Is this final? Has this been decided?"

"I thought you'd see it my way, Anna. I thought you'd understand. Like Tim says, it's a poster. You still have your book."

"Is this what you all think? You all think this is right?" Anna glances around the room nervously.

Rita lowers her head. The guys nod theirs. Tim throws up his hands.

"How will I explain this to Bess Milford?"

"That's your job," Tanya says. "Ours is to market it, and I think the boys here did a fine job. I think the book will be a success. Cheer up, Anna. Smile."

Paul Bishop calls while Anna is in the conference room. She gave him the date of her arrival in New York, but has not yet contacted him. Was she waiting for him to call her? She is a grown woman, and it's silly to play such a game. She likes him and he likes her. She does not need to test his affection for her to know he is likely to be as anxious to see her again as she is to see him. Still, she is reassured by his call. He leaves a message with her secretary. He will be in surgery until five but he has sent her an e-mail. Anna switches from the company's server to the one where she gets her personal e-mail and logs on. There have been more than a few scandals in the office when personal e-mails were retrieved on the company's server. There are rules, but people break them. Laziness? Out of foolhardy wishful thinking that out of all the e-mails flying through the Internet space, it's a trillion-to-one chance theirs will land on their boss's desk? And yet a marriage ended in divorce when an office affair was uncovered through the company's e-mail; one man barely escaped jail in a Ponzi scheme.

Paul's e-mail is brief. He misses her. He would have called last night, but after eight hours of surgery, he fell asleep, exhausted. Can they meet for early dinner, say about six? He names a Midtown restaurant, near to her office.

She wants to see him, needs to see him. She put on a brave face when she left the meeting, but her hands are still shaking. She was not cheered up by Tanya's baseless promises. The book will be a publishing failure. Tanya knows it, and if she doesn't, Anna thinks she's less informed about the market for literary fiction by black writers than she should be. They have joined forces against her, the boys in the art department, the people in sales. Rita was sent to pacify her. They have hemmed her in and left her no choice. She is glad Paul contacted her; she needs a sympathetic ear.

Anna taps out a message on her keyboard:

Isn't six too early? Can you realistically get here by then? You said you'd be in surgery until five.

Ten minutes later comes the response from his BlackBerry:

Manhattan is just over the George Washington Bridge. I can make it.

Let's say six thirty. It'll give you more time.

I don't want you waiting for me, Anna. Your work ends at five, no?

How about six fifteen?

The same man who put her at ease on the island is already sitting at the table when she arrives at the restaurant. He stands up to embrace her; his soft paunch pressing against her midsection feels warm and comforting. This is not a young man, a man inexperienced in the ways of the world. This is a man who has lived long enough to have survived the disappointment of a lost love, a marriage undone, a man who has been in the real world for years. He knows life can be unfair. When he nuzzles her ear, the tension of the day leaves her, relaxing her muscles. She likes that he does not use the newfangled scents touted by celebrities that suffuse the hallways of modern offices. She likes the gray hair at his temples. She likes that he has not dyed it.

"So here we are," he says. "Fish out of our tropical waters."

"Fish in cold water," she retorts.

"Come now, it's only fall." He grins, white polished teeth against dark-plum skin. "Winter is still waiting for us." He holds out the chair for her. An old-fashioned man. Tony, her ex-husband, was not an old-fashioned man. He wanted her to get on with the times. *Isn't that what you women want?* he would say. *Didn't you want to be treated like men? Doesn't feel good, does it, when it bites you on the ass?*

Tony was crude and inconsiderate; Paul is refreshingly polite and thoughtful. He stands up when she comes to the table. He pulls out the chair for her. He arrives early at the restaurant so she will not be kept waiting.

"So, how was your first day back at work?"

She wanted a sympathetic ear when her secretary gave her his message, but now in the intimate setting of the fancy restaurant Paul has chosen for them, she does not want to recall her humiliation from the conference room. She remembers their last night together, his arms around her when they danced on the deck of the restaurant, the sea below them glittering in the moonlight. What happened at work should not spoil her personal life. There is Paul sitting across from her, happy to see her again. There is her mother to worry about, the surgery she will face soon, her life hanging in the balance. There is the apartment to prepare for her mother and father. A plan gone awry in the office should not unsettle her; the novel will gather dust once the first three weeks of flurry in the sales department dies down and their misplaced marketing strategy back-fires. But Paul asks his question again, and all the hurt of the day returns to her.

She has been disregarded, disrespected. They did not consult her. They made their decision with no consideration for her input. She should have been involved from the beginning. Now she is expected to accept the decision they have made for her, to be satisfied with Tanya's patronizing remark. *It's the same book*, Tanya said. But it will never be read as the same book, Anna knows. Readers who are interested in literary fiction will pass over a book with such a sexually explicit cover. Readers who simply want to be entertained and not challenged will discard it after the first page when the sentences become too complex, too intricate, too long, when the ideas they are invited to ponder are too complicated.

"It was hell," she says.

"Your first day?"

She tells him about the book cover, the decision they made for her. "They could have called me. E-mailed me. Anything. They were all gloating, all those puffed-up boys in the art department."

Paul listens quietly as she spills out her anger and frustration, and when she is done, he asks, "And your mother? Have you heard from her?"

For a second the questions jar her and her anger rises again. Her back stiffens and she pushes her chair back, widening the distance between them.

"But Anna," he croons, leaning toward her, "in the long run, what does it matter?"

"What does it matter? Would you have liked it if the same thing was done to you? You are the head of surgery in your hospital. Would you have liked it, while you were away, if one of your doctors made a decision on your patient without consulting you?"

"No. I would not have liked it. I would not have liked it because it could be a matter of life and death for my patient."

"And don't you think it could be the same for my writer?"

"Anna, I think you're being a little melodramatic, no?"

Old-fashioned. Why had she not considered the downside of being old-fashioned?

The waiter approaches their table. "I'm not hungry," she says spitefully, and the waiter's face crumbles. He has just finished reciting a list of culinary wonders the chef is famous for. She has not eaten all day; her stomach is growling, but she says, "I'll have the soup and salad."

"That's it?" The waiter stares at her, refusing to believe she has been able to resist his litany of mouth-watering treats.

"That's it," she says.

Paul orders from every category on the menu: appetizer—he chooses smoked salmon; soup—he'll have the hearty lobster bisque; entrée—he selects steak, medium-rare; dessert—chocolate cake à la mode. But when the waiter leaves, he begins an apology of sorts. "Look, Anna," he says, "I'm talking about perspective. I know what happened hurt you a lot, but you'll get to live another day, to have another chance with another writer—perhaps even the same writer—to make things right again. In my profession we don't always get that other chance. A patient may not be alive the next day for me to correct a mistake."

He is right, but he hasn't considered that she may be right too. He doesn't understand. Scientists rarely do. In high schools and colleges, the humanities are expendable. When funding is questionable, courses in literature are among the first to be eliminated from the curriculum. Who took us to the moon? the scientists ask. Certainly not the novelist. Who discovered the human genome, the potential cures for devastating diseases? Administrators in business departments are no less distrustful of the usefulness of made-up stories, their term for novels. How do stories help the economy? they ask. Who invented the Internet? Not the storyteller. And so on and so on they prattle, until humanities courses become an indulgence to be endured on the way to serious studies.

"Books," she says, "have influenced every great movement in history. Even atheists today are shaped by the stories Luke, Mark, and John told." She goes down a list, incomplete she knows, but she wants to make her point. She names Homer, Sophocles, Machiavelli, Shakespeare, Tolstoy, Camus, Sartre. "And where would the civil rights movement have been without the inspiration and prophetic words of Ellison, Baldwin, Hurston, and Wright?" she tells him. "And without de Beauvoir and Audre Lorde, how long would it have taken the women's movement to get off the ground? C.L.R. James gave us stories that helped us in the Caribbean begin to free ourselves from the shackles of colonialism. What our society needs is to be inspired again, to be reminded of the values that have sustained the human race over the centuries. Politicians cannot do that for all their talk of family values. Look where they've got us. Bickering in camps as to who can keep his pants on and who takes them off at the drop of a hat when a pretty girl passes by. It is writers who remind us of our human condition, that we are all in the same predicament together, all banished from Eden, all condemned to die, all flawed creatures who should be tolerant of flaws in others. That we should be our brother's keeper."

She is aware he is listening intently to her. His soup has arrived but he has not touched it.

"Where did you learn this?" he asks.

"Graduate school. I was an English major."

He picks up his soup spoon and twirls it around. For a while he says nothing, his eyes fixed on the movement of the spoon. Then abruptly his hand is still. He looks over at her. "Then, Anna," he says, his voice grave, "you must fight for your writer."

The tension between them dissipates. They are friends again. Their conversation afterward is low-keyed. They do not talk about her troubles at work; he makes no attempt to compare his profession to hers. He seems to be mulling over what she has said to him, but they do not go over that ground again. They talk about her mother, her parents' impending arrival. He says he will come with her to meet them at the airport. He will arrange a car service to bring her mother to the hospital when the surgery is scheduled.

After dinner, he drives her home. He walks with her up the stairs of her building but he does not go in. He kisses her on the mouth. It is a satisfactory kiss, but not a passionate one. He is an old-fashioned man, but even an old-fashioned man would have pressed her to spend the night. Lying in bed alone, she wonders if she might have turned him off with her rage, with her pedantic arguments, thoughts long shuffled to the back of her mind since she handed in the last paper for her final class in graduate school. It has surprised her how much from those days returned to her, and with such force. How now, in the darkness, curled up in bed, her mind's eye recalls the professor who brought her class to misty-eyed silence with his recitation of Hamlet's speech to Rosencrantz and Guildenstern: *What a piece of work is a man! how noble in reason! how infinite in faculty! in form and moving how express and admirable! in action how like an angel! in apprehension how like a god! the beauty of the world! the paragon of animals!*

She chose a career in publishing because she likes books, because she wants to be among writers of books, but where has that gotten her? She edits work by writers who care only for the profit their writing garners, brought out by publishers with their eyes on the bottom line of their ledgers. Bess Milford cannot be compared to the Greats, to the writers who have sustained civilization through times of despair. It would be ludicrous to make such a comparison. But Bess Milford has written a novel that is more than plot driven, more than about an adulterous man getting it on with his sexy mistress. Her novel tells a story, but it also tells the truth about the human condition, about the universality of temptation, about the unending battle between reason and passion, about our proclivities toward the carnal in spite of our best intentions.

FIVE

Paul calls early the next morning. Anna is still in bed but she tells him she has been up more than an hour. It is not exactly a lie; she is awake if not out of her bed. She did not sleep well, her mind sifting through a sequence of images, none of which she can recall now. The sun was not up when she reached for the book on her bedside table, *The Collected Works of Jane Austen*. For years she has turned to Jane Austen when her nights are broken with dreams that trouble her sleep. The world seemed safe in Austen's times, safe and regulated. Families stayed together in the same village, in the same country. Even when children became adults and married, they did not move far away. They did not immigrate to foreign countries unreachable except by long hours on an airplane across miles of ocean. Parents could be counted on. Neighbors could be counted on. No one died alone in city apartments, their bodies left for days, crawling with maggots, until the putrid stench of rotting flesh insinuated itself up the noses of the people who pass by. Women had disadvantages in Austen's world, but in the end there were men with fortunes who married them and promised them good lives.

"What were you doing up so early?" Paul asks.

"Reading," she says.

"Manuscripts for work?"

"Jane Austen. I find her stories soothing."

"I know what you mean," he says, surprising her.

"Mind you, I didn't read Jane Austen on my own. We were made to in school back home. *Pride and Prejudice*, that's the one we studied. I remember thinking it was the British plan to make us passive colonials. Give us their stories, tell us how admirable their people are, and we'd be lulled into forgetting our stories, forgetting our histories, forgetting how they stole our island. All we would want is to be like them."

"Don't spoil Jane Austen for me, Paul," Anna says, swinging her legs out of bed.

"How do you think they built those mansions they lived in? The famous Darcy! How do you think he got so rich? The slave trade. That's how."

"You don't know that."

"What I know is that it's how England got rich."

She has not seen this side of him, and though it irritates her that he has poked holes in her fantasy, she cannot say she hasn't had similar thoughts herself.

"Well, I like Jane Austen."

"Watch it," Paul says, but he is laughing now. She laughs too. Would she have laughed if Tony had criticized her in this way, warned her of the perils of admiring the old colonizers? They have taught you self-hatred, Tony once said to her. But she and Paul share their island's history of negotiation rather than confrontation. Their compatriots may have adopted British customs, but they did not give up their own. They have passed on their stories to their young; they have maintained their rituals, their dance, their art, their music. They are the creators of the only significant musical instrument invented in the twentieth century. Their steel pan is played all over the world, outdoors to the beat of soca and calypso; indoors at stately concert halls, mesmerizing audiences with symphonies by some of the masters: Beethoven, Mozart, Tchaikovsky, Bach.

"I'm careful," she says.

"About last night . . ." His tone has changed. It's softer, warmer. "I meant what I said. I called to wish you good luck. With the book," he clarifies quickly.

She is pleased he hasn't forgotten. "I think I'll stay home today," she says.

"They haven't beaten you down, have they?"

"I need to get the apartment ready for my parents," she says. But she does feel beaten down. She had closed the book long before the telephone rang, Elizabeth Bennet's cool defiance in the face of Darcy's arrogance no longer boosting her confidence. She knows the story will end well: Elizabeth will see her error; Darcy will apologize; together they will ride into the sunset. This morning the happy ending is not enough to raise her spirits. She has been cornered. Paul says she must fight, but it is far too late. The die has been cast; Tanya Foster has made up her mind.

"Good idea," Paul says. "In the final analysis, family is what counts."

Family. Hers is so small she must do her best to preserve it. Grandparents on both sides dead; aunts and uncles in England, cousins she wouldn't recognize if she met them in the street. She must make her parents welcome, do her best to ensure they will be comfortable.

She begins with the den—a second bedroom, the real estate agent claimed when she showed her the apartment. A bedroom fit for a child, she would agree, but Tony has left her, and she is thirty-nine, unlikely to have a child even in the unlikeliest chance she would find someone to marry again. She has made the child's room into an office of sorts, shelves against the wall piled with books and manuscripts for work. A desk more neatly organized: inbox, outbox, a ceramic jar filled with pencils and pens, an electric pencil sharpener, a cordless phone on its base, a monitor on a stand, the computer on the floor next to a printer. Opposite the desk is a folded futon where she sits when she wants to be more comfortable. She has put a pillow and a thick quilt on the futon. Some nights she has fallen asleep there, her head on the pillow, the quilt drawn up to her neck. She opens the futon now. She will sleep here and let her parents have her bedroom.

She spends the day moving books from her bedroom into the den, washing the linens at the laundromat three blocks away, making the beds. She cleans the stove and refrigerator, mops the kitchen floor. The room facing the kitchen, which is painted off-white, serves as both dining room and living room. In the dining room are two chairs and a small table; in the living room, on either side of a glass-topped coffee table, are two brown leather armchairs and a matching leather couch with decorative pillows on either end. Colorful prints and posters on the wall are a perfect balance for the browns and beiges in the apartment. Anna dusts, she vacuums, she polishes. By late afternoon, her apartment is thoroughly clean. Her parents will arrive in six days, but tomorrow she must return to work and she will not have time to prepare her bedroom again, so tonight she will begin sleeping in the den. She makes one final inspection. Her apartment is attractive, better than most she has seen. She was foolish to panic at the thought of her parents staying here. Paula is right: they will be proud of her, or should be. She owns the apartment, and the neighborhood is fashionable. Or becoming fashionable.

At work the next day she calls Bess Milford. She tells her she has good news and bad news. The good news is that the salespeople are excited about her novel. They think it will sell well.

"And the bad news?" Bess Milford asks.

"You may not like the cover," Anna says.

Anna faxes the cover, and, as she predicted, Bess Milford blows up. "I thought writers had input about their covers!" she yells angrily into the phone. It is clear she means to implicate Anna.

Anna reminds her that she signed a contract giving the publisher the rights to market her novel.

"Aren't you the bigwig at Equiano?" Bess Milford sneers. "Do something!"

Anna says she'll try, but she's not sure that whatever she does will make a difference.

"The cover is a lie," Bess Milford says, her voice terse with indignation.

Anna knows her author is right but she also knows her salary is paid by the company that has decided on the cover for the novel. "It's a poster, Bess," she hears herself saying. "It's an ad to draw readers to your novel." Her words fall back on her ears. She is a hypocrite. She is trying to pacify Bess Milford with the very lie Tim Greene thought would mollify her. Anna had resented his patronizing solicitude and can imagine that Bess Milford resents hers too. Yet she does not want to raise her hopes. Tanya Foster makes the final decisions for the company; Anna cannot override her. She tells Bess Milford she will do what she can to change the cover. "Let's see what happens," she says.

Later she busies herself answering e-mails, avoiding contact with Tim. She knows he's in the office. She hears the rustle of papers and the swishing of the wheels of his desk chair, back and forth in the cubicle adjoining her room. Her door is open and the sounds filter in. What work can he be doing? Anna does not know. He is an assistant editor assigned to her but she has not yet given him books to edit.

Tanya calls. She wants to see Anna in her office. She does not say why. Anna hangs up the phone and walks down the corridor.

"Sit, sit." Tanya indicates the chair facing her desk and gets straight to the point. "I've given Raine's books to Tim."

Anna sits down and composes herself. She folds her hands tightly on her lap.

"I thought you'd like that. I know how you feel about Raine's books."

Books like Raine's are not the ones she wants to edit, but books like Raine's are the ones that pay her salary.

"I know you didn't like editing her books," Tanya continues when Anna does not respond.

Anna crosses her legs. "What about B. Benton?"

"I've given B. Benton to Tim also," Tanya says. "Tim has a feel for those books, if you know what I mean."

Anna tells her that she does not know what she means.

"He's African American," Tanya says.

"And?"

"And you are from the Caribbean."

"What difference does that make?"

"Tim understands African American readers. He knows what they want."

"And what is that?" Anna asks.

"I read the bottom line, Anna. That's all. People tell me what they want; I don't ask them what they want. The sales numbers give me all I need to know. Here, here." She rifles through a stack of papers on her desk as if searching for proof, for the report on sales figures.

"You don't have to bother," Anna says. "I read the sales report."

Tanya lays her hand flat on top of the papers and fixes her eyes on Anna. "You're not upset, are you?" She wrinkles her forehead as if perplexed. "Because I thought . . ." Her voice drifts.

Anna is sure she is feigning bewilderment. She decides to ask the question that has troubled her since Tim arrived. "Is Tim Greene to be my assistant editor or yours?"

"We work for the same company, Anna," Tanya says, smoothing back the furrows on her forehead. "There's no yours and mine. There's only what's best for the company."

"For Windsor or for Equiano?"

"Anna, Anna," Tanya coos.

"Equiano is my responsibility," Anna says.

"And I am the publisher of Windsor. Equiano is an imprint of Windsor. I don't think I need to remind you of that, do I?"

"So that is it?"

"You surprise me, Anna. I thought this would be what you'd want."

"I want to publish more literary fiction, but that does not mean—"

"But that does not mean what, Anna? Are you saying you want us to publish more novels like Raine's?"

"I'm aware those books keep us afloat," Anna says.

"More than afloat," Tanya says sternly.

"I'm aware they are profitable." Anna cools down her tone.

"Good, good. Then you understand." Tanya stands up. "If you take your emotions out of this, Anna, you'll see this is a win-win for both of us. Tim knows the territory; he has a feel for the kind of books Raine and Benton write. He'll make money for the company. It will be good for you and for me. I'll have a better bottom line and you will have a better bottom line. Think it over. You'll see how this makes sense." She comes around her desk and places a hand on Anna's shoulder. "Look, I didn't mean to upstage you or usurp your authority or anything like that by speaking to Tim. It's just that I thought it would be better if the assignment came from me. It wasn't easy getting Tim to leave his company for us. I wanted him to know we appreciate having him here."

An apology. Anna is not convinced it is sincere. Even if she suppresses her emotions, the fact remains that twice Tanya has bypassed her and made decisions that should have been hers to make.

"You are still in charge, Anna," Tanya says as if reading Anna's mind. "I've made that clear to Tim. You have to approve the final edits. No manuscript from Equiano goes to the printer without your approval." Her hand remains resting on Anna's shoulder; she squeezes it playfully. "This will be good for you, Anna. You'll have more time to concentrate on what you enjoy. You'll like Tim, you'll see. He'll expand your list. Equiano is going to get even bigger."

Back in her office, Anna e-mails Paula who responds right away. She'll come over to her apartment after work. They'll sort this thing out.

What Paula notices first is Anna's tan. "God, I miss the sun," she says, flopping down on the couch. "Look at you. You're golden brown."

Anna has taken off her workday suit and changed into blue jeans and a white T-shirt. The bright whiteness of the T-shirt is a strong contrast to her sunburnt skin. "And you are warm chocolate," Anna says.

Paula grins. She is already dressed for fall in an olive-green cardigan and matching full skirt which she pulls tightly around her large though shapely thighs. Anna wishes Paula would go on the diet that worked for her, but Paula dismisses the idea. She has one life to live, she says, and she won't deny herself the pleasure of good food. She has been denied other pleasures. She means sex, she means a meaningful relationship with a man, but Anna thinks Paula has given up too soon. Thirty-nine is not old, she tells her. Thirty-nine is ancient in the dating game, Paula responds, and quotes a Harvard study. "A woman my age has less than a 3 percent chance of finding a husband," she says.

Anna does not give up. Paula is a curvy woman. There are men who like curvy women.

"In Africa," Paula says. They both burst out laughing.

"Back home too," Anna says.

Home. They are no longer laughing.

Now Paula surveys the living room. "Everything here is virtually sparkling. The parents?"

"I'm getting ready," Anna says.

"Looks like your mother's house."

"And ten times smaller."

"You have her taste. There's nothing in here she won't love."

It is true; her taste in decorating has not strayed far from her mother's. Her style is conservative and muted, the colors in her living room a palate of earth tones: taupes, deep browns, beiges, off-whites. Even the prints on the wall are understated: watercolors by Jackie Hinkson, her favorite artist, of the sea and the mountains at dawn, fishermen pulling in seines on the beach at the end of the day. There is one exception. It is a painting of La Diablesse by Boscoe Holder, the colors intense, smoldering. But her mother would approve of this one too. She has the original in her living room.

While Anna puts on the kettle for tea, fills a bowl with brown sugar and the creamer with evaporated milk, they talk about her plans to take her mother to the hospital. Paula recommends a car service that she swears by, but Anna says that won't be necessary, since Paul has offered to arrange for a car to bring her mother to the hospital.

"Paul?"

"Dr. Bishop," Anna says, and brings cups, saucers, and cutlery to the cocktail table.

"So he's Paul?"

"The son of a family friend. My father worked closely with his father years ago."

"I like him already. Paul, the male counterpart to my name. You have chosen well, Anna."

"Don't." Anna wags her finger at her friend and returns to the kitchen.

"So I take it this Paul is not simply the doctor who will do your mother's surgery."

"I told you who he is," Anna says. She drops two tea bags in a teapot and fills it with boiling water from the kettle.

"But you didn't tell me he's Paul."

"Black cake." Anna returns with a tray bearing the teapot, a cake, two plates, and two forks.

"Black cake!" Paula is immediately distracted.

"My mother's helper made it. Here, try it." Anna puts a forkful in Paula's mouth.

"My God, it's practically dripping with alcohol."

Lydia, her mother's helper, promised it would be. She had soaked the fruit in rum and cherry brandy for weeks before she folded it into the cake mixture.

For the second time Paula says, "I miss the sun. I miss all this." She takes the fork from Anna's hand and pulls apart another piece of cake. The sounds that come out of her mouth when it reaches her taste buds are sounds of pure, unadulterated pleasure. She sighs. "Why are we here, Anna? Why?"

"Because we are here," Anna responds.

Few immigrants will open the Pandora's box of the whys—why they left behind familiar lands, familiar faces. They ride the waves of nostalgia, hoping they will not last. There is the road ahead; America promises rich rewards if they are patient, if they work hard. It's futile, a waste of precious time, to look back.

"Come, sit next to me," Paula says, and she makes space for Anna on the couch. "Let's hear what happened today at work. Tell me everything."

But Anna takes the armchair. She does not want to be coddled; she does not want Paula to agree with her just because they are friends. She wants her to be objective, to support her because she is right: Tanya Foster will damage Bess Milford's novel with the sexually explicit cover she has approved.

"The guys in the art department think I'm an old fuddy-duddy," she says. "They think I don't know anything about what people want to read. They think their youth gives them special access to the times. But the times are constantly changing, constantly evolving. If you are a slave to the times, you'll always be playing catch up. Styles come and go. What's trendy today is already on its way out, another trend pushing behind it to take its place. But human nature is human nature. That has not changed. All of us are flawed; all of us have the same basic desires, needs, fears. Between birth and death our lives are a constant struggle to stay alive. A novel about our human condition, regardless of the color or ethnicity of the characters, is one that will last."

Paula concentrates on the cake she is eating and listens without interruption. Anna tells her about Rita, whose only desire seems to be to figure out what Tanya wants and give it to her. She says Tanya tried to apologize. "As if she could pacify me. This morning she told me that I'll see. That it will be a win-win situation for both of us." Anna leaves Tim Greene for last, saying simply that he's a new assistant editor assigned to her. He won't take the chance of disagreeing with the publisher of the company who hired him.

"What exactly did he say?" Paula sits forward on the couch.

"He said a book cover is a postcard."

"Did Tanya agree?"

"She informed me that Tim Greene is African American."

"Oh?"

"As if I couldn't see that. More tea?"

Paula nods.

Anna rises and walks toward the kitchen, taking the teapot with her. Almost there, she turns back abruptly. "I haven't told you everything. Tanya has given Raine and Benton's books to Tim Greene. She says I'll have the final approval, but I know she says that just to keep me quiet. Tim Greene will make all the decisions on those books, I'm sure of it."

"That should be okay by you, right?" Paula knows Anna's views on the books Raine and Benton write.

Anna hugs the teapot to her chest. "They are our best sellers," she says.

"But not the books you want to publish."

"Tanya says Tim Greene knows what African American readers want. She says he'll make money for the company."

Paula puts down her plate with the cake. "You understand what she's really saying, don't you, Anna?" she asks gently.

Anna does not turn around from the stove. "I brought back some tamarind balls too. Would you like some?"

"But you must, Anna," Paula insists. "You have to understand that while we may have passports, politicians are not talking about us when they talk about real Americans. We are not on their radar screen. Never forget that, Anna."

The week passes uneventfully, or at least without the major upheavals or confrontations that Anna certainly thought possible when she informs Bess Milford that the final decision on the cover for her novel has been made. Bess says simply, "The more things change . . ."

She does not finish the sentence but Anna knows the ending well: *the more they stay the same.*

The despair in Bess's voice cuts a wound in Anna's heart. Months ago, when Anna called with the good news that Equiano would make an offer for her novel, Bess Milford was beside herself with joy. "This is the best day of my life thanks to you." Anna felt like a fairy godmother then. "Things are different now for writers like me," Bess had said, "because there are black editors in charge like you." And what difference had that made? It's all business, according to Tanya Foster. Race has nothing to do with business; the bottom line alone is what counts.

For the most part, Tim Greene stays out of her way. Anna continues to hear noises drifting out of his cubicle: papers shuffling back and forth, the thud of something larger hitting the floor, the computer keyboard tapping furiously, sometimes low murmurings when he speaks on the phone, sometimes outright laughter. Once or twice he pops his head into her office to apologize. "Sorry, boss," he says. "Old friend with a joke not fit for ladies' ears."

He continues to address her as boss: Boss, I'm going out for lunch. Can I get you anything? Boss, let me take that for you, as he reaches for a stack of manuscript papers she is carrying. Boss, nice morning! Never does he ask her a question about work, not a word about the books assigned to him. He never mentions Raine, he never mentions Benton. Magically, overnight—for Anna is sure it was at night, when she had left the office—their manuscripts disappeared from her shelves. She had almost finished editing Raine's manuscript and is sure Tim Greene has seen her blue pencil markings. Either he disagrees with the changes she recommends, or he means to ignore her opinion completely. But he is always polite to her; always greets her with a smile. When she says, "You don't have to call me boss," he smiles coyly and replies, "But you are my boss, boss."

He continues to wear suits to work. Sometimes he wears a sports jacket, but whatever he wears is always in style, from the fashion pages of *GQ* magazine. He changes the color of his shirts from one day to the next—white, then pale yellow, blue, and pink. Always they are carefully matched with designer ties.

Anna spots him one day having lunch in a café with a man equally decked out in sartorial splendor. They are sitting next to the window. She is walking down the street to a nearby deli. He is looking in her direction. She waves, but he does not wave back.

"Gay," Paula speculates, but Anna saw when he touched his friend's arm that he was not looking in her direction at all. He was looking at a young woman, half her age, strutting across the street. She was wearing a tight-fitting sweater and a miniskirt. Her four-inch spike-heeled black boots reached up to her thighs.

A couple of days later Anna sees him again with the same man, and again Tim Greene does not notice her when she passes by. This time he and the man are huddled over a stack of papers, what seems to her like a manuscript.

The receptionist on the ground floor of the building tells Anna that Tim Greene is the last to leave the office. He says twice that week Tim Greene left the building as late as ten o'clock.

"Watch out for that one," Paula says to Anna.

SIX

Anna has more pressing matters on her mind. Her parents will arrive on Sunday. On Monday, she must take her mother to the hospital for her pre-op tests. Paul Bishop has arranged with Dr. Ramdoolal to have most of the tests done on the island and the results faxed to him, but the hospital in New Jersey wants additional blood work and cardiology exams. For insurance purposes, Paul explains to Anna. He has full confidence in the accuracy of the tests Dr. Ramdoolal has sent to him—but patients sue, occasionally without cause. He has some influence in the hospital, he says modestly. He is the head of the surgery unit. He can get the results of the pre-op tests almost immediately, and, if all goes well, her mother can have surgery as early as Tuesday morning.

Tanya is sympathetic, more than sympathetic, when Anna asks for two days leave while her mother is in the hospital. "This is the age of the Internet," she says to Anna. "You don't need to take time off. You can work from home. E-mail me, use the fax. I can reach you on your cell when you're not at home."

Anna has stocked her kitchen with the food she thinks her parents will like. For breakfast she has bought salted codfish, smoked herring, and sardines, food her stomach can no longer tolerate in the morning. On Friday she goes to the West Indian market in the Flatbush section of Brooklyn. There she buys ground provisions, the vegetables grown under the earth that her father likes, *blue food* he calls them: dasheen, edoes, yams, sweet potatoes—not the yellow American kind of sweet potatoes, but the whitish ones with bluish streaks running through them. She buys calalloo leaves, fresh pigeon peas, pumpkin imported from Puerto Rico, and grated coconut for the pelau Paula will remind her how to cook. She buys tropical fruits: mangoes, sapodillas, pomme cythères, pommeracs. For dessert she gets tamarind balls, sugar cakes, coconut fudge, coconut ice cream.

It surprises her how so many of the foods and sweets they eat on the island are readily available in Brooklyn. She would not have known if Paula had not directed her to the West Indian shops. There are parts of Brooklyn, Paula says, where except for winter and those gloomy brownstones you would not know you've left the islands.

"People live the same way they lived back home," she explains to Anna. "They eat the same foods, play the same music, dance to the same beats. They raise their children the same way and send them home for the summer vacation so customs and traditions will get passed to the next generation."

"What's the point?" Anna asks. "They are not going back and this is their children's country."

"I plan to go back when I retire," Paula says.

"You might as well assimilate in the meanwhile. Life will be easier for you. You'll find all the foods Americans eat in your supermarket. You won't have to make the trek to Flatbush."

"Assimilation is a pipe dream," Paula says.

Anna does not reply that the pipe dream is planning to return home when you retire. The statistics are there for Paula to read. Of the few who go back home, many return to the States when they discover that time has marched on: the place they returned to is not the place of their dreams.

"America is a salad bowl," Paula says when Anna does not respond. "It's not a melting pot as the politicians want us to believe. A tomato is still a tomato in the salad bowl. And who'd want to melt anyhow? You'd lose your identity if you melt."

"You'd become an American," Anna counters.

"Impossible! I'd know one of us no matter how long we had lived in this country. I can tell just by the way we walk and talk. All that hand gesturing, the sing-song accents."

"But not our children. They won't speak with our accents and they'll walk like John Wayne," Anna says.

Paula slaps the side of her thigh and bends over laughing. "John Wayne? You can't be serious, Anna! Who'd want to walk like John Wayne?"

"If you and I had children . . ." Anna pauses. They are both childless but they are not menopausal. Perhaps there is still time. She starts again. "The children of people like you and me walk as if they have the right to be, the right to exist. They have ingested America's ideas about freedom and individuality."

"They swagger as if they own the world," Paula says.

It is a criticism Anna is familiar with; she has heard it many times before. "Still," she responds, "I like the freedoms Americans take for granted. I like the way they believe in the sanctity of the individual."

"Sanctity? Are we talking about religion here?"

"I mean the fact that the individual has inalienable rights."

"The right to pursue individual happiness even when that pursuit is damaging to the community?"

They have reached their usual impasse, Paula not budging on her conviction that the rights of the community must have priority over the rights of the individual. Anna accuses her of advocating socialism. "Even the communists know that while socialism may be a good idea in theory, in practice it does not work," Anna says. "The Berlin Wall fell; the Soviet states have disintegrated."

But Paula responds that it is the "me, me, and me alone" generation that is eroding family values.

"I like having the freedom to be me," Anna says. "I like having the right to pursue my happiness. That's what I want for myself."

"Well, you don't have to stop eating Caribbean food to want that," Paula answers irritably.

But Anna has not stopped eating Caribbean food. Not entirely. She has simply expanded her tastes. For her parents, she will keep a Caribbean kitchen. While they are here, she will cook Caribbean food.

On Saturday Paul Bishop calls. He thinks it will be better if her mother comes directly to New Jersey from the airport. He can arrange for her to stay in one of the apartments the hospital keeps for out-of-town families. She and her father may stay there too, of course. From there they can easily get to the hospital for her mother's pre-op tests on Monday, and he'll send one of the nurses to accompany them to the hospital on Tuesday. Tomorrow he will take her to the airport to meet her parents, and, if she agrees, he will drive them directly to the apartment in New Jersey.

Anna is overwhelmed by his kindness. The arrangement he proposes is perfect, more than perfect. Her parents will be extremely grateful to him, she says. She will never be able to repay him for being so kind to them.

"I don't know about that," he says jokingly.

Her heart flutters. She reminds herself that the kiss he gave her on her lips was a chaste one. She should not read more into his words than light banter. "Oh, is there a fee?" she asks, her tone as light as his.

"Time will tell," he replies enigmatically.

He arrives the next day at the time they agreed upon. He is dressed in a light beige knit polo shirt tucked at the waist in tan slacks. He looks relaxed, happy to see her. He kisses her on the left cheek, the right cheek, and then on her mouth. The kiss on her mouth lingers. Suddenly shy, she backs away; he does not try to hold her.

She is already packed, ready to go: two changes of clothing, her laptop, her notebook, the final chapters of a manuscript she is editing. She has prepared a fruit basket to welcome her parents, with apples and grapes and the tropical fruit she bought at the West Indian market. She has added a package of Crix biscuits, a jar of orange marmalade, a box of Lipton tea bags, and a can of Carnation milk. Her parents will want tea in the afternoon, as is their custom. She will serve them tea with the biscuits and marmalade at four. She adds bread and butter and two tins of sardines, breakfast for her father. Paul has told her that there will be no need for her to make dinner. "Breakfast or lunch, for that matter," he says. "The hospital has a great cafeteria." But she will stick to her plans.

Paul helps her carry the basket and her luggage to the car. His fingers are on the handle of the car door when he hesitates, turns, and pulls her to him. He kisses her again on her lips. This time she does not back away. "You look lovely in red," he whispers in her ear. She has dressed for her mother in her favorite red sweater and black pants, but she is glad he likes her outfit. If he thinks red looks good on her, then her mother will think so too.

On the drive to the airport Paul reassures her that her mother has a very good chance of remission after the surgery. Estrogen feeds most breast cancers, he says, but her mother's body has long since stopped producing the level for a woman of childbearing age. He admits the tumor in her lymph node under her arm is worrisome, but he believes it will be contained.

"Is your mother a praying woman?" he asks.

Anna tells him that her mother is devoted to the Virgin Mary. She prays the rosary several times a day.

"That's good," he says. "My patients who pray recover faster. Praying gives them hope, a positive attitude that helps them heal. The ones who don't pray often sink into despair."

But for more than two years, locked up in the darkness of her bathroom, her mother prayed to the Virgin Mary. Still, the tumors kept on getting bigger and bigger until the one on her breast erupted and bled.

"Mummy might have gone to the doctor earlier if she had not relied so exclusively on prayer," she says.

"Yes," Paul concedes. "That's the other side. Sometimes religion gives them false hope."

"So much false hope that they wait too long to see a doctor," Anna says wryly.

"You mustn't blame her. Your mother was afraid."

Anna is afraid too. Her mother's mother died of breast cancer; and now her mother has breast cancer. The arrow is pointing directly to her.

"What about you?" Anna asks. "Are you a praying man?"

"Me? I'm a believer in a general sense. I suppose you could say I am spiritual rather than religious. I believe there is a power, some entity greater than us that rules the earth. It keeps the planets from colliding into each other; it keeps us from destroying each other."

"It doesn't stop wars," Anna says.

"I believe in cosmic justice. Do evil and it will come back to you."

"*Evil on itself shall back recoil, and mix no more with goodness.*"

"Something like that."

"John Milton," she says. "A poet. He wrote that."

"Hmmm." He is looking straight ahead at the road before him. Then, as if her words have finally penetrated his mind, he says, "The power of books. Yes?"

"Of good literature."

"Milton was a smart man."

"A brilliant poet."

"I see what you mean," he says. He turns briefly to her, smiles, and then his eyes go back to the road. "He's right, Milton. If somehow you escape paying for the evil you do, your children will surely pay, and if not them, your grandchildren, and so on. I believe that."

"Me too."

"Are you religious?"

"I do not disbelieve," she says

He grins and plays with her words on his tongue. "I *do not disbelieve*," he murmurs. "The double negative." They speak no more about religion or their beliefs.

Her mother is wheeled through the gate at the airport. She sits with her back erect in the wheelchair, her head held high, a proud brown-skinned woman cognizant of her worth, seemingly unaware she is in a country where white skin has more value than hers. Her father lags behind the agent who pushes his wife up the ramp. From where she stands waiting for them, Anna sees her mother beckon her father. He comes to her, she whispers something to him, and he reaches for his wallet. The agent shakes her head, her mother says something to her, the agent shakes her head again. She has probably offered the agent money, Anna thinks. Her mother is a woman accustomed to paying for service: for Lydia who cooks and cleans for her; for the woman who comes once a week to iron her clothes; for Singh who tends her flowerbeds; for the boys who mow the lawn and weed; for a driver when her husband is unavailable to take her to appointments. Her father tries to take the handles of the wheelchair from the agent and when she does not allow him, her mother smiles graciously at her and gets out of the wheelchair. She places her hand on her husband's arm and walks toward them. But she does not need her husband to support her; her gait is strong, steady.

For a woman inside whose left breast and under whose arm malignant tumors throb, she appears to be in remarkably good health. Her skin is silky smooth, unlike the skin of so many women her age who live in temperate climates where heat flowing out of ducts beneath the floor sucks moisture from everything, leaving faces pinched and parched, wrinkled like prunes. At seventy-two Beatrice Sinclair could well pass for a woman of sixty or younger. Her head, bald from weeks of chemo, is covered with a soft navy-blue fleece hat. In the absence of hair, her deep-set eyes and prominent cheekbones are more pronounced. Around her neck she has loosely tied a silk Hermès scarf. Anna recognizes it as the one her father bought for her mother on their last visit to Paris. In all, her mother has three Hermès scarves. This one has a pattern of gold and brown horseshoes scattered across a navy background. The color matches the brass-buttoned navy cardigan and navy slacks she is wearing, and the crisp white shirt beneath the cardigan makes a stunning contrast, brightening her complexion.

Where has her mother learned to dress so appropriately for the fall? She should not be surprised. Her mother has traveled often with her husband to the States and Europe. In spite of herself, Anna feels proud she has such a stylish mother.

Paul thinks her mother is stylish too. "You look wonderful, Mrs. Sinclair," he says, and shakes her hand. "You are such an elegant lady."

Her mother flashes him a wide smile. "Thank you. I feel wonderful. I don't know why they insisted on making me sit on that wheelchair. Dr. Ramdoolal must have said something to the ticket agent. But, as you can see, I didn't need it."

Anna comes closer and brushes her lips across her mother's cheek. It is the only embrace she gives her. Her mother does not expect more. But her father reaches for her. He wraps his arms around her and draws her to his chest. Anna has to hold back tears that begin to well in her eyes when he whispers in her ear, "Thank you."

"And you too, Mr. Sinclair," Paul says. "You look like a million dollars."

Her mother has probably dressed him. Her father would not have picked out the fawn-brown sports jacket or the light beige scarf around his neck. He is not a man who cares about fashion. He would wear the same clothes forever if his wife didn't stop him. If his clothes are not dirty, he sees no need to change them, he tells her. Every day Beatrice must remind him that in the hot sun he gets damp and sticky. He smells. And yet John Sinclair is a meticulously neat man. In his closet shirts are lined up by color, pants hung the same way. His socks are balled in a neat pile in his drawer next to his handkerchiefs which he carefully folds, though occasionally they are sticky with the peppermint sweets he eats, sometimes as many as ten a day, throwing the transparent wrappers all over the lawn even when there is a dustbin nearby. It is a habit that infuriates his wife, the one idiosyncrasy that belies his neatness.

He looks tired, drawn, Anna thinks, the circles under his eyes darker than she remembers. The skin on his face is slack, his long nose more beaked. He has already lost most of his hair and now her mother has lost hers too. No strands peek out from under her hat, not even wisps and tufts left after her last chemo treatment, but without hair her mother's features are stronger, more defined. Her father's bald head, circled at the base with a sparse scattering of gray hair, is the head of an old man.

He had not seemed this old when she left the island, and guilt stabs Anna's heart. *She should not have left so soon.*

"It was a long trip," her father says. "Your mother slept on the plane, but I couldn't find a way to get comfortable."

Perhaps that was all, the tight seating in the plane that made it impossible for him to relax. But they have traveled in first class, where the seats are wide and comfortable.

Anna tells him about the apartment Paul has arranged for them. They are relieved, grateful to learn they will be staying on the hospital grounds. Her mother says she was worried about how they would get from Brooklyn to New Jersey. John Sinclair places his hand on Paul's shoulder. "Your father raised a good son," he says.

The apartment is small but tastefully decorated. There are two rooms, a bedroom in the back and an open space in front with a kitchenette, a small table and four chairs, an armchair, and a couch. The couch opens up into a narrow bed and Anna tells her parents she will be more than comfortable sleeping there; they can have the bedroom. Her parents do not protest. In more than forty years of marriage, they can count on their fingers the number of nights they have not slept together on the same bed.

Paul reviews the list of pre-op tests Beatrice will have to take the next day. John Sinclair says he will go with his wife and stay with her until all the tests are done. Anna says she will stay with them too.

When Paul leaves, John Sinclair tells Anna it won't be necessary for her to accompany them. They'll be fine, he says. He has noticed her laptop and the manuscript pages she put on the table. "Stay here and do your work. Your mother and I can manage."

Beatrice Sinclair waves away Anna's objections. "It's settled," she says. Anna can walk with them to the hospital in the morning, but she should return to the apartment to do her work. "You have an important job. Head of a publishing company."

"Head of an imprint in a publishing company." Anna is quick to correct her.

Later, just as she is about to turn in for the night, her mother remarks that Paul seems taken with her. "He admires you," she says to Anna. "I think things will work out between you two."

"He's doing this for you," Anna says. "Because Daddy was so good to his father."

Her mother does not try to dissuade her. "If you say so," she responds, but there is no conviction in her voice. As Anna turns to leave, she stops her. "You looked lovely today in that red sweater, Anna. Red suits you, so becoming for you." And blood rushes to Anna's face.

SEVEN

True to his word, her father manages. Anna leaves her parents at the department where her mother will have the first of her pre-op tests. The nurse tells Anna her mother should be ready to return to the apartment around three. She will call her when the tests are done. Anna tells her father she will collect them in time for tea together at the apartment. "At four," her father says and winks at her. He is a stickler for punctuality, for the routines that mark the passing of his day: breakfast at seven-thirty; lunch at twelve-thirty; tea at four; dinner at six. At night he crosses off another day on the calendar he keeps in the drawer of his bedside table. He quotes Yeats. "*An aged man is but a paltry thing*. I shall sail to Byzantium," he says.

Her mother does not approve. She tells him he is too morbid. "You have life now, and the promise of eternal life with God and the angels afterward."

"I want eternal life here," he says.

"Think of the promise."

Now it is she who is facing the possibility of the imminent fulfillment of that promise.

"Oh, your mother can't have anything to eat," the nurse says to Anna. "Surgery tomorrow."

Surgery tomorrow, but today Anna knows she must focus on work. Tanya Foster has been patient, but soon her patience will grow thin. She had already given her an extension on her vacation, two more weeks that allowed her to be with her mother until she had her last chemo treatment, but she cannot expect Tanya Foster to be as generous after her mother's surgery.

At the apartment she opens her laptop and logs on. An e-mail from Tim Greene is waiting for her. It begins with a long preamble. He wishes her well. His prayers are with her that her mother's surgery will be successful. He knows it will be, because the mother of his good friend was in a similar situation and she survived; now she is in total remission. He gives more details about the friend, about the mother. Blah, blah, blah . . . Anna skims through the lines. Her eyes catch the name *Raine*. She stops and goes back. He has finished the edits of Raine's new novel and will meet with the author later in the afternoon. He has a few ideas on how Raine can make the novel more marketable. He makes no mention of Anna's notes, her edits on the novel. He does not ask for her opinion. *I have some thoughts on how we can make the novel a big seller*, he writes.

Is that all that is needed? All that has to be done is to make the novel marketable, make it a best seller, and to hell with making it a better book? Anna reaches for the phone and begins punching the numbers for Equiano but before she gets to the last one, she presses the off button. What's the use? she thinks. He has already been given the authority. Raine has been assigned to him. It is obvious he does not intend to consult her.

There is more in the e-mail. She reads the last lines: *Of course, you will have the final word. I'll be sure to let Raine know that.*

The final word about what? About how to make the sex scenes steamier? About how to make the women more alluring? Bigger breasts here, firmer legs there? About how to make the men sexier? Rippled pecs there, stronger thighs here, organs bursting out of skin-tight pants? A man rips off the bodice of a ludicrously curvy woman. He slits her skirt and exposes a thong barely covering the triangle of her private parts. The story is predictable: the woman struggles, but yields eventually. For the man is really a good man who is plagued by the demons of a deprived past. The woman is really a good woman; she will help him overcome his past. Together they will ride into the sunset. All the characters are stock figures mined from the erotic dreams of lonely women. They are beautiful, they are sexy, and if they are not rich at the beginning of the story, they will be at the end. And is that not the point? Is that not what lonely women want to read, curled up in empty beds with only the comfort of vicarious pleasures? For black women the statistics are grimmer than those the researchers at Harvard report. White women have until forty, but the axe falls on black women barely out of their twenties.

Is that what Tony wanted her to understand when he told her she was lucky? "Look around you. How many black women do you see who have a man?" he said to her, his lips curled in disdain. "How many have a husband?"

Did he expect her to stay silent and do nothing while he cavorted with his mistress? Paula had warned her when she said yes to Tony. "He is an American," Paula said. "You are entering territory you know little about." But Anna believed she knew all she needed to know. American men are monogamous; American men are happy to grow old with the woman they married. Before cable TV would expose this lie, such were the stories from America that her newly independent island aired on TV and showed in the movies. A well-ordered family is a mirror to a well-ordered government; one woman for one man and it follows, like day follows night, one nation under one God. That seemed the philosophy fueling the prevalence of these fairy tales.

Anna was a child. Rationally, as an adult, she knew those stories of monogamy in America were false, but such is the power of lies imprinted on an impressionable young mind. They become myth, a sort of truth. An American husband would be faithful, and when her father betrayed her mother, she made up her mind she would not marry a Caribbean man; an American man would have kept his vows.

Her father loved his wife, yet he had a mistress, fell in love with another woman. Her name was Thelma. That was what he said to Anna the day his traitor's gift rolled off her mother's skeletal arms. It was a diamond-studded bracelet he had given her mother for her birthday, not seeming to notice the veins that rose on her arms like hard wires or the two knots protruding at the top of her breast bone, or that her cheekbones had become scaffolding for her slackened flesh and her eyes were sunk in pools ringed with black circles. He was in love and that was all that mattered.

When her mother had enough, she fought for him and won him back. He was remorseful; she was forgiving. Now he is an attentive husband, a loving husband. While his wife undergoes the pre-op tests for the mastectomy the doctor will perform on her left breast tomorrow, he waits for her in the lobby of the hospital. He is anxious, he is nervous, he is afraid. He does not want to lose the wife he has loved for more than forty years. *Loves*, he says now to Anna, emphasizing the tense. Loves as he had always loved her, will love her until the end of time.

"My father was the last person in the world I expected to cheat on his wife," Anna once said to Paula. "All that talk he gave me when I was growing up about integrity and character. And yet he couldn't keep the vow he made to his wife before the church and the law. He expected me to empathize with him because he was unhappy, because in spite of years of happiness with my mother, he could not manage one brief spell of unhappiness. He could have turned to her; they could have worked out their problem together—whatever it was—but no, it was easier to get sympathy from a woman who had never lived with him, who had no idea what it was like to live with his flaws. Like a child, he laid his head on the breast of another woman instead of facing his problems."

"You're too hard on your father," Paula had responded.

"I've forgiven him."

"It doesn't seem that way."

"I just haven't forgotten. I won't make the same mistake my mother made."

"And what is that?"

"Marry a Caribbean man."

"American men are no better," Paula said.

"At least they believe in monogamy."

"Serial monogamy," Paula said. "They marry, divorce, marry again, divorce again."

Tony is marrying again. An affair was the reason their marriage ended in divorce. He did not deny the affair; he did not apologize. He was unhappy, he said. Unhappy as her father claimed he was unhappy. But her father apologized. He did not leave her mother. Now her father does all he can to convince his wife of his remorse, to prove to her his undying love and devotion.

Tanya gave Tim Greene the manuscripts from Raine and B. Benton but she has not taken the others Anna acquired. By two-thirty Anna finishes the edits on one of them. It's a story about a black surgeon in Georgia who saves the life of the wife of a prominent white official in the Jim Crow

South when black doctors were not allowed to touch white women, even in an emergency. Anna is proud that she will be publishing this novel. She believes publishers should be the guardians of our culture and history. The novel about the black surgeon in the Jim Crow South is not one of those mindless books that Tanya Foster seems to think black readers yearn to read. It is a good book. It fills the missing pages of a history yet to be fully unearthed. Anna believes that if this novel is made available, there will be readers for it. *If you build it, they will come.* A line from a movie. It is her credo too.

She e-mails her notes to the writer, turns off her computer, and goes to the kitchen to prepare tea for her parents. She finds cutlery, cups, saucers, and plates in the kitchen cupboard. They are clean, neatly stacked on the shelf, but she washes them, conscious as she squeezes liquid soap onto the dish cloth how she is not unlike her mother. Lydia cleans the house, but Beatrice inspects with a duster in her hand. From the basket she brought with her Anna takes out the package of Crix biscuits, the marmalade, the box of tea, the Carnation milk, and the sugar. She places them on the table. Her mother can have the tea with them but not the biscuits. She makes a place for her mother between her father and herself. She has fifteen more minutes before she leaves for the hospital. She flicks open her laptop again and logs on. There's an e-mail from Bess Milford: *You don't mean to just give up. I hate the cover. I HATE, HATE, HATE IT. It's insulting to me.*

She cannot deny that Bess Milford is right. The cover is insulting not only to her but to every black writer who thinks of himself or herself as a writer who is black and not merely as a black writer. Anna e-mails a response: *I will do what I can.*

She closes the laptop and reaches for her jacket.

Through the window she sees her parents. Her mother's tests must have finished earlier than expected, as they have decided not to wait for her to accompany them back to the apartment. They are walking arm in arm, close to each other. Her mother's head is resting on her father's shoulder. Anna cannot recall ever having seen them display such intimacy in public before. They are private people, people who subscribe to the conviction that character is built on a person's ability to control their private thoughts, their private feelings. They believe excessive displays of emotions are character flaws. Nobody likes you to bleed all over them, Anna's mother once said to her. She was only eight years old. *Keep your skeletons in the closet. Wash your dirty linen in private.* So Beatrice Sinclair did not tell her husband that tumors were growing in her breast and under her arm, and even when they bled on her husband's vest that she wore to bed, she kept her silence—though by then she knew he knew. Her husband too would wait until she gave him permission before admitting what he knew.

> *Give thy thoughts no tongue,*
> *Nor any unproportioned thought his act.*
> *Be thou familiar but by no means vulgar.*

Vulgar was the word her mother used to express her disapproval of couples who embrace in public. Now there she is, leaning heavily against her husband, embracing him in the open where everyone can see.

Is it age that has softened them? Fear that there may not be much more time left for them, time for proprieties now seeming foolish, inconsequential, given the brevity of life? Days and hours count for them now; they cannot waste them.

A sudden wind sweeps through the trees. The leaves shudder and turn on their backs; some flutter to the ground. Fall will not be far away. Her father pulls her mother closer to him. Perhaps she should not have tried so hard to persuade her mother to come to this strange, cold land, Anna finds herself thinking. Perhaps in spite of the inadequate hospitals on the island, the services that can be erratic at best, it would have been better for her mother to have surgery there. Perhaps on the island with her mind more at ease, comfortable in familiar surroundings, her mother would have a better chance for recovery.

Anna grabs her jacket and a coat she has brought for her mother. It was warmer when they left early that morning, and her mother had refused to put on the coat. "I'll look like an old lady in that thing," she said.

Had she looked like an old lady in that thing when she wore it two seasons ago? Anna wonders. Is that why Tony felt justified in walking out on her? "You've changed," he had said. "You used to be so . . ." He did not need to finish the sentence. She used to be so stylish. She used to laugh. But it's hard to be stylish or to laugh when in the third year of your marriage your husband loses his job, when your income spirals down and you can no longer keep up with the payments for the expensive condo your husband bought, or the Benz he liked to drive. She had to work harder, to earn her way up the corporate ladder. And didn't she win the prize with her position at Equiano? She pooh-pooh'd Paula when she waved the flag of a vice presidency before her, yet it was exhilarating for a brief second to entertain the possibility. But Tony left her for someone younger, someone prettier, and in the end, he blamed her.

She runs out to meet her parents, the coat bundled in her arms. Her mother raises her head when she sees her and slips her arm out of the crook of her husband's elbow.

Her father quickens his pace. "We didn't want to disturb you," he says as he reaches her. "You needn't have come. It's short walk."

Her mother makes burring sounds with her lips. "My God, it's freezing," she says.

It is not freezing. The weather has turned, but for the beginning of fall it is still a relatively warm day. Anna wraps the coat around her mother's shoulders and buttons it at the top.

Her mother continues to blow her lips. "I don't know how you can stand it, Anna." She clutches the collar of the coat and brings the ends together at her neck.

An old bitterness threatens Anna's determination to be the good daughter. *How can she stand it?* Soon it will get cooler and then cold. When the temperature drops lower, water pooled in crevices will freeze, icicles will hang down from the tops of buildings. People will slip and slide, some will break bones. The wonderland of white snow will turn to filthy slush when cars drive by and trucks trundle through the streets. Trees will be stripped of their leaves, left naked, their limbs exposed. Everywhere brown will replace green. Days will be shorter. It will be dark in the mornings when she leaves for work, dark when she returns. *How can she stand it?* How can she turn her back on warm days, on sunshine all year round, on green trees? How can she bear the layers of clothing that weigh her down? Her mother had never asked. Not once.

But her mother is ill; tomorrow she will have surgery. Anna bites her lip and releases it. "It's not so bad," she says. "It's beautiful when it snows."

Inside the apartment she prepares the tea. Her mother

observes her every move. "It's good to see you haven't lost our customs, Anna," she says.

Tea at four is not their custom, at least not their custom originally. It is a legacy of colonial rule, so precious to the British they made addicts of a country. Two wars, spanning more than twenty years, in 1839 and again in 1856, because the British discovered that if the Chinese became addicts, they could keep their silver and get the tea for free. So they went to war with China and forced her to open her ports and import the resins from the poppy seeds they grew in India, one of their colonial outposts.

The addiction of a country because the British liked the custom of four o'clock tea. It has become a custom too on the English-speaking islands.

Anna pours tea in a cup for her mother and adds evaporated milk, Carnation, the brand she likes. She serves her father the Crix biscuits and orange marmalade. Her mother is impressed. "Where did you find the Crix?" she asks.

Anna tells her about the West Indian markets. "It's how immigrants can stand it," she says, still bristling from her mother's words.

Her mother raises her cup to her lips, stops, and brings it down again. She turns to Anna. "I was wrong about America," she says. "The Americans were all very nice to me. All the nurses, all the doctors, they were very kind."

EIGHT

Her mother had doubts before. Before she came to the States, she believed what she saw on the American TV channels beamed to the island and she was afraid. She had seen black people handcuffed by the police, black people on drugs, black people screaming in rage and horror when an innocent man was shot down. Forty-one bullets aimed at twenty-three-year-old Amadou Diallo when he reached into his pocket and pulled out his wallet. It was dark; the NYPD believed he had taken out a gun. Nineteen bullets entered his body. Beatrice Sinclair did not want to come to a country where her color would define her, where the density of her melanin would determine the treatment she would receive. She is here because she loves her husband, because Dr. Ramdoolal has convinced him that in the States his wife will have a good chance for recovery, because Dr. Paul Bishop, a son of the soil, offered to be her surgeon. So it is with a measure of awe and disbelief that later that night she relates to Anna what transpired in the hospital that morning. Some of the nurses were Latino, some were black, but both the lab technician and the nurse who treated her were white. "They were caring," she says. "They knew I was afraid and they put me at ease."

This is no time for Anna to say to her mother that the story of America is complicated; America is a work in progress. There are black people who own mansions, who are heads of large corporations, who are highly respected professionals in every field. The richest and most powerful person on TV in America is a black woman; the most powerful person in the government is a black woman. Americans are the most generous people in the world. If there is a catastrophe anywhere in the world, the victims can count on the kindness of Americans. Ordinary citizens give millions within hours. The government sends money, supplies, manpower. And yet America has supported some of the world's most vicious regimes, the world's worst dictators. And yet in America there are places where black people are corralled in drug-infested ghettos. It is not the time to say America is both selfless and self-serving. Her mother has seen the better side. And perhaps that is enough. She does not need to know more.

"So considerate," her mother says. "I could not wish for better."

In the morning she is ready, so confident and upbeat that though Paul Bishop has asked an attendant to bring her by wheelchair from the apartment to the hospital, she insists on walking. She is not afraid now. She has prayed the three mysteries of the Rosary—the Joyful, the Sorrowful, the Glorious. "We do not always understand God's way," she tells Anna, "but no doubt the universe is unfolding as it should." The Desiderata. Her mother has a framed needlepoint copy of the prayer on her wall.

Paul Bishop is also confident. While her mother is being prepared for surgery, he speaks to Anna and her father. He has done this surgery hundreds of times before. Beatrice Sinclair is a strong woman; she will pull through fantastically, he promises. The chemo she was given in the previous weeks has worked; her tumors have shrunk considerably. In the presence of Anna's father, Paul Bishop is all professional, but he speaks like a friend too. He says to Mr. Sinclair that he will care for Mrs. Sinclair as if she were his mother. If Mr. Sinclair wants, he can arrange for him to spend the night in the room with his wife.

John Sinclair is grateful; he wants to be in the same room with his wife.

Paul Bishop takes Anna aside. He'll be free in the evening, he says. Perhaps they can have dinner together.

The surgery is successful. Two hours after her mother is wheeled to her room, they are given permission to see her. Her head is propped up on white pillows, her body covered with white sheets that reach to her neck. Surrounded by all that white, her mother's brown face shines as if bathed in a sort of celestial light. She is bald, there is not a trace of makeup on her face, her skin is slack, the muscles still loose after hours of sedation, but to Anna her mother seems more beautiful than she can remember.

"Mummy," she whispers. Their eyes meet. Anna wants to say more. She wants to say: I was so afraid. I was so worried. I am so glad, so relieved this is over. The words do not come. Years of restraint between them stifle her impulse to show affection, to tell her mother how much she loves her. She cannot, she does not know how to breach this barrier. She smiles; her mother returns her smile, and then her eyes drift away. She is searching for her husband. He is already next to her, holding her hand. Her mother feels his touch and turns her head toward him. John Sinclair steps closer to his wife.

"John," she whispers, "it wasn't so bad."

He repeats what he said to her when she confessed her most personal fear. She would be deformed if she has a mastectomy, she said then; he may be repelled by the scar on her chest. Now, in a voice loud enough for Anna to hear and for the nurse and the male attendant in the room to hear, he says: "From now on, Beatrice, you and I will have our showers together."

In the evening at dinner with Paul, Anna is withdrawn. She gives one-word responses to most of what Paul says to her. When he explains that though it is too early to tell, he has seen little evidence that her mother's cancer has metastasized, she responds, "Good." When he gives her the prognosis for her mother's recovery, she murmurs, "Hmm." He says her mother will probably live to be ninety and Anna replies, "She prays." She moves her food around her plate with her fork and puts little of it in her mouth. He asks if she would rather order something else, and she says, "It's fine. Really." He does not believe her. He takes her hand in his. "What is it?" he asks.

She does not know herself. She does not understand why her mood has sunk so low. She was looking forward to dinner with him; she wanted to celebrate the day that has turned out so well for all of them. Her mother's surgery was successful; she could live for many more years. Her father is happy for his wife, elated he can spend the night with her. His wife is happy her tumors are gone, happy she will not be alone tonight. Their daughter is happy for them, happy too to be with a man she is growing to like, a man who has been kind to her parents, who has removed the tumor from her mother's breast and the one in her lymph node. And yet she cannot shake off the gloom that has settled over her, the dark cloud that has enshrouded her.

"Is it your job? Are you worried about your writer, what's her name?" Paul asks.

"Bess Milford," she says. She has not forgotten Bess

Milford. The unspoken accusation still rings in her ear. She has let her down; she has let down all the Bess Milfords of the world. Bess Milford expected more of her. A black editor should have brought a different sensibility to her work, should have known the importance of publishing a novel like hers, and should have insisted. But she is not thinking of Bess Milford now.

"It couldn't be her that has you so gloomy, could it?" Paul Bishop withdraws his hand.

"No," she says quickly. "It's not about my job." She puts down her fork.

"Is it the chicken?" He is looking at her plate. She has barely touched her food. "Is it tough?"

She shakes her head. "It's been a stressful day."

"That has ended well."

She has been ungrateful. She apologizes. "We can't thank you enough," she says.

"I wanted to help." He reaches for her hand again. "But, of course, I had another motive."

"I'm glad," she says. And indeed she *is* glad. After Tony, she has been reluctant to risk romance again, but Paul Bishop is a good man, a kind man.

The waiter clears their table and offers them dessert. She forces herself to smile. She wants to show her appreciation but the dark cloud lingers. She chooses the most sumptuous dessert on the menu, a triple-chocolate cake. She'll have the ice cream too, she says.

Paul Bishop is not fooled. He asks her one more time. "Tell me, I want to know. Perhaps I can help." She still has no answer that satisfies him, so he says what he believes will comfort her. "Your mother's going to be okay. All she needs is love and attention. You and your father are the best medicine for her now."

And suddenly, without warning, the dam she has plugged cracks and tears stream down her cheeks. They begin with a trickle but soon the tears are fatter. They pool in the neck of her blouse. She cannot stop them. Paul Bishop hands her his napkin and she presses it to her eyes. The tears do not stop. She is crying quietly, without sound, as if her heart will break. Paul signals to the waiter to bring the bill. He gets up and moves to her side of the table. He puts his arm around her shoulders. "We'll leave now," he says. He guides her out of the restaurant.

They make love. She is about to put her key in the door to the apartment when he pulls her to him. This time there is no questioning the passion in his kiss. His mouth still on hers, she opens the door. He slides one side of her jacket off her shoulders and she wriggles it free; the other side falls to the floor. Leading her backward, he takes her across the room, undressing her, unbuttoning her blouse now, reaching for her bra. "Not the bedroom." She tugs his hand. He releases her and breathing hard (he is not a young man), he throws the cushions off the couch and unfolds the bed. He reaches for her again and she stops him. "Wait!" She presses the palm of her hand against his chest. These are new times, times when sex can be life threatening, but he is ready.

"I have one," he whispers.

Afterward, lying next to him, she asks. "How did you know to come prepared? Or are you always prepared?"

"I'm a doctor," he says. "We know the cost of not being prepared."

Still, she wants to know. "Did you think we would make love?"

"If not today, some day soon. I knew it the moment I saw you."

"In New York?"

"No. On the island. Didn't you know that was why I stayed an extra day?"

She snuggles close to him. It has been so long she has forgotten how wonderful it feels to lie naked with a man you like, may possibly love. His body feels warm. Soft. Tony worked out; the muscles in his arms and legs were firm, taut, the contours of his chest defined, his thighs hard. He made love to her with an urgency she once thought was passion, but which left her frightened by his greed, his ravenous desire for her body. She could have been any woman; it was her body he wanted, not *her*, not her body and spirit. But Paul made love to the whole of her, to her body, her mind, her spirit, pacing himself, waiting until she felt what she had never felt with Tony, a slow, growing fire rising deep inside of her. When it exploded she fell against him, spent, her head on the cushion of his chest.

He strokes her hair and she slides her hand over his middle-aged paunch. This is the first time they have made love, but it feels to her as if it is one of the many times she has lain next to him breathing in the musky scent of his body.

"So tell me now, why the tears?" His mouth is in her hair.

The tears surprised her too, but now, her body limp, encased safely in his arms, she does not want to remember.

"Was it something I said?"

She snuggles closer to him, boring her nose into the side of his chest.

Tenderly, he places his fingers on her chin and lifts her head. "You must tell me, Anna. You shouldn't keep whatever it is bottled up. It isn't healthy. I want to know. I want to help." His fingers brush her cheek. "Are you worried about your mother? Is that it?"

She shakes her head.

"Because there's no need to worry. The surgery was successful."

A multitude of reasons get tangled in her head like strings wound around each other into a tight ball; she cannot distinguish one from the other. "No. That's not it," she murmurs.

"Then what?" He kisses the top of her head. She tries to move away and he tightens his arm around her shoulders. "Don't be afraid," he says.

But she is afraid. Of what, she does not know. It is a familiar fear that has taken refuge in the pit of her stomach for so many years, it refuses to be acknowledged.

"You began to cry when I said that what your mother needs now is your father's love and your love. Why, Anna?"

"It's all over now," she says. "See. I've stopped crying."

"Tell me." His lips are on her forehead. "Tell me, Anna."

One strand slips out from the mass of tangled strings. "I don't know how to love her." She says this quietly, so quietly he does not hear her.

"What?" He bends down, his ear close to her lips.

She repeats her words; they are more audible now.

"You don't mean that, Anna." He raises himself up against the headboard at the back of the couch and pulls her up with him.

She has told him what he wants to know. She does not want to say more, but he prods her. "Everyone knows how to love their mother, Anna. Babies know."

"Babies begin with a blank slate," she says.

"And what could have been written on your slate that time could have wiped away?"

"My mother was not very demonstrative."

"Those were the times, Anna," he says gently. "My mother was not demonstrative either."

"She hugged and kissed you."

"I was a boy. My father didn't approve of all that kissing and hugging for his sons. He said my mother was going to make us into mamby-pamby boys if she kept on kissing us." He pokes his finger in the fleshy spot below her waist. "And there it is; I am a mamby-pamby boy, mamby-pamby over you." He nuzzles her neck.

She moves her head away from him. "I bet she hugged and kissed your sisters," she says.

"Not as much as mothers do today." His arm remains around her shoulders.

"My mother didn't."

"Not even when you were a baby?"

"I don't remember her kissing me at all."

"Not at all? You must be mistaken, Anna."

"I would remember," she says.

"All mothers kiss their young children."

"Then she must have." Anna says this in a voice thick with resignation.

Paul shakes his head slowly. "Well, you're grown up now. You can kiss her, show her how much you love her."

"You have to be taught," she says.

He wriggles his nose and does not respond.

"You have to be taught to love your mother," Anna says again.

"All children love their mothers, Anna," he responds with strained patience. "I know you love yours."

"I don't know how to show it."

"You show it just fine. Look what you've done. You stayed with her on the island and now you are here. You took a risk. You won't lose your job, of course, but you were willing to take that chance. Come, don't be so morose." He tickles her under the arm. She squirms away from him, but he pulls her back down on the mattress. "Smile, Anna. Everything will be all right. Loving your mother is the most natural thing in the world."

Loving. He is easy to like, easy to open herself to the possibility of loving. In five years of marriage to Tony, not once had she told him of this pain buried deep inside of her. She and Paul have come from the same place, they share the same culture. Their roots go far down in the ground on their island. He understands. His mother was not demonstrative. Those were the times, he says. You're grown up now.

Is growing up all it takes? Should she be mature and teach herself to unlearn what she has never chosen to learn?

No one quarrels with the lyrics of *South Pacific*. No one disagrees that you've got to be taught to hate and fear; it's got to be drummed in your dear little ear. Why not to love?

Her mother was kind to her. She cared for her as any good mother would. She was well fed, well clothed. There were parties for her birthday. Presents. Presents again at Christmas. What more could a daughter want?

Paul does not spend the night. He has surgery the next morning. Before he goes, they make love once more. It is good again, comforting again, but when he leaves she is restless, the question their talk has raised still haunting her: what more could she have wanted?

She wanted to be touched, to be told she was loved. Only once did her mother try to explain. Her prayers had not stopped the relentless march of the malignant cells multiplying under her arm and in her breast. One tumor was the size of a plum, the other as large as a lemon. If there was ever a time to explain to her daughter, it was now, to tell her why that afternoon, when Anna was a mere child, she had turned away from her.

Anna wants to forget but that day returns to her in nightmares. She was seven years old. All her father wanted her mother to do was kiss her when she came home from school. Her mother had recoiled. *What's this? What's this, John?*

It was only very recently that her mother confessed she had learned from her own mother not to show her feelings. Her own mother had not hugged and kissed her. She learned from her not to hug and kiss her daughter. Her mother adds more. She blames the colonial times. The Queen of England was not demonstrative. She did not hug and kiss Charles and Anne, not in public, and not in private either, it was commonly believed. Poor Lady Diana, Anna thought. How she must have disgusted her mother-in-law with all those gushy kisses she planted on the cheeks of William and Harry.

Anna wants to forgive. She fills her ears with the words of an old man's prayer: *Change ah we heart, O Lord. Change ah we heart.* Her mother tries, but the habit is ingrained. They continue the way they were before. They are kind to each other, but they do not touch, they do not say affectionate words to each other.

Paul Bishop says loving your mother is the most natural thing in the world. It is not to her. Yet this is what her mother needs now, what the doctor says will speed her recovery. So she will try. When she visits her mother in the hospital, she will kiss her.

NINE

She makes breakfast for her father, sardines she knows he likes. She has brought two tins of sardines with her but not lettuce, tomato, and avocado. Her father is finicky about the presentation of his meals. The eye increases the pleasure of the taste buds, he says. When Lydia serves her parents at home, their meals are works of art on a platter. Sardines covered with translucent rounds of raw onion are nestled on green lettuce leaves and surrounded by wedges of red tomatoes, the glistening yellow centers of hard-boiled eggs and slices of avocado, lemony yellow on top, green on the bottom. Anna does what she can and aligns the sardines carefully on a white plate, placing their silvery heads next to each other. She finds a basket in the cupboard and lines it with a napkin. When her father comes she will toast the bread and put the slices in the basket.

He is in the lobby when she arrives at the hospital to meet him, on his way to have breakfast in the cafeteria, he says. She tells him she has prepared sardines, his favorite breakfast, at the apartment. He doesn't want to leave her mother alone too long, he says. She didn't sleep well last night. "Of course she didn't complain. But that was major surgery she had. Your mother is stoic, Anna. She suffers in silence."

He means to praise his wife. There is no irony in his intent though he is a man fascinated with the ironic. The stories he tells of his life in the colonial days, when the Englishmen ruled the island, always begin the same way, with a low guttural guffaw gurgling up his throat. "Life! It's so ironic," he would say, recounting his rise from chemist assistant to personnel manager and, before he retired, to director of the island's major oil company. In the old colonial days, skin color was a barrier to the climb up the ladder for local men. Then, when Independence loomed, his dark skin became a life raft for the Englishmen. "Better to have a local man at the helm of the company when they negotiated their exit from the island," he used to say, his eyes dancing mischievously. But when he relates the details of his wife's night in the hospital there is not a shred of irony in his voice. On the contrary, his voice is weighted with awe as if he has chosen to obliterate from his memory that it is her very silence that has brought them to this day. Now they must depend on the hope that aging cells are slow to multiply and that the estrogen that feeds the young breast dries up in the old.

"Stay with her until I return, Anna," he says. "She'll be happy to see you."

Her mother is lying propped up on the bed, her eyes closed, when Anna enters the room. She is breathing evenly. Air moves slowly up her nose and is released quietly through her slightly parted lips. Her mother's face, relaxed, is that of an innocent woman, a woman incapable of causing pain to anyone, especially to her daughter. Anna draws near and is immediately filled with remorse. She has behaved like a child. She has not lived her mother's life; she does not know how much her mother has been scarred by the pain she suffered in her childhood. She needs to forget *What's this? What's this, John?* How foolish she must have seemed to

Paul. He is right. She needs to grow up. She needs to act as the grown-up adult she is.

Anna stands silently at the railing of her mother's bed. She does not move, staying rigid as a statue. Only her eyes travel up and down the length of her mother's body. Her mother is asleep; she cannot see her daughter. Then suddenly, without warning, Anna is overtaken by an impulse she is unable to control. Her head is thrust forward; her body, as if by a will of its own, bends itself at the waist, over the railing on her mother's bed. Her mother's breath rises and falls. Anna hovers over her, her breath upon her mother's breath, her lips almost on her mother's cheek.

"Anna!" Her mother's eyes shoot open.

Anna flinches. Her spine, on automatic, is ramrod straight again. She takes a step backward, adjusts her face. There were tears that had begun to surface; she blinks them away.

"You're here." Her mother attempts to pull herself up on the bed and Anna places her hand on her shoulder and gently guides her back down. "Don't, Mummy," she says. "It's too soon."

Her mother settles back on her pillow. Her eyes rove seemingly aimlessly over Anna.

Anna grips the bed railing. "How are you, Mummy?" With effort, the words leave her tongue.

Her mother looks away and sweeps her left hand across her face. "I'm here," she says. No sentiment is registered in her voice. "And the cancer is gone."

Anna does not contradict her; she does not say that the tumors are gone, but time will tell if the cancer is gone. Her mother is a woman who looks forward; she does not look back.

"Your father?" her mother asks. "Have you seen him?"

"He's having breakfast in the cafeteria. I made sardines, but . . ."

"He's a stubborn man. I told him you'd want him to have breakfast with you in the apartment."

"He didn't want to leave you that long," Anna says.

A wan smile creases her mother's face. "He's a good man, your father."

Anna nods. "A good husband."

"Eventually," her mother adds.

Anna does not press her to explain.

"And what about you? Can you be away from work that long?" her mother asks.

Anna tells her that she can do all the work she needs to in the apartment. She has her laptop. She can e-mail, send faxes. She can call her boss on her cell phone if she has to.

Her mother fixes the sheet that has slipped below her collarbone. The bandages are visible, but there is no blood.

"Does it hurt?" Anna asks.

Her mother shrugs. "They have given me painkillers. It's hard to know if it hurts." She pats the sheet in place close to her neck and peers up again at Anna. "E-mails and faxes," she says, and sighs. "What a world! When I was working we had none of those. We had to be there, in the office. We couldn't work at home."

Her mother was fired when her pregnancy began to show. She did not have the choice of working at home. Her boss had not wanted to let her go. She was an excellent executive assistant; she wrote his letters, edited his reports, but a rule was a rule under the colonial government. When her suits no longer fit, she would be questioned. In those days a woman was expected to submit her resignation when she got married. She had a spouse, a partner with a job. Hers could be assigned to a woman without a partner, a woman who did not have a job. But when a married woman got pregnant things were different: the expectation then became a requirement.

"It's a different world now for women," Beatrice says to her daughter. "A woman can be at the top of the ladder. Like you, Anna."

"It's only an imprint, Mummy," Anna reminds her.

"The top of an imprint. That's where you are." Her eyes move past Anna to the back of the room.

Her husband has returned, his breakfast in a paper bag. His wife has just had surgery. Ten minutes away from her is an eternity for him.

The phone is ringing when Anna opens the door to the apartment the hospital has loaned her parents. It is Paula.

"How's your mother?"

"Her usual self," Anna says. "She was practically sitting up just hours after the surgery."

"Your mother belongs to the old school. Women like her just suck it up. You can never tell how they are really feeling. Sucking it up is their badge of courage."

Is that what she should have thought when her mother tried, when it took her years, her daughter already married and divorced, a year shy of forty, to explain *What's this? What's this, John?* Then, for one brief moment, tears in her eyes as she remembered her own mother, remembered her own childhood, her longing for her mother's touch, she had said: *You cannot imagine, Anna, how many times I have wanted to tell you how much I love you.*

But courage does not warm the heart of a child; love does. It is the courage to love that should have been the badge of courage for the old school, the courage to break down walls no matter how constructed, no matter *why* constructed. It is the courage to reach beyond the self, to take the risk, to expose your vulnerability for the sake of the ones you love, that should have merited praise.

Paula notices her silence. "She doesn't want your father to worry," she says. "Nor you."

Why can't she be more sympathetic, more understanding? *Lieben und Arbeiten.* Loving and working. This is Freud's answer to the question of what is most necessary for the child to grow up to live a happy life. *Lieben,* the more important of the two, according to a decades-long study of hundreds of Harvard graduates.

"My father says she is stoic."

"Courageous," Paula says.

The word lingers between them. Seconds pass and then Anna clears her throat. "Mummy will sleep most of the day, so I thought I'd get some work done here, and afterward have lunch with my father."

"You're a workaholic, Anna."

"I have responsibilities."

"You're not still worrying about Bess Milford?"

"I'm going to try one more time to persuade Tanya to change the book cover," Anna says.

"Be careful."

"You think I shouldn't?"

"You may be stepping into waters too hot for you."

Anna bristles. "I've been in this business a long time, Paula."

"I don't doubt you know your business. There's no way Windsor would have made you head of Equiano if you weren't one of the best in the publishing industry—but like I always say to you, we may have the passport, but we are hyphenated citizens. They know the terrain better than we ever possibly could."

TEN

Until she reminds herself that she does not share Paula's pessimism, her friend's warning has made her uneasy. Paula has long decided that the bridge between immigrants and Americans born in America is a wobbly one. You can fall off any time America wants to shake it, she claims. But Anna will not allow Paula's despair to infect her. She has been in the publishing business for close to ten years. Tanya Foster knows her worth and will not discard her, hyphenated citizen or not.

She began on the ground floor, working her way through the slush pile at Windsor. Manuscripts poured in, sometimes as many as one hundred a month, most of them so poorly written it took only a reading of the first page to pass on them. Yet Anna admired the spunk of these writers. Clearly no agent had taken them on; possibly their work had been rejected by several publishers, but they had not lost hope; they kept on trying. It was virtually a miracle to find a decent manuscript in the bunch. "Like finding a needle in a haystack," the woman who hired her said. The company had little expectation of discovering a publishable manuscript this way. Literary agents are the front guards for publishing companies. They work on contingency; if a writer does not get a contract for her manuscript, they do not get paid. So editors feel confident that they can rely on them; agents will only take on a client if they believe the manuscript is marketable. Yet the manuscripts kept pouring into Windsor, unsolicited, unheralded by agents. Anna's job when she worked with the slush pile was simply to adjust the company's form letter of rejection to the individual writer so it would appear as if an editor had actually read the entire manuscript.

It was finding that needle in the haystack that got Anna noticed. Unlike her coworkers whose maximum was ten pages, Anna sometimes read far more of the manuscripts assigned to her from the slush pile. She had become quite good at giving advice, offering helpful editorial direction to the writers. She felt sympathy for them and wanted to give them some hope. Perhaps another publisher would take a chance on their revised manuscripts.

Then two things happened, one of which could have caused trouble for her had it not been for the second. A writer had taken her letter seriously, revised her manuscript, and sent it to another publisher who released her novel. The novel was a hit. Within the first six months of publication it sold seventy thousand copies. Grateful, the writer sent her a thank you letter, with a copy to Tanya Foster. Tanya was furious. She had not hired Anna to solicit books for her competitor, she said, and probably would have fired Anna had one of the editors not told her that she was reading a manuscript Anna recommended to her from the slush pile. It had promise, she said. In fact, the novel had so much promise it sold out its first printing within a month.

Anna's efforts did not go unrewarded. She was hired full-time as an assistant to the editor and it didn't take long before she was promoted to editor. When other publishers decided to go through the door Terry McMillan had opened with her national best seller *Waiting to Exhale*, Windsor created Equiano, an imprint for books by writers of color, and Tanya Foster appointed Anna to head the new company. Terry had proven there was a market for books by black writers. Black women had bought her novel in the hundreds of thousands. Windsor believed that with Equiano it would create a gold mine.

Within a short time books by black writers became a genre. There was literature and then there was black literature. Literature encompassed different genres: romance, tragedy, melodrama, comedy, satire, epic, and so on. Black literature was any literature written by a black writer, the expectation being that it would have relevance only to black readers. Bookstores and, unfortunately, too many libraries organized themselves according to this new genre under the pretext of accessibility, that much misused word. There was fiction separated by genre—romance, mystery, etc.—and then there was fiction by black writers under the caption *Black Literature.*

Curiously, when white writers wrote about the experiences of blacks, or when their main characters were black, there didn't seem to be any need for accessibility; their fiction could be found in the stacks for general fiction, alphabetized by their surnames. Academia followed suit. There was *Nineteenth-Century American Literature* and then there was *Nineteenth-Century African American Literature*, as if African Americans were not also Americans. There was an exegesis on Milton under the category of *Seventeenth-Century British Literature*, and then, in stacks with the heading *Black Studies*, was an exegesis on Milton written by a black man.

The first black writer that Anna published refused to have her photograph on the jacket cover. She is a writer, not a black writer, she said. She writes novels, not black novels. She wants her novels to be read by any reader, not exclusively by black readers. Bess Milford's argument to

Anna is the same. She wants a jacket cover for her novel that reflects the subject and theme of her novel. The people she writes about are human beings. As far as she knows, she shouts out at Anna, black people are human beings, white people are human beings, and so the novel she has written will have meaning for black readers *and* white readers. But the jacket Equiano has decided upon for Bess Milford's novel is for the kind of novel the sales force at Windsor assumes a black writer writes and which a black reader will want to read; it is a novel whose genre is *Black Literature*.

Anna has promised Bess Milford that she'll try, so she will e-mail Tanya Foster again. Perhaps it is not too late to persuade her to redo the cover for the novel. She will not talk about its literary merit, about the importance of publishing books by black writers that reflect the universality of the human condition regardless of differences in skin color, culture, class, age. If there is hope for the world, Anna believes, it is in our ability to see ourselves in others, in persons who do not look like us, do not talk like us, do not live like us, but who in every essential way are exactly like us. People who desire the same things all people want: above all to survive, above all to be happy, to love and be loved; who fear the same things: above all their mortality, the end of a knowable life; who hope for and dream of the same things: above all justice, for many an afterlife where good is rewarded and evil punished.

You cannot hate the person who mirrors your hopes, fears, and dreams, Anna tells Paula. If hate is what you need, if power is what you desire, you must invent lies; you must create blindfolds that will block your sight, that will prevent you from seeing yourself in the person you hate, that will blind you to similarities.

Paula agrees. In a utopian world we would live in harmony, she says, but here, in the real world, we are competitive; we crave power. We need others under our feet so we can stand tall above them. She returns to her disillusionment over the hope she once had of remaking herself in America. "Americans born here need to flex their muscles over immigrants. It makes them feel powerful."

"All Americans were immigrants at one time," Anna reminds her. "Except, of course, for the aboriginal American Indians and the Africans brought here in chains."

"The oppressed are sometimes the most rabid of oppressors," Paula responds. "They want their turn too. Watch your step. You are an immigrant; you are disposable. Don't go overboard fighting for Bess Milford."

But Anna wants Equiano to tell the truth. She will not deny that novels like Raine's and Benton's reflect reality, but they do so only partially. They tell convenient truths. They perpetuate stereotypes, myths that justify the cravings of the economically and socially privileged for power over the poor, over the disadvantaged. She will choose her words carefully when she e-mails Tanya. She will speak her language, use terms that will be meaningful to her. She will speak about the bottom line. She will argue that the present cover will not be good for sales.

Subject: Jacket cover for Bess Milford

Dear Tanya,
Thank you for the flowers and basket of fruit you sent for my mother. The surgery went well and there is every indication that my mother will have years ahead of her. She has age on her side and we are told that her tumors were contained. We expect she will be discharged from the hospital in two days so I

should be back in the office by Thursday. I really thank you for your patience and for giving me the time to be with my mother.

I have been in communication with Tim Greene. I expect to hear from him later in the day and hope to wrap up the final edits on Raine's novel by tomorrow. I remain concerned about Bess Milford. I know you love her novel as much as I do, and like you, I want it to sell well. The more I think of the jacket cover the salespeople want, though, the more I'm convinced that it's the wrong cover for the novel. I don't just mean it's inappropriate. You already know how I feel about that. What I mean is that I'm not sure that cover will actually sell the book as the salespeople think. The people who will be attracted to the novel because of the cover will soon discover that it is not the kind of novel they were expecting. Bess Milford doesn't write chick lit, as you well know.

We really have no definitive idea on how books sell, but the general opinion is that books sell by word of mouth. So the people who find out that the cover on the novel promises something that the book is not will spread the word—do not buy this novel!! I think they may even get angry that we are trying to pull something on them. Then there are the readers who like to read the sort of book that Bess has written. Those readers will never pick up a book with such an explicitly erotic cover. I think we will be making a mistake to go ahead with the cover. I think it would make sense financially, bring us more profit, if we change it. Of course, you have the last word, but I feel very strongly about this.

All the best,
Anna

She has been careful not to give the slightest indication in her e-mail that she suspects Tanya has not read the novel. Tanya has said she loves the novel, and though it could be implied she has read it, Anna has no evidence of this. "I trust your judgment," Tanya said, when she accepted Anna's recommendation months ago to purchase the novel for Equiano. Since then she has offered no comment other than her endorsement for the jacket cover. It is likely all Tanya has read is the synopsis and concluded that this time Milford has added some spice to her novel to make it more marketable. And wasn't that what she intended? Anna berates herself bitterly. Wasn't that the effect she wanted when she e-mailed the synopsis along with the entire edited manuscript? She had highlighted the salacious parts of the novel, the sex scenes, particularly the one where the man makes love to his mistress in the tight confines of a bathroom stall. So isn't she just as guilty as the guys in the art department? *Man trying to get away with keeping the wife satisfied at home and getting it on with the girlfriend.* Are the means justified by her goal to get more marketing dollars for Bess Milford's novel? Well, the plan backfired and here she is at the mercy of the salespeople who, she is certain, have not read the novel, who rarely read more than the blurbs the editor sends to them. They make decisions on trends they determine from the numbers they gather on what sells in which bookstores, in which areas. They are not readers, most of them. They are businessmen, businesswomen. They would just as well sell a pharmaceutical as they would sell a novel. But Anna cannot let them have the upper hand here, not for this novel.

In minutes Tanya responds to her e-mail:

Subject: Re: Jacket cover for Bess Milford

Dear Anna,

What you said makes a lot of sense, but I think you should have more faith in our sales force. They really know their business. Maybe to you and me the cover is a mistake, but we don't know the market as they do. I think this is going to be a win-win for you and for Bess. Cheer up. You have lots to be cheered up about. Your mother is doing well and Tim told me that he had a good meeting with Raine yesterday. I'll let him tell you about it.

There's some news about me. It's not official yet, but I may be going to another company. More when I see you.

Yours,
Tanya

Anna tries to quiet the fear that has set her right eyelid twitching. She has nothing to worry about, she tells herself as she rereads the last lines of Tanya's e-mail. Successful publishers are always in demand. And Tanya Foster is a successful publisher. Windsor is doing well, but the Equiano imprint is turning in the stronger profits. Equiano was Tanya's brainchild and Anna has no doubt that the returns on the investment in this imprint have made Tanya attractive to other publishing companies. But what will happen to her when Tanya is gone? It is Tanya who appointed her to her position. Will a new publisher support her the same way?

She has been suspicious of the sudden hiring of Tim Greene. What is to be his position when Tanya leaves? She had asked for a replacement for Tammy Mohun. Tammy was her assistant, her secretary. She answered the phone, checked the mail, filed, sorted. Sometimes Anna asked her to research some arcane point when she questioned the accuracy of the fact-checker. Sometimes Tammy took manuscripts home and returned them with extensive notes that Anna had to admit were very astute, but the young woman had not been hired as an editor. Tim Greene was. He was to be her assistant editor, Tanya Foster said, though Anna had not asked for an assistant editor.

The more Anna thinks of Tim Greene, the more incensed she becomes, and the more worried too. She e-mails him. She asks about his meeting with Raine and tells him to e-mail the ideas he indicated he had for improving the novel. She will take control of the books published under the imprint she heads, she tells herself, determined not to be undermined by a newcomer, an upstart. Let him send his notes. If he has disregarded her edits, she will demand that he retract whatever he has said or sent to Raine. She won't be petty; she will consider his recommendations, but she will not allow him to disregard hers.

She finishes the e-mail and reaches for the phone. She must let Bess Milford know the jacket cover will not be changed. She has done her best, and there is nothing more she can say to Tanya that will make a difference. She begins to dial Bess's number and she loses her nerve. She cannot bear to hear the disappointment that will certainly be there in Bess's voice. Bess has pinned her hopes on Anna. Perhaps she should not have been so enthusiastic. Perhaps she should have been more discreet with her praise of the novel. Even a senior editor, the head of an imprint, must work with a team. The decision to acquire a novel and the approval of the budget to market it do not rest on a single person. Perhaps she should have explained these constraints to Bess Milford from the beginning. Instead she had been excessive with her compliments: *The best novel I've read in years. This is a story that will resonate with people all over the globe.*

She had used that deceptive "c" word. "It's a crossover novel," she said. "People from every ethnic group, class, gender, and age will find something of themselves in your story. We all face this conflict between our private desires and public responsibilities, and your story gets to the heart of our dilemma." But now she knows the novel will not be marketed as a crossover novel; it will be marketed as a black novel and there is little she can do to change that reality.

She takes the easy way out. She e-mails Bess. You can avoid the sting of direct confrontation on the telephone, but e-mails allow an even greater distance when the message you have to deliver is an unpleasant one. You can frame your words exactly as you want; no one will interrupt you; no one will point out your hypocrisy, the lie in what you say, at least not until you are done, not until you have had the chance to invent your defense.

Her e-mail to Bess is brief. She apologizes; she promises to make certain that the cover for her next novel will be appropriate. She is aware she cannot make good on such a promise, but she means to try. She ends the e-mail with what she knows is not the truth: *Your novel is going to reach a diverse readership, Bess. Have no fear.*

Afterward, she works on letters she will send to two of the other writers on her list. She is careful to boost their confidence and so she begins the letters with the usual praise that editors send to writers to nudge them into rewriting their novels, but she is also cautious. She reins in her enthusiasm. *I like your novel very much and readers will like it too. Your characters are engaging and you hold the reader's interest,* etc., etc., but . . . She writes three paragraphs of buts.

It is close to midday when Anna finishes the letters and makes the last of her business calls. She logs on to her e-mail again. There is no response from Tim Greene. He has read her e-mail; of that she is certain. She signs off, closes her laptop, slips on her jacket, and leaves the apartment to have lunch with her father.

It is a glorious day, the sort that causes inconvenient thoughts to drift through the mind of the unbeliever, tempting the unbeliever to reconsider firm convictions and entertain the possibility of a Prime Mover, some intelligent, supernatural force that has set in motion the Big Bang and the unending cycles of evolution that have created order and beauty in the world. It is the sort of day when, gilded by the sun, refuse assumes a strange beauty. Garbage bags heaped on sidewalks and even the slats of boarded-up windows of abandoned buildings in neighborhoods collapsing under the terror of crime and drugs seem to shimmer under a spreading arc of golden light. The sky is an infinite blue, clear and bright. The leaves on the trees will soon wither and die, but for now they glitter in the breeze in a kaleidoscope of reds, pinks, oranges, and golds.

Anna's father too is struck by the gloriousness of the day. She finds him walking on the hospital grounds. "Anna!" he calls out to her. He is holding a plastic bag. Under his arm is a folded newspaper. "Your mother sent me to the gift shop to get a magazine for her," he says when he catches up to her, "but I couldn't help going outside. What a beautiful day!" He lifts up the plastic bag in his hand for her to see. "I hope I got the right one." The right one would be a scandal magazine about American celebrities, one that gives her mother vicarious pleasure scoffing at stories of scantily clad, rich American women whose fourth or fifth husband has left them for a young starlet.

"It may be the richest country in the world," she has said to Anna, "but they can't do something as simple as keep a family together." True or false, Anna often thinks this barb is directed to her. She couldn't keep her family together. Her husband left her; she is childless.

Anna peers into the bag. "You've got the right one," she says.

"I bought the *Times* too," he says. In the evenings he reads sections of the newspaper to his wife before they go to bed. He wants to keep her current on the happenings around the world, he says.

"Did you sleep well?" she asks him. Her father's pants are creased and the collar of his shirt has disappeared under the neck of his sweater, but for someone who slept in his clothes, he still exudes the air of a man of substantial social status. At home her mother chides him for wearing days-old clothes stained with the rind of oranges he picked from the trees in their garden, or from the pellets of dog food he fed to the fish in his pond, and yet no one would mistake him for other than a gentleman. He walks with his head held upright, and in his eyes one sees the confidence of a man aware of his worth and dignity as a human being.

"Like a baby," he says. He is lying, of course. He cannot have slept well on the armchair next to her mother's bed.

"And Mummy?"

"She woke up only once. The nurse helped her to the bathroom and then she slept until the morning."

In the lobby of the hospital, they wait for the elevator. When the door opens, a young man stands aside to let them in. "Hope you have a good morning, sir," the man says to her father when he exits. *Sir.* Even here people defer; they recognize John Sinclair as the gentleman he is.

Her mother is sitting up, her head turned toward the window, her fingers pressed to her mouth. She does not change her position when Anna and her father walk in the room. "I didn't believe the sky could get so blue here," she says. "Just like the sky at home." The soft lines at the sides of her eyes fan out and the skin on her cheeks spreads upward.

Anna bends down over her and her mother raises a limp hand and touches her face. "You're a good daughter, Anna," she says. Anna brushes her lips against her mother's soft skin. Her father, looking on, grins. Then in an instant her mother is her old self again. "Go, Anna." She leans back on her pillow. "Take your father with you. He's itching for a break."

Her mother's hand is no longer on her cheek yet Anna can still feel the traces of her fingers on her skin.

"Your father was all cramped up on that chair last night," her mother is saying.

Anna is barely listening to her, her mind drifting inward.

"Did you hear me, Anna?"

She refocuses and is in the present again. "I'll take him for lunch if he's ready to go," she says.

Her father drops the newspaper on the armchair where he slept and takes the magazine to his wife. "I wasn't cramped up, Beatrice," he grumbles. "It's a comfortable chair."

Her mother waves him away. "Take him to lunch, Anna. He needs the exercise. If he doesn't need a break, I do. They'll be bringing my lunch soon and I want to take another nap."

"Still ordering me around, Beatrice?" her father says.

Her mother shakes her head and rolls her eyes. "Just leave the magazine, John."

She will have to wait until he returns to read it. She has movement in one hand, but it will be difficult for her to turn the pages with the other hand connected to an arm that must be aching from the severed muscles on her chest. Anna winces. Below the bandage poking out of the neck of her mother's hospital gown are the sutures that close the skin left gaping apart after Dr. Bishop removed her mother's left breast.

"Go on, John!" For all the harshness in her mother's words and for all the rolling of her eyes there is tenderness in her command. She has sent her husband out to get a magazine she cannot read without his help and yet she is sending him out again because she's worried about him, more worried about him than she is for herself. He needs the exercise, she says. Her husband is not a young man. The joints in his limbs get stiff.

"Go on!" she says again, and chases him away. "Anna must have things to tell you." She wants her daughter to distract her husband. Anna must talk to him of things other than his wife's illness.

Her father is a willing coconspirator. It is love that causes her mother to care for his welfare, love that causes her husband to do as she asks, but it is also character, a quality Anna fears has outlived its time. To have character is to have fortitude; it is to have courage, discretion—the better part of valor. But in these days, to value discretion is to be mocked at, to be laughed at. For husbands and wives openly discuss the most intimate aspects of their lives— what they do in bed and afterward—before millions on national TV and do not seem to care.

Her parents value privacy. If her father is worried about

his wife, he does not reveal those fears to Anna. Whatever he and his wife have discussed will remain between them. At the hospital cafeteria, he inquires instead about Anna's job. "Did you get much done this morning?"

"With the computer it's almost the same as if I were in the office," she tells him.

"The computer is beyond me. I'll never be able to understand those newfangled machines. The fax was enough of a mystery for me."

She laughs, remembering how he called her in New York from his home on the island to tell her that one of the companies that kept him on retainer for his management advice had given him a fax machine. "It's amazing," he had said. "You put a letter in one machine and it comes out in another, thousands of miles away."

"Like the telephone," she replied.

"At least I can understand the telephone. Voices transmitted through the airwaves make sense to me, but written words? It's unbelievable."

He still refuses to get a computer or communicate with her through e-mail or fax. He uses the telephone and occasionally sends her letters by post.

"You know," he says "you shouldn't work too hard." Anna has bought a ham sandwich, but her father, accustomed to a full meal at lunchtime, has chosen meatballs and spaghetti. He is using his knife to cut the spaghetti strings. Anna watches as he patiently slices the strands into small bits, cuts the meatball, spears a piece of it with his fork, and loads the spaghetti on top of it with his knife. He will not eat the American way, with a fork, resting his knife on the side of his plate. This way of eating with the knife and fork may be a colonial import but he has lived all his life under colonial rule.

"I don't work too hard," she says.

"You are a grown woman. It may not be my business to give you advice, though . . ." He glances up at her.

She touches his hand. "I'll never stop wanting advice from you," she says reassuringly.

He casts his eyes back down on his plate and concentrates on maneuvering the spaghetti on the back of his fork. Some of the strings slide off the tines.

"Swirl them," she says.

He looks helplessly at her.

She reaches over the table to his plate and shows him how. "Try it. There is no other way."

He tries. "I guess I'm being pulled into these modern times," he says, and swirls the spaghetti on his fork.

"I don't think Italians would agree this is a modern way to eat." Surely he must know this, she thinks.

He sighs. "How things have changed since Independence." His mind has drifted to other times, to the passing of an era. "Now the young people back home do whatever they want. They don't care what the British think. *Which is good.*" He says these last words emphatically, repeats them, and adds, "This is the way it should be." He wants to be sure she understands he is not a mindless Anglophile. He has neither forgotten nor forgiven the brutality of slavery under the British, the torture of Africans, the genocide of Amerindians who once populated the chain of Caribbean islands. He will never accept the arrogance and greed of the British that led them to assume they could own his island and the people on it. He puts another forkful of spaghetti in his mouth, and after he has swallowed, dabbed his lips with his napkin, he says, "But you don't throw the baby out with the bathwater."

For her father, the baby is the British system of laws,

the British system of government, the British system of education. The British system of table manners. It would be futile, Anna knows, to engage him in an argument that there could be, and are, other ways better than the British ways.

"What's the advice you wanted to give me?" she asks. "I interrupted you. You were saying something about working hard."

"Life," he says and sighs again, this time deeply. His shoulders collapse when he exhales. "It's short. One minute you're a boy in short pants, next minute your knees lock when you try to get up."

"Oh, Daddy."

"It's true. I'm an old man and it seems that only yesterday I was climbing coconut trees."

"You're not an old man."

"I'm eighty-two."

She cannot deny that eighty-two is old, but she does not want to go down the road with him that starts with his age and leads to his mortality and inevitable death. "I enjoy my job," she says.

"Yes, but you must take time to smell the roses."

"*You* worked hard."

"I also hunted and fished. Your mother and I traveled."

"I don't have a husband."

She silences him with this swift retort and is immediately remorseful. He worries about her. He worries that without a husband she may end up a lonely old woman in a foreign land. He has told her he read somewhere that married women live longer than unmarried women; they are happier when they have a companion. But he is not as direct as her mother; he does not try to find a husband for her. It is of no concern to him whether or not the doctor who will operate on his wife is married. His interest is in the doctor's surgical skills, his ability to save his wife's life. Her mother wants to know. *Does he have a wife?* She presses her husband to give her the answer.

But now Anna detects the slight strain of anxiety that enters her father's eyes and it makes her uncomfortable. She does not want to give him false hope, just enough hope to put the light back in his eyes. She tells him she had dinner with Paul Bishop the night before. She expects they will see more of each other.

"I like him," her father says brightly, clearly relieved. "Paul's a good man. And a good surgeon."

"Mummy couldn't have been in better hands."

"He's a good friend for you too. It makes me happy to know you don't spend all your time working."

"I don't." She is aware she says this too quickly, too harshly. The clatter of dirty dishes and cutlery piled up on trays as people make their way out of the cafeteria fills the empty space that opens up between them. When her father speaks again, he has returned to the question he asked her when they sat down to eat. "Tell me about your job. Are you happy at Equiano?"

She does not want to tell him about Tim Greene. She does not want to give voice to suspicions that may yet be unfounded. She tells him about Tanya Foster. "She's leaving the company," she says.

"Is that anything you should be worried about?"

"No."

"No?"

He is quizzing her. A man as brilliant as her father, who has spent years in the maze of labor relations, can easily detect the undercurrent of concern coursing through the single word she used. "Only that she's the one who hired me," she says, hoping to cover up her gaffe.

"Sometimes we make too much about the importance of our jobs in our lives. Have you read *The Iliad*?"

She is puzzled by this curious detour. "Yes," she says cautiously.

"And what do you make of Achilles?"

"The best of the Greek warriors. He lived for the glory of war."

"Most people think so. But he preferred life to the glory of war." He sits back in his chair and closes his eyes. "*O shining Odysseus, never try to console me for dying. I would rather follow the plow as thrall to another man, one with no land allotted him and not much to live on, than be a king over all the perished dead.*" He opens his eyes. "Enjoy your life, Anna. Don't set too much stock on your job. Enjoy life while you are still young."

ELEVEN

Her father does not spend the night in the hospital. It is not by choice. He would have if his wife had allowed him. He would have stretched out on the armchair near her bed, his legs propped up on the footstool the nurses have given him, and declared he was as comfortable as if he were in his own bed. Indeed, this is what he tells his wife. "I like it here," he claims.

"Don't be silly, John," his wife responds. "Your old legs must be cramped by now. You're not a young man. And besides, you smell."

Her husband does not take offense. He kisses her on her forehead. "And you smell like an angel," he says.

Beatrice grimaces. It's a pretense, Anna knows. She is pleased by the compliment, the reassurances her husband gives her of his undying love. "Take him away," Beatrice says to Anna, who has come to fetch him for dinner. "And don't bring him back until tomorrow morning. Make sure he takes a shower and changes his clothes. He's worn the same pants for two days now."

John Sinclair does not give up. "I'll come back after dinner."

His wife faces him. Anna is startled by what she sees. Her mother's eyes are misty; the hand she raises trembles slightly. "I know, I know," she whispers. Her father grasps her raised hand. No more words pass between them and yet everything they need to say is said. When her mother finally slips her hand out of his and waves toward the door, her father leaves with his shoulders slumped.

It is a moment of intimacy that is too raw for Anna. She walks quickly out of the room.

The next morning Dr. Bishop comes to check on Beatrice. She is sitting up, waiting for him. She is ready to go home, she says. "I feel fine." The nurses cannot deny she is telling the truth. They are amazed by her rapid recovery. She was walking up and down the corridors of the hospital the day after her surgery, stopping to chat with the other patients.

Paul Bishop says he cannot make promises, but he'll see what he can do. When he leaves, Beatrice grumbles that all the hospital wants is her money. There is no reason for her to take up a bed that someone else might need.

Anna is surprised to hear her speak of money. Her husband handles all her affairs. He denies her nothing. She asks and she receives. He keeps accounts for her in the best stores on the island. She simply goes there and orders what she wants or needs. He leaves the running of the house to her, and has set up an account for that purpose. Yet she makes him pay the salaries of their housekeeper, the gardener, the boys who mow and weed the lawn, the woman who washes and irons their clothes. On the matter of laundering clothes she is consistent with the philosophy she and her husband share. They believe a person's privacy is inviolate, to be honored and respected. They will brook no intrusion into their private lives. So her mother will not allow the woman who comes twice a week to launder their intimate apparel. She herself washes the undergarments she and her husband wear. She washes their towels, washcloths, bed linens, any fabric that has touched their private parts. Though her husband provides her with a sizable account for the domestic affairs of her house, Beatrice Sinclair keeps a private account inaccessible to her husband. Every week she takes a little something from the house account and puts it in this private one. A woman would be foolish not to keep a little something for herself, she tells Anna. John Sinclair is a very generous man, but it's important for a woman to have money of her own. Just in case, she says.

Just in case what? Anna has never been able to get an answer from her. But perhaps now is such a case, such a *just in case*. They do not have insurance. On their island, the government pays for the medical treatment of its citizens. The downside, of course, is high taxes. Another downside is that without the motive for profit, hospitals are poorly supervised. Equipment is not properly maintained or disappears outright. Doctors make little more than university professors and, envious of their counterparts in America, they either emigrate or supplement their salaries by collecting fees from patients they see separately in offices they own or in the private hospitals managed by businessmen. The affluent are willing to pay the fees and the cost of a private hospital. Beatrice and John Sinclair are among the affluent, but Dr. Ramdoolal has little confidence in the private hospitals, *nursing homes* they are called, no irony intended. "Go to the States," he urged them.

So perhaps Beatrice has discovered the cost of medical treatment in America. Perhaps on one of her walks down the corridor, she has inquired and has been told of the enormous fees the hospital charges for each day she remains in her room. John Sinclair can pay these fees, Anna is certain, but her mother will not put this burden on him. She feels well, she says. It's time for her to leave the hospital. She wants to go home.

When he makes his rounds later in the afternoon, Dr. Bishop agrees to discharge her. "But you'll have to stay in the country a little longer, until I can be sure your sutures have healed."

He has misunderstood her. Beatrice Sinclair does not mean her home on the island where she lives with her husband. "I want to go home," she says. "To Anna's."

So the day has come, the day Anna fears. In the morning her mother will come home to her Brooklyn apartment.

She should be pleased. Her mother's decision should relieve her. She has spent two days with her parents in New Jersey, and now she needs to return to work. Tim Greene has made her wait a full day before he answers her e-mail and when he does, he ignores the one she sent him. He does not forward the edits he recommends for Raine's new novel. He writes not one word about his meeting with the author. His e-mail is brief. It begins with the usual deference he extends to her as the head of Equiano. He is sympathetic, concerned for her mother's health, upbeat about the future of the company.

Subject: Tim checking in

Dear Anna,
I don't want to be presumptuous. You are my boss and if you take offense by my addressing you by your first name, please let me know. I wouldn't take that liberty except that Tanya Foster insists I call her Tanya. She says things are informal in the company. They do not wait on ceremony here. But, of course, if you prefer, I will absolutely call you Ms. Sinclair. No offense will be taken.

I suppose you've heard that Tanya is leaving. All is uncertain here, but with you at the helm, I know we have nothing to worry about.

I hope your mother is doing well. I don't mean to be selfish. I know you have to take care of her, but we want you back in the office. Everything is going well. We have a great list of books for this season and with you nudging us along, I think Equiano will have its most profitable year ever.

Sincerely,
Tim

Her blood boiling, Anna clicks the delete icon on the computer and then rethinks her spontaneous impulse. She should keep a record of this e-mail Tim Greene has sent to her. It reeks of insincerity, not even measuring up to syco-phancy. She needs to keep Paula's warning in mind: Tim Greene is not to be trusted. She recovers the e-mail from the trash folder and reads it again. He is toying with her. In the office he addresses her as boss—*Good morning, boss. Have a nice evening, boss*—but he uses her first name in the saluta-tion of his e-mail, ready to apologize if she objects. Tanya Foster, however, is plain Tanya to him. He knows she is leaving the company, though Tanya claimed she has not yet made the announcement of her departure official. They are friends, Anna is certain.

Already anxious about her mother's arrival in her apartment, Anna busies herself packing her things and her parents' things for their trip back to Brooklyn in an attempt to keep her mind off Tim Greene's e-mail. Perhaps she is wrong. Perhaps Tim Greene does not even intend to stay with the company. She doesn't think of herself as a person inclined to paranoid thoughts or conspiracy theories, yet she finds herself unable to dismiss the possibility that Tanya intends to take Tim Greene with her when she moves to the new company. Perhaps Tim Greene has not responded to her queries about Raine's new novel because he plans to poach Raine for the new company. Let him do that! Anna is suddenly elated. Her body shudders with a perverse feeling of satisfaction. Let them both do that, she says to herself, finding relief at last from the thoughts swirling in her head. Let them take Raine, and Benton too. Raine will have to honor the contract she has with Equiano for her next novel, but then Raine will owe them nothing except the right of first refusal. And Anna will make sure Raine will not have to wait long. If her suppositions are correct, she will refuse the author's next book. She does not want to publish books like Raine's. She will take advantage of Tanya's departure. She will turn Equiano into a company she can be proud of, a company that will publish the kinds of books by black writers who do not play into the stereotype of black people as oversexed, grossly materialistic, money-grabbing, greedy individuals who might seek violent ways to get what they want. She will shepherd the company toward fulfilling the promise of its namesake, Olaudah Equiano, an African who survived the brutality of slavery in America and went on to write an inspiring autobiography that at once exposed the cruelty of the slave owners and revealed his own extraordinary fortitude and brilliant mind.

Her anxiety now greatly reduced, Anna picks out a change of clothing for her father. Her mother has packed her own clothes in the valise she brought to the hospital. She will not leave in the same clothes she wore when she arrived. She is a woman who is fanatical about cleanliness, particularly regarding her person. On the island, she changes her clothes at least twice a day. She will not have four o'clock tea with her husband in the same clothes she wore to breakfast. She would have been in the garden all morning supervising Singh, and her clothes would be damp with perspiration from the broiling sun. For hours she would have trailed behind Singh instructing him on how to pot the seedlings, how to trim the orchids, how to replant the impatiens that are wilting in the sun. There is nothing she says that Singh would not have already known—he has a magnificent garden of his own—but between them there is an understanding that continues to baffle Anna. When her mother issues orders, Singh complies. It is as if nothing has changed for them since colonial times except for the skin color of the colonizer. Then Anna is thrown into confusion when she sees them laughing together, playing games in the sunlight with the garden hose, her mother spouting water on Singh, Singh running across the lawn, her mother right behind him giggling like a schoolgirl.

Anna knows it will not be easy to persuade her father to wear the clothes she has set aside for him. He will argue that what he is wearing is just fine for the trip to New York. She cannot disagree, but her mother will be annoyed if he is wearing yesterday's clothes when they come to fetch her.

Paul Bishop calls later in the evening. It's Beatrice's last night in the hospital and he wants to take Anna out to dinner. He hesitates and then adds, "With your father, of course." When Anna gives her father Paul's invitation, he politely declines. He's had a big lunch in the hospital cafeteria, he says. He doesn't think he can fit much more in his stomach. He'll have some Crix biscuits and tea for dinner and turn in early.

Anna is not convinced. She thinks he and her mother

have talked about Paul. She thinks her mother is already planning her marriage. She is angry that her father has succumbed to this fantasy. "I like Paul," she says, "and I think he likes me, but we are just friends."

"Dinner together twice since we arrived?" Her father grins mischievously. "You must be more than friends."

"Mummy has set you up to this."

He denies her mother has anything to do with his decision not to have dinner with them. "You're still young, Anna," he says. "Seize your time. Carpe diem."

Paul confesses he is not disappointed. He wants to spend the evening alone with her. He will order Chinese, he tells her, and they can have dinner in his apartment. That is, if she doesn't mind. It is what she has secretly hoped for.

His apartment is sparsely furnished. A round table with two chairs and a leather couch are the only pieces of furniture in a fairly large space that serves as kitchen, dining room, and living room; the bedroom is in the back. He apologizes for not having a more attractive apartment. When he and his wife parted, he explains, he took only his clothes; he left everything else behind.

Anna does not think he is lying, but still she finds this difficult to believe. Tony had drawn up an extensive list before they separated. He seemed to know to the last penny what each of them had purchased in the five years of their marriage. She could have half the wedding gifts—half the china, half the silverware, half the stemware—but the furniture was all his, bought with his money when he supported her. It was futile to oppose him, to point out that though he made much more than she did when he worked at the brokerage house, he never did support her. She had a job at Windsor.

It was Tony's idea that they keep separate bank accounts. She had no access to his and he never added anything to hers. She cannot disagree that he paid most of the bills for the mortgage, the furniture, the Benz, but when he lost his job he had to depend on her. She wanted him to give up the Benz. He could get a smaller car, something they could afford, but he refused. He said she was jealous; he had something she couldn't use, which was true since she didn't know how to drive. "Nonsense," Paula had scoffed. "The Benz just made him feel like a big man." Ultimately, it was for that reason Anna indulged him. His pride was hurt when he lost his job; she could not bear to see him suffer more. Then one day she found a phone number in his jacket pocket. She called and a woman answered. He said if she had paid more attention to him, if she had made love to him when he wanted, if she had been a better wife, if she had had a baby like he wanted, if she had . . . The list of ifs went on until for the sake of peace she conceded.

"My husband was more calculating," Anna admits to Paul. "He said marriage is a business and we were business partners."

"Marriage is not a business for me," Paul says softly.

"That's the way it seemed once the lawyers got involved. Tony handed my lawyer his list, but I had nothing to give to his lawyer. The whole process was humiliating."

Paul has his arm around her waist. He removes it and walks away from her toward the kitchen. Anna remains where he left her, unable to shake the past out of her head. "I found an apartment and moved in," she says. "I left everything behind. I had to start all over. I remember I got a call from Fortunoff." She chuckles, but the expression in her eyes remains grim. "They were wondering if someone had stolen my credit card. I had purchased so many things in one day: dishes, cutlery, glasses, sheets, towels. I hadn't counted on how much I would need when all I took were my clothes."

Paul picks up the take-out menu from the Chinese restaurant that is lying on the kitchen counter. "What would you like? This place is the best. Anything you order will be terrific."

He does not manage to distract her. "I will say this much. It felt good to walk out and leave Tony with his petty little list."

Paul puts down the menu. "Is that how your father sees marriage? Is it a business to him?"

"It's different for my father," Anna says.

"How?"

"He loves my mother." Unexpectedly, her voice wavers and Paul reaches for her and folds her in his arms.

"That's the way it should be, Anna." His mouth is in the well of her neck. He draws her closer and she hears the thump, thump, thump of his heart. "Don't you believe otherwise. We should marry for love."

She feels, and knows she is not imagining, that an unmistakable change is occurring between them. He tightens his arms around her. Thump, thump, thump. Her heartbeat matches his. *For love, he said. We should marry for love.*

He calls the Chinese restaurant and orders their food but they make love before it arrives. It is gentle love, sweet love, nurturing love. When it is over, she feels restored, the past retreating until all that remains is the present, she with her head on the shoulder of a man who makes her feel safe, whole.

They eat in bed. Paul brings the shopping bag with the food to the bedroom and they spread an old quilt on the bed and sit cross-legged facing each other. Except for two stemmed glasses Paul has filled with white wine and placed on the bedside table, everything they use is disposable. They eat directly out of the cardboard containers from the Chinese restaurant, plucking out the food with wood chopsticks. Paul has ordered chicken for himself and shrimp for her, but he insists that she taste the chicken. He clasps a piece between his chopsticks and brings it to her mouth, but when she parts her lips, he withdraws the chopsticks. She opens her mouth again and he withdraws the chopsticks again. Two more times he does this. Shivers of pleasure ripple down her back. She closes her eyes and throws back her head. He circles her lips with the chicken, the warm flesh titillating against her moist mouth. When the hard wood of the chopsticks touches her tongue, her body quivers. He pulls her to him and pushes aside the cardboard containers. They make love again.

Afterward, when she gets ready to leave, he reverts to being her mother's surgeon. He has agreed to discharge her mother, but he tells her he will do so only on the condition that she is prepared to follow his instructions to the minutest detail. The dressing on her mother's chest must be changed every morning and every evening. He explains that there is an intricate web of blood vessels lying beneath the breast. He has sutured them, but fluid and blood sometimes collect beneath the stitches. He has put a drain at the end of the incision. It looks like a straw for drinking soda, and it will drain the excess fluid and blood onto the dressing. So she must change the dressing to prevent infection, he says. Every morning, every evening, and whenever it is feels too wet. "Can you do this, Anna?"

She has lost her voice.

"Because we cannot take the chance of infection. Your mother is strong, but she's not young."

Sound rises up her throat, indistinct, neither affirming her willingness to do as he asks nor objecting.

He asks the question again. "Will you be able to do this, Anna?"

Her stomach is churning, but she forces herself to nod in agreement.

"If you can't . . ."

But she must. "Mummy wants to leave the hospital," she says.

"I have to be sure."

She composes herself; she masks her fears. "I'll do it," she says, erasing all traces of hesitation in her voice.

Her father is asleep when Paul brings her back to the apartment. She hears him snoring lightly in the bedroom. How well her mother knows him! In spite of his determination to spend the night with his wife in the hospital, insisting he would be as comfortable in the armchair as if he were in his own bed, the joints in his eighty-two-year-old body would have stiffened. In the morning they would have creaked and hurt when he tried to unlock them. *For love. They married for love.*

It is divorce that is a business, Anna thinks. The first lawyer she hired was a woman well into her fifties. She wanted a retainer. "Just so we don't have to talk about money until this is over." Four thousand dollars. Anna dipped into her savings. Every time she called, the lawyer was ready with advice, none of it about the law or her rights, all of it intended to pacify her as if she were a prepubescent girl unable to control her emotions. "These things take time, Anna. Go out and enjoy yourself. Take a vacation. Leave the worrying to me." Three months later, her lawyer was giving the same advice and by then Tony's lawyer had added new demands. Anna was making more money now than Tony and it was only fair that she pay a small alimony until he could return to the lifestyle which he had so generously provided for her during their marriage. Her lawyer was incensed but all her vitriol was for Anna's ears. She did nothing to counter Tony's demands. So Anna engaged another lawyer. This one, a man, wanted a retainer of ten thousand dollars. Once he had it, he rarely answered her phone calls. Fortunately, an arbitrator eventually dismissed Tony's claims.

She was grateful to Paula for holding her tongue, for not gloating, for not saying she was right: Anna should not have married out of her culture. "In America," Paula had said, "skin color is identity. Skin color is all it takes to box you into a category. People here think that since Tony is black and you are black, you should understand each other, that you are a good fit. But it is culture, not color, that gives us our identity. Tony may be black but he is American, he does not share your culture. None of his forefathers were raised in the Caribbean. You are as different from him as if he were a white American."

She is thinking of Paula now, thinking that it is only to her can she confess that while Paul Bishop was describing how she must take care of her mother at the apartment, her heart sank, her legs felt weak.

Paula says her mother is courageous. Paula says her mother belongs to an age when women rarely revealed their true feelings. It is this learned restraint that got them through the worst of times: through unfair treatment because of their gender; through the infidelity of husbands which had to be endured for the sake of the children. It is learned restraint that allowed her mother to endure in silence a tumor blooming in her breast.

Mothers, Paula says, are free to love their sons but they must raise their daughters. They must prepare their daughters for a world that may not be fair to them. They must toughen them. Too much coddling will give their daughters false expectations of opportunities that in reality will be available only to men. But Anna thinks the world her mother experienced was not unfair to her. Her husband provided for her every need; he denied her nothing. She was a full partner in their marriage, not an inferior.

"Women had to learn not to complain," Paula said. "They had to learn to suck it up."

But how to release inhibitions when one has been taught restraint by a mother who has learned to suck it up? How to look upon her mother's breasts, to touch them, when her mother conceals her naked body from her daughter?

She sleeps fitfully and calls Paula first thing the next morning. "Paul says I must change her dressing. Every morning, every night. Sometimes more if it gets too wet. How can I do that, Paula?"

"You're like your mother—squeamish," Paula says.

Paula knows Beatrice's history. She knows that Beatrice Sinclair could not bear to be in the same room with her mother when she was dying of breast cancer. The stench of rotting meat put on her mother's leaking tumor · revolted her. For it was the prevailing wisdom then among the women on the island that since cancer eats flesh, it will be satisfied by any flesh, even cow's flesh.

But Anna does not share her mother's squeamishness; she is not repelled by blood, or by a leaking wound. It is her mother she fears, though she cannot name precisely

what about her: whether it is rejection, her mother turning away from her—*What's this? What's this, John?*—when her
father insists that a daughter should kiss her mother, or
whether it is habit calcified that will not loosen the muscles in her fingers when she reaches for the bandage on her
mother's breast. She does not know if longing penned up
for so many years behind a façade of stoicism will explode,
break loose from its dam, and leave her exposed, vulnerable, powerless.

Anna, the stoic. There: her father's word said in praise
of her mother! Is she, after all, her mother's daughter? Has
she learned the same restraint?

"I'm not like her," Anna says defiantly. "I'm not afraid
of blood."

"Then what?"

"We haven't been that close."

"The heart does not recognize physical distance," Paula
says. She means the years she has not lived on the island;
she means the years she has not lived in her parents' home.

"That's not it," Anna says.

"So what is it?"

"We don't hug and kiss like I suppose you do with your
mother."

Paula bursts out laughing. "You're just afraid, Anna.
Get over it. Your mother won't bite you."

And her mother does not bite her. Beatrice's compliments are excessive, over the top, when she walks into
Anna's apartment. She loves the brown leather couch and
the two matching armchairs, the taupes, beiges, and off-
whites everywhere; the way the colors contrast against the
decorative Aztec-patterned pillows with their bright hues
and geometric shapes. She loves the glass-topped coffee
table. A bit modern for her, she concedes, but she belongs

to another generation. Her gaze slides over her daughter. "You're a young woman, Anna," she says. Her gaze slides away. "Well, not young. But you are nowhere close to middle age. You have a bright future ahead of you."

Anna does not remind her that at thirty-nine, she is at the age when the descent can be predictably shorter than the ascent, the fabled trigger of the midlife crisis. Her mother does not want to be told that she is almost forty; she does not want to be reminded that at almost forty, her daughter is unmarried and childless.

"I have the same Boscoe Holder." Her mother is standing in front of the painting of La Diablesse, the elegant seductress of the rainforest feared by mothers of boys on the verge of manhood. Holder has dressed La Diablesse in a white Victorian gown, the high collar, puffed sleeves, cinched waist, and pleated flounce flowing over a high bustle in the back, capturing in detail the repressive style deemed fashionable for women of that era. He has not painted her cloven foot, but her eyes, shaded by a white lace parasol and a hat brimmed with a large pink flower in full bloom, are ablaze with erotic desire. She stands against a background of dense forest and bright green ferns, the earth around her painted in shades of burnt orange. John Sinclair likes the muted seascapes of Jackie Hinkson's watercolors, but Beatrice Sinclair chose this painting. Was it the cloven hoof ever more present for its absence, the elegance of the gown, hat, and parasol failing to distract the eye, that drew her in? Or was it the hat and parasol suggesting the modesty of the wearer that the smoldering eyes belied? Anna thinks it is the latter that fascinates her mother. Her mother is a modest woman, her father says, but he confesses it was her swaying hips and seductive stride that made him lose breath when he first saw her.

"She's lovely," Anna says. "I couldn't resist getting the print."

Her mother's eyes remain fixed on the painting. "We have the same taste," she murmurs.

"And she'll inherit the original." They turn around in unison, surprised by the sudden intrusion of John Sinclair's voice. They had not noticed him standing behind them. He had been back and forth taking the suitcases to the bedroom. He had not seemed interested in what they were saying. "That's our plan," he says now to Anna. "Your mother and I intend to leave the painting to you."

Beatrice steps away. "Hopefully not too soon," she says quietly. And in that instant Anna is reminded of her illness. Her color is vibrant. Not a hint of pallor mars her brown skin. She is wearing a festive fuchsia-pink cotton dress, the fabric too light and too bright for the fall weather, but it drapes over her body and hides the bandaged wound on her chest. How deliberately she must have chosen this dress, Anna realizes now. The color warms her mother's face so convincingly that Anna has been deluded into forgetting the major surgery just three days ago.

After lunch, Anna settles them in her bedroom. Her mother says she'll take a nap and urges her husband to do the same. John Sinclair does not object, but Anna suspects he does so because he doesn't want to get in his daughter's way. "You must have work to do," he says to Anna.

It is two in the afternoon; the workday is almost over. When Anna calls her office, Tanya Foster tells her there's no need for her to come in. The following morning will be just fine. "There's nothing happening here that can't wait until tomorrow," she says.

Anna does not detect the slightest trace of insincerity in her tone, and yet she is troubled by a nagging sense of foreboding. Perhaps it is the lively chatter and laughter in the background that make her wary; she is certain she hears Tim Greene's voice shouting out, "Tanya! Come look at this."

Something is happening, there is no doubt, but whatever it is, Tanya Foster seems to think that for Anna, it can wait until tomorrow.

At ten to four Anna boils the water for tea for her parents. When the kettle whistles, her mother comes out of the bedroom. Her gait is steady, her face animated. "Anna! How nice of you. Tea at four. You remembered."

Anna is flustered, amazed at her mother's strength and confounded by the sweetness in her voice. Since they have arrived, it is her mother who has been nice, complimenting her on the apartment, now praising her for remembering tea at four. She planned to serve them in the bedroom. She has already prepared a tray with guava jelly, slices of the coconut bread she bought in the West Indian bakery, cheddar cheese, milk, sugar, cups, saucers, cutlery, dessert plates. "You shouldn't have come out," Anna says. "I wanted you to have your tea in the bedroom."

Her mother pulls out a chair and sits down. "I feel fine. The nap was all I needed. I have had enough meals in bed in the hospital. I want to sit on a proper chair and eat at a proper table."

Anna begins to unpack the tray on the table. "Here, let me help you, Anna," her mother says, but as soon as she extends her right hand for one of the cups, she winces and the cup clatters to the saucer. The tumor was not in her right breast, but her right arm is weak and it is too soon for her to stretch it.

Anna moves the tray away from her. "Let me serve you, Mummy."

Her mother allows her arm to drop to her side. "In the hospital, I fed myself," she murmurs. Anna looks away, embarrassed for her, though she empathizes too. Her mother is woman whose husband feeds her illusion that she depends on no one. She is accustomed to having full control of her household. If her father were with them, Anna thinks, he would know what to do to erase the fear gathering at the corners of her mother's eyes.

"It's my turn," Anna says. "You took care of me when I was child. Let me. I'll set the table for you and Daddy."

Her mother yields; her face relaxes. "You know, Anna," she says, sitting back in her chair, "I told your father that the happiest day of my life was when we got married. But the truth is, the happiest day of my life was when you were born." Her eyes drift dreamily and out of her mouth comes a sound that is mirthless, though her lips are spread in a smile.

Anna moves the tea things from the tray to the table. The knife slips off the cheese board in her hand and falls to the ground. She bends down to pick it up and when she stands up again, the flash flood that swept through her body, heating her face, subsides. "Is that why you sent me away?" Her voice is modulated to a harsh whisper.

Her mother peers up at her, genuine surprise in her eyes. "Oh, Anna, why do you say such things?"

She says such things because she cannot stop herself from thinking such things. She says such things because she cannot prevent herself from thinking that this was what her mother wanted, that she wanted Anna out of the way so she could have her husband to herself and the social life she craved: the cocktail parties, the dinner parties, the trips around the world.

"I didn't send you away," Beatrice says when her

daughter does not answer her. "You wanted to go away."

"How do you know what I wanted?" Anna places a plate in front of her. "You never asked."

"I know what I wanted for myself. I know I wanted more out of life than to be a wife."

Anna does not believe her. An old pain gnaws at her heart. "And more than to be a mother," she says, finishing what her mother has not said.

Her mother does not back down. "Yes. And more than to be a mother. I wanted it all: marriage, motherhood, and meaningful work. But I couldn't have it all. Not in my day. So I wanted to give you the chance I did not have. Now you can have it all, Anna—a job, a husband . . ." Her eyes brighten. "Oh, I know you'll marry again and you'll have children. I believe that, Anna."

And what is she to believe? Is she expected to believe that this was her mother's grand plan? But the plan did not work. Her daughter is divorced; she has no children. Well, let her mother believe what she wants to believe. This is not the time to open that wound. There will be other times after her mother has fully healed.

"Where's Daddy?" Anna wants to turn her mother's attention away from her. She puts three tea bags in the teapot. She will add the boiling water when her father comes and give him an extra tea bag, for he likes his tea strong.

Her mother seems to welcome the distraction. "Oh, I told him to put on another shirt," she says. "That shirt he wore to the hospital this morning was ripped at the pocket."

Anna had seen the tear on her father's shirt, but it was miniscule, so tiny she would not have noticed it if her father had not stood before her and asked, "Do you think your mother will approve?" He was asking about the color of the shirt, whether it was a match for the brown pants he was wearing. He had not noticed the rip on his shirt and Anna had not bothered to point it out to him.

"I always have to check him before he leaves the house," her mother says irritably.

The irritation is a pretense her mother has long nurtured. The checking began after her father had an affair, after Thelma, after he said his wife wasn't fun anymore, after she forgave him. And after his wife was fun again, John Sinclair happily submitted to her inspections.

"I should have shown him the tear at his pocket," Anna says, "and fixed it for him."

Her mother narrows her eyes and smiles slyly, grateful, it seems to Anna, for the part her daughter has willingly played in her game. She adjusts the folds of her dress over her knees and exhales. "I wonder what's taking him so long," she grumbles.

Their quarrel is over. Anna is relieved she has succeeded in diverting their slide down a precipice that surely would have ended in shattered bones on the rocks below.

"John, come!" Beatrice calls out to her husband. "Anna has fixed tea for us."

They do not talk about her mother's illness at teatime. They do not talk about it at dinnertime. They talk about domestic matters, about the home they left behind, about Singh and Lydia who are now in charge. Her father launches into his usual argument. It is time they retire Singh, he says. Singh hardly does anything in the garden. They hire boys to mow the lawn and weed the flowerbeds. Beatrice reminds her husband that Singh is younger than he is. John Sinclair snorts: "He is seventy-eight! Seventy-eight is not young, Beatrice. Sixty is the retirement age on our island."

Anna knows how this argument will end. Her father will give in, as he usually gives in to her mother, but not before he forces her to make a concession.

Lydia also has no work to do since her employers are not on the island. Beatrice has not been unreasonable. She has agreed to pay Lydia her full wages while they are gone, but she insists that the woman keep her regular hours. She wants Lydia to come to the house at five, as she would normally. "To do what?" John Sinclair asks.

"People get lazy when they have too much time on their hands," Anna's mother says dismissively. She recites the list of duties she has left for Lydia: Every day Lydia must dust and vacuum. On Mondays and Wednesdays she must mop the terrazzo floors in the passageways and in the covered veranda. On Tuesdays and Thursdays she must clean all the kitchen cabinets and the linen closets. It's not enough work to fill the hours of the three weeks the Sinclairs are expected to be away. Still, Beatrice tells her husband, she expects Lydia to keep the same work hours.

John Sinclair seizes his chance to underscore his point. "Lydia'll get a lot of time to sleep in the veranda," he says, "and to watch the soaps on TV in the den." Beatrice throws him a withering glance.

Anna is glad for the domestic chatter, glad to put a bandage on the sore that had begun to bleed moments ago. But she must ready herself for the feelings to return in the evening. For tonight, before her mother goes to bed, she must change the dressing on her chest; she must remove the drain the surgeon has inserted at the end of the sutures to release the blood and fluids that have collected there. Her mother must expose her body to her. She must touch her naked skin.

TWELVE

She has nothing to fear. Later that night, steeling herself for her duty as a daughter, Anna knocks on the bedroom door. "Come in," her father calls out. Anna opens the door and what she sees bolts her feet to the floor.

On the island her father has the reputation for being a man's man, admired not only for his intellect, for his quick wit and laser-sharp ability to make heads of private companies, local and English, yield to his persuasive arguments on matters of labor negotiations; respected not only for the high lifestyle he has provided for his wife, who has never had reason to work, but also because he is a man who can sit with kings and yet is at home with peasants. For years he hunted and fished with people from the countryside who could neither read nor write. There are stories about how he led his fellow hunters through a dangerous rainstorm in the forest, how he narrowly escaped being swallowed by a macajuel snake. Fishermen tell how in the gulf connecting the South American continent to the island, where an oil belt runs under the water from shore to shore, he dared to fish close to the forbidden line where Venezuelans soldiers trained their guns on islanders trespassing on the side of the gulf they claim is theirs. It was rumored her father yelled out "¿Qué pasa, amigos?" when the soldiers threatened to gun him down. With a broad grin plastered on his face, he held up a case of beer. "For you."

The soldiers pulled up alongside, and still unnerved, refusing to be intimidated, her father pointed to the bottles of whiskey and rum under a bench in the boat. "For you too," he said, disarming the soldiers and forcing smiles across their stone faces. Few know why he stopped hunting and fishing. Few know that it was the pleading eyes of a deer within his shooting range that made him put down his rifle. Few know it was the death of his friend in his arms, in the pirogue where they had spent many happy hours on the sea, that had made him stop fishing. Anna knows these stories, yet she is still unprepared for what she sees when she steps into the bedroom.

Her father does not acknowledge her presence. He is standing in front of her mother, fully dressed, concentrating on what he is doing. Her mother is sitting on the edge of the bed, her back to the door. She is naked down to the place when the slit begins on her backside. Her husband towers over her, her head barely in line with his shoulders. She too does not utter a word; she too does not turn her head when Anna's footsteps reverberate through the room. It is a tableau of a husband and wife in a scene so unbearably intimate that tears puncture Anna's eyes. She stands there transfixed. Time freezes, stops still for the image to be indelibly imprinted in her mind.

She would not have believed her mother's body so exquisite. It is not a young body. Her mother is seventy-two. Already time has destroyed much of the elasticity in her skin; it sags, but it does not crease. There are no wrinkles on her back. The skin is smooth, fluid, butterscotch-brown flowing from fleshy shoulders down to a certain defined, if thick, waistline, flaring out to voluptuous hips. It is not a body to be found in fashion magazines; it is the body of a mature woman who has not denied herself her passion for mangoes or coconut ice cream, a body softened by fat, a body that would arrest a painter's eye.

Symmetry, Anna believes, defines beauty for many artists, the alignment of curves and planes and lines that cannot be altered without the risk of shattering its perfection. Her mother has no hair on her head, the follicles deadened by the toxins meant to halt the growth of the tumors. But even her bald head held erect as she faces her husband—regal, it appears to Anna—is essential to the symmetry of the curves, lines, and planes of her body, fixing the point from where the eye is compelled to descend, and rendering the viewer, like Anna, breathless.

What her father is doing is what Paul Bishop has instructed Anna to do. Although she cannot see her father's hands, Anna is certain he is removing the blood-stained dressing from her mother's wound, cleaning the drain attached to the last of the sutures.

A man's man. She had thought her father squeamish as a man's man is supposed to be. When they took Beatrice to the doctor on the island, her father's friend Neil Lee Pak had warned him, "Woman's business." Neil Lee Pak advised him that Anna alone should be with her mother when the doctor examines her.

A man's man remains outside, waiting for the results. A man's man leaves matters of a woman's bodily functions to the business of women. But it is her father who does this woman's business; it is Anna who stands outside in the waiting room.

"If it should happen to me, if the gene passed down from my mother's mother to my mother should be in me, waiting to erupt, I will know how to handle it," Anna says to Paula when at last the emotions that tightened her throat loosen their grip and she is able to call her.

"Where are they now?"

"Sleeping. They were so . . ." Anna breathes in, exhales, and tries again. "I wanted to serve her tea in bed this afternoon, but she was out of her room before I could get there. I knew she was in pain, though she never said a word. She acts as though nothing really major has happened to her, as if losing her breast is no big thing. I don't think I'd be able to do that. I don't think I'd be able to suffer in silence."

"She's not suffering in silence," Paula says.

"She hasn't complained."

"To you."

"I don't think to my father, either," Anna says.

"It's her faith."

Anna does not understand.

"The faith that had her praying for the tumors to go away is the same faith that consoles her now. She doesn't need to tell you or your father about her pain. She speaks to the Virgin Mary. She puts her suffering in Mary's hands and so her burden is lightened."

Paula's response surprises Anna. "Since when have you become religious?"

"Oh, I didn't have a conversion, if that's what you mean. I'm a believer, but I don't have your mother's faith. I admire it, that's all."

"She spent months locked up in her bathroom praying to the Virgin and all that happened was that the tumors got bigger," Anna says. "They didn't go away."

"Your mother believes her prayers were answered."

"And exactly how were they answered? She had to have chemo to reduce the tumors before a doctor could operate. They had grown so big."

"Her prayers were answered when your boyfriend came to visit her," Paula says.

Anna brushes her comment away. "He's not my boyfriend."

Paula chuckles. "I stand corrected. When your lover came to visit her."

Anna does her best to ignore her. "So tell me, Miss Soothsayer," she says, "how were her prayers answered?"

"You need to have faith like your mother that things will turn out well for you with your Dr. Bishop," Paula chides her.

"Things didn't exactly turn out well for my mother," Anna responds.

"Your Dr. Bishop persuaded her to come to the States. She had surgery here. It was successful. Your mother believes her prayers were answered and she is cured. She acts the way she does because she believes she has nothing to worry about now. The cancer has been removed— not the way she wanted at first, but the tumors are not there anymore. She has faith that her prayers have made it possible, that the Virgin Mary acted in her own way and in her own time. The universe is unfolding as it should."

The Desiderata. Her mother quoted these same lines on the morning of her surgery.

"Your mother's religion may have saved her," Paula says.

"Most of the sins in the world are committed in the name of religion," Anna replies defiantly.

"And most of the good too," Paula counters, silencing Anna. She has been critical of her mother's attitude toward the people who work for her. She has accused her mother of neocolonialism, of bossing Lydia and Singh with the same high-handed, superior manner that the white colonial bosses used to humiliate the people they colonized in the days when the island was a colony. She seethed at the hypocrisy of her mother's devotion to religion while she continued to belittle those she considered her social inferiors. Then Anna discovered that all she thought was real was not real, that she had used the eyes of an outsider to judge her mother. For she had seen her mother scamper across the lawn with Singh. She had caught Lydia sprawled on the floor in the den watching the soaps. *As the World Turns.* "Madam and I does talk about it," Lydia had said.

"You may want to deny it," Paula says now, "but you're just like your mother." Anna begins to object, but Paula cuts across her stammerings. "She's probably in pain as you say, but your mother wants to protect you. She doesn't want you to suffer because of her. And look at you. You spent your entire vacation with her. You drained her sutures and changed her dressing though you didn't want to. You sucked it up."

She could have told Paula right then that it was her father who drained her mother's sutures and changed her dressing. She could have admitted that before she knocked on the bedroom door, she had stood there, minutes passing by as she tried to build a wall around herself, a barrier that would shield her from longing, or perhaps rejection, and would not leave her exposed, vulnerable. It is shame now that seals her lips, shame for the relief she felt. For it is her mother who has had the generosity of spirit to deny herself for the sake of her daughter. Her mother exercises restraint. She withholds her suffering from her daughter. Is this the lesson she has to learn? Like a wall, is restraint a barrier that protects while it excludes?

"Don't you have to get back to work soon?" Paula asks, changing the subject.

"Yes," Anna says. "Tomorrow."

"Be prepared."

They are not in the same room, but Anna is sure if they were, if she could see Paula, her friend would be wagging her finger in warning. *Be prepared.*

THIRTEEN

But Anna is not prepared. There is a bouquet of bright orange tulips with yellow tips in a glass vase on her desk. Immediately, she thinks they are from Tanya, a gift to welcome her back to work. More than once she has told Tanya that her favorite flowers are tulips. There is a card next to the vase. She puts down her briefcase and opens it. The tulips are not from Tanya; it is Paul who has sent them to her. Warm feelings of gratitude escalate to rapturous joy. Paul had practically accused her of placing her priorities in the wrong order, putting work before her family, and yet he has cared enough to let her know he still supports her. She has never told him tulips are the flowers she likes best, and yet, of all the flowers in the world he could have sent her, he has sent her tulips.

She is a practical woman, a realist. She has been impatient with her mother for placing her faith on hope, on prayers alone, when science, years of medical research, could have helped her. She has taught herself to rely on reason and on observable fact. Now a vase full of yellow-tipped orange tulips jettisons lessons she was forced to learn when Alice abandoned her and she found herself alone in a foreign country without family or friends. *If he should ask me to marry him, I will say yes.* The words come to her with unshakeable certitude.

Glued to the outside of the card is a photograph of a beach. She recognizes it. It is on the eastern coast of the island where the Atlantic is a roaring cauldron, smashing glistening waves against towering black rocks that will eventually be broken into bits by her awesome power, and leaving winding banners of frothy white surf along the shoreline. A forest of coconut trees bend toward the coarse-grained sandy beach, their trunks bowed by the force of trade winds. Paul has sent her a reminder of the history they share: tulips that grow in the country where they live, a photograph of a beach in their homeland. Inside the card, he has written just a few words:

> Dear Anna,
>   You remain in my heart.
> Love,
> Paul

She stands in front of her desk, her eyes closed, her back to the door, the card pressed to her chest. So full of warm affection for this man who has come into her life, a man straddling two worlds like her, she does not hear when Tanya knocks on her office door or when she walks inside the room. Only when Tanya taps her on her shoulder is she jolted to the present.

"Flowers!" Tanya cradles the petals in her hand. "An admirer?"

Anna slips the card under a pile of papers on her desk. "A friend," she murmurs.

"Must be a special friend."

"Yes, a special friend."

"Lucky you."

They kiss each other on both cheeks, and when they part, Anna bends down to pick up her briefcase that she has left on the floor.

Tanya steps back and apologizes. "Good Lord. I haven't even given you a chance to get settled."

But Anna is grateful for this moment to remake her face, to suppress the joy that had brightened her cheeks, to dampen the sparkle in her eyes, and to put on a smile that Tanya will recognize, the bland, friendly smile she wears at work. "I can't tell enough how much I appreciate the time you gave me," she says. "My parents are thankful too, especially my mother."

"It was the least I could do," Tanya says.

"And now you're leaving. Things won't be the same here without you."

Tanya sits in the chair next to Anna's desk and stretches out her legs. "I wish I could take you with me. You are a treasure, Anna. Equiano would not be where it is today without you."

"I can't take all the credit," Anna says. She is facing Tanya now, sitting on her side of the desk. "Without you, I don't think we would be so successful."

Tanya crosses her hands over her thighs. "Yes, you have a good editor's eye. You can find them even if they are buried in the haystack. I told Tim how we found you."

Anna's back stiffens. "How is he doing?" She hopes her tone is casual and does not betray the anxiety that has snaked up her spine.

"You probably already guessed that we never intended for him to be an assistant to you the way Tammy Mohun was," Tanya says. "I figured you'd be the best one to teach him the ropes."

"The ropes?"

"The business. What we do here."

"I thought he already had experience in the publishing industry," Anna says cautiously.

"Yes, but not in a company that is organized as we are. They didn't have a special imprint for writers of color where he was."

"So you're taking him with you? Is that what you want to tell me?'

Tanya brings her chair closer to Anna's desk. "Look, Anna, there are going to be some changes here. I think they will be good for you. I think you're going to like them. Tim's a good guy. He's smart, a Cornell graduate."

"Cornell?" Anna is mildly surprised. From the way he dresses, the way he seems to keep his thoughts in check, she would have thought Howard, the Ivy League of the black colleges.

"That's another story," Tanya says. "How he got there. Oh, I don't mean he didn't have the grades, but it costs a lot of money to go to Cornell."

"I suppose as smart as you say he is, he must have had a scholarship," Anna remarks.

Tanya purses her lips, and then, seeming to decide to ignore the sarcasm in Anna's tone, her lips relax. "Yes, I suppose you can say he had a scholarship. A sort of scholarship anyway. But he earned every penny. That's what they said about him at his last job. They said he earned his pay. All the books he edited did well. He knows about sales, what people read, what people want. You're going to find him great to work with, Anna," she says brightly.

"Work with?" The muscles around Anna's mouth tense.

"I wanted to tell you about this a long time ago." Tanya is leaning over the desk, her hand extended, but Anna has rolled her chair backward. "Windsor is expanding," Tanya says.

"Expanding?"

"This is going to be good for you, Anna. You are in the right place at the right time."

"The right—" Anna stops herself. She has been repeating Tanya's words like an immature child who is unable to fully process what she has been told. "What does this expansion have to do with me? Or with Tim for that matter?" she finally says, hardening her voice.

Tanya withdraws her hand. She crosses her legs at her knees. A dark shadow seems to loom over her eyes, her eyebrows contracting. "It's all business, Anna. I may be the publisher, but I work for the company and for the investors in the company. I . . . You too, Anna, must comply with the board's decisions. They want to expand. We're going to merge with McDuffy. I'm not really leaving the company. I am going to be the head of the new merger, the head of Windsor-McDuffy."

Anna stands up and gathers the shreds of her self-control that had begun to unravel. She stretches out her hand to Tanya across her desk. "Congratulations. That is good news for you, Tanya. And well deserved."

Tanya slides to the edge of her chair and takes the hand Anna offers her. "Good news for you too, Anna. Sit, sit. Let me tell you."

Anna settles back in her chair and waits.

"First, we are not going to move you. But now Equinao is going to be more specialized than it was before. You know, our original plan was that Equiano would handle all the books by writers of color. That meant Asian, African, Latino, Indian, Korean, Caribbean, African American, what have you. But as you can see, the African American books took over. That list has just grown and grown, and Windsor has had to handle the spillover. Not doing a good job at it, if you ask me. So when we agreed to merge with McDuffy, we decided to create a specific publishing house for all writers of color, not just an imprint in another company. We're going to call the new publishing house TeaHouse Press and merge McDuffy's list of writers of color with our list. It's going to be big, something that the publishing industry has never seen before." Tanya's voice strains with excitement, her eyes sparkle. "We're going to take over the market of books by writers of color. This is going to be huge!"

Anna's spine begins to tingle again. "You can't be serious," she says.

"As a heart attack. Think of it, Anna. Every writer of color will have to come to us. We are going to be the experts. We will corner that market. All the Asians, all the Africans, all the Latinos . . ."

"All the what-have-yous," Anna says quietly.

"What did you say?" Tanya is staring at her.

"It's racist," Anna says.

"What?"

"What you plan to do is no less than racial segregation."

"We're not talking about people here, Anna. We're talking about books."

"People write books."

"Of course people write books, but we are in the business of books, not people. We are publishing books, marketing books, selling books."

"That people write."

"I think if you open your mind, Anna, you'll see how this is a good thing for the people who write books. They need us. We know the business of getting books to readers. With this new press, we will be able to focus all our attention on promoting and distributing books by writers of color. We can reach out to specific demographics. We can design print, electronic, and television advertisements targeted to specific groups. This will increase our market share. Writers will get better returns, higher royalties. Isn't that what writers want?"

"They want to write good books."

"Don't be naïve, Anna. The only problem writers have with us is about money. They say we're not promoting them enough, distributing their books widely enough. But bottom line, they are talking about money. That we're not making enough money for them is their real complaint. You think if we made a lot of money for them they'd still complain? No, they'd be praising us to the hilt—it wouldn't matter what we do, what we call ourselves. With TeaHouse Press we'll be in the best position to sell their books, to make more money for them."

"The name is racist," Anna says.

"TeaHouse Press? You must be joking."

"It sends a not-so-subtle signal that the books published here need not concern white readers."

"Come on, Anna. Everybody drinks tea. Why, English people love tea. They drink it all the time. You can't be more Anglo than the British! They drink tea in China, in India, on your islands in the Caribbean, right? They drink tea in Africa. Even in South Africa, those Afrikaners drink tea. What could possibly be racist in the name TeaHouse Press? Someone suggested Molasses House Press and Cocoa House Press. I could see how you could complain about those names. I mean molasses is definitely black and cocoa is brown, dark brown to be sure."

"And so is tea," Anna says, keeping her voice even.

Tanya plants both elbows firmly on top of the desk. She points her finger at Anna. "That's your problem, Anna. You don't understand niche marketing."

"I understand that a well-written book is a well-written book regardless of the color of the writer's skin."

"That may be true, but a well-written book by a writer of color is more meaningful to a reader of color."

"No more meaningful than to a white reader."

"I disagree," Tanya says. "People like stories that reflect their similar experiences. Readers of color get to see themselves in books where there are characters of color."

"I see myself in Jane Austen," Anna says.

"You're educated."

Anna's head burns. "Careful, Tanya."

"I mean, you're a special reader. You're different from the average black reader."

"Careful, Tanya," Anna says again.

"People like to read about themselves and people who are like them," Tanya insists.

"People learn more from people whose experiences are different from theirs. You may be comforted to know that someone just like you has managed to overcome some adversity or has triumphed in some way, but you learn a lot about yourself, what your true values are, what your real positions are on issues, when you are out of your comfort zone. Like Brutus said to Cassius—"

Tanya throws back her head and laughs. "You're proving my point, Anna. You're an elitist. That's your problem."

"*The eye sees not itself / But by reflection, by some other things.*" Anna does not allow Tanya to derail her.

Tanya stands up. "I didn't come here for a lecture, Anna." Her eyes narrow to slits before they open again. "Anyway," she says, more calmly now, "I've never heard you object to Equiano, and Equiano is an imprint for writers of color."

At Windsor. But Anna holds her tongue. There is something in the way light blazes from Tanya's eyes that warns her to say no more. Tanya Foster is still her boss. But if she dared, she would tell Tanya her hopes. She would tell her that she saw Equiano, and imprints like Equiano, as a transitional phase in publishing, a way to bring attention to the works of writers of color to publishers and readers. All readers. Eventually, imprints for writers of color would no longer be needed, their lists of books fully integrated with the lists of mainstream publishers. Equiano would be merged into Windsor, she thought, contracted, not expanded to a house of its own.

Tanya waits for her to respond, and when Anna doesn't, she looks directly into her eyes and says, "I came to let you know what's happening. I don't want you to be surprised when you hear the news later today."

More news. Anna tenses but keeps her lips firmly closed.

"Tim Greene has been appointed to head TeaHouse Press." Tanya frames the words as an announcement of an irrevocable decision.

Paula warned her. Still Anna is not prepared to hear this news. In all her suppositions of what might happen when Tanya leaves the company, she had not considered this one. Even as Tanya disclosed that she would head the newly formed Windsor-McDuffy Publishing Company, her brain continued to write the script she had rehearsed: Tim Greene would join Tanya. Didn't Tanya admire him, praise him? "Where will that leave me?" She is aware she sounds nervous.

"You'll have your position." Tanya lowers her eyes. She slides her hands down the sides of her narrow skirt and twists it at her hips as if to adjust it. But her skirt does not need adjusting; it falls perfectly straight to her knees. "Equiano will be an imprint of TeaHouse Press," she says.

"You mean I'll be working for Tim Greene?"

"You're smart, Anna. You read tea leaves." She turns to leave, stops, and turns back. "Tea leaves, TeaHouse." Her face breaks into a wide smile. "That's a good one." She is laughing when she opens the door. "Tea leaves, TeaHouse. Funny!"

Her day is ruined. Less than an hour ago she was filled with such joy, such hope. She had allowed herself to make a cataclysmic leap to her past, reading meaning in signs, finding her future in a bunch of tulips, allowing herself to hope though she had no real evidence. Cataclysmic because she had long broken the habit, instilled in her from childhood, of believing in a world of spirits that existed side by side with the natural world, making their presence known by signs and symbols that warned of dangers or pointed the way to happiness.

She had grown up with stories of the spirits that roam the island, the soucouyant, the douen, La Diablesse, stories she breathed in like air and which permeated every segment of the island, sparing no one. Her mother is Catholic, but when Anna was a child, sick with fever, the chicken pox, or measles, she burned orange peel for the spirits to heal her daughter, and lit candles to the Virgin Mary. When Beatrice woke up one morning with black and blue marks on her arm during a week-long holiday the family was spending in the country, she swore a soucouyant had sucked her blood in the night. John Sinclair, who had converted to Catholicism to please his wife, tried to dissuade her, but all his patient reasoning about bats in the fruit trees that must have bitten her arm could not change Beatrice's mind. She believed, as many others on the island believed, that the soucouyant lived under the silk fig tree. At night she shed her skin and sucked the blood of her victims before turning into a ball of fire. Anna has a vague memory of her paternal grandmother, who was not Catholic, reducing her mother to tears when she claimed that there was not one ounce of difference between Catholicism and obeah. The followers of both believed in the magic of transubstantiation, though that was not the word she used. As Anna remembers it, her grandmother, Mrs. Henrietta Sinclair, told her mother, Mrs. Beatrice Sinclair, that she knew good Catholics who did not swallow the Communion the priest placed on the tongues. They put it in their pockets and at night used the Communion in their obeah rituals to awaken the dead.

Anna has told Tanya this story. They laughed. Now Tanya has used it against her. "You read tea leaves," she said sarcastically.

But she has not read the tea leaves. The fingers on her right hand twitched when she first met Tim Greene, but she dug her nails into the palm of her hand and let her brain determine what she should think. This morning was an aberration, reading her future in tulips, orange ones with yellow tips, her favorite. Now she must prepare herself for Tim Greene. He is to become her new boss. This is the reality she must face. How foolish she was to let her brain delude her into believing that he was no longer going to be with the company, that Tanya would take him with her when she left.

Perhaps if she had read the tea leaves she would have made more of the omissions in Tim Greene's e-mail. Not one word about Raine when she had asked him to send her his notes and recount his meeting with the writer. But the boss does not have to report to his underling.

Tim Greene does not gloat. His manner is deferential toward her. He approaches her as he has always done. He does not call her boss, but he does not use her first name either. "Ms. Sinclair," he says, offering his hand. "How good to see you. We missed you. We've put practically everything on hold, waiting for you to come back."

She resists the temptation to ask, *What things? What have you put on hold?* Instead she shakes his hand. "Congratulations," she says. "Tanya tells me you are to be the new boss."

He smiles and squeezes her hand reassuringly. "You are still the boss of Equiano," he says.

"And you are going be the boss of the company that houses Equiano."

"You've done good work here." He pats her on the shoulder. "Nothing to worry about."

She shivers at his touch though she has the presence of mind to pull herself together before he notices her reaction. *Nothing to worry about?* His rapid advance up the company is everything to worry about.

"When is the merger expected to take place?" she asks.

"The stockholders will vote tomorrow."

"So soon?" Her eyes shoot open wide. It is too late to hide her dismay.

"It all came together very quickly."

Anna can hardly believe this is true. "Is that why you were hired?"

"Tanya thought I'd be a match for the company. Help her improve sales." It is a criticism aimed at her, she is certain. There is no need for him to be diplomatic—he is in charge now. She has argued against the books that put Equiano in the black. She wanted to change the cover of Bess Milford's novel. She objected to the picture of the scantily dressed voluptuous black woman in the arms of a half-naked man. It is too explicit, she complained. Too erotic. It cheapens the novel. But this is what sells, what made the company rich, and Tim Greene was hired to make the company richer.

He is American, born here, African American, Paula reminded her. He knows the terrain better than she ever could.

"Hey, take that frown off your face," Tim Greene says. "Everything will work out all right. We'll talk. You'll see."

But see what? He does not say. He has to go to a meeting. To get things ready for the merger tomorrow, he tells her.

FOURTEEN

She does not discuss the changes in her office with her parents. She tells herself she will not add to the difficulties they are facing. The surgery was successful but there are no guarantees. Doctors are not deities; they are not God; they cannot guarantee the future. Yet if thoughts of uncertainty run through her mother's mind, her mother conceals them well. The circles below her eyes are darker than usual and she cradles her left arm under the sling drawn across her shoulder, but these are the only observable signs she allows of the disease that had terrified her for months. Years, Dr. Ramdoolal said.

She is sitting comfortably on the couch when Anna comes home, her legs propped up on the footstool, her eyes glued to the TV, the channel turned to *As the World Turns*. She is addicted to this soap opera. "Going to watch some sinning," she says when she retires to her bedroom after lunch every day on the island. She is a good Catholic. She believes premarital sex is a sin; she was a virgin when she married. She believes adultery is a sin worse than premarital sex. Her husband went to confession after he ended his affair and she forgave him. Now they take Communion together in church on Sundays, proof of his fidelity.

Anna sometimes wonders if her father's dedication to her mother is not part of the penance the priest imposed on him in the confessional, but such an idea is laughable; she has witnessed too many tender moments between them.

The expression on her father's face when he changed the dressing on her mother's wound stirred her to the depths of her heart. Would that she could marry a man who would feel the same about her! If her father's devotion was imposed, it is an imposition he has willingly embraced. He does not want to lose this wife he adores.

Her mother turns away from the TV when Anna greets her. "I can't believe what those women get away with," she says. She decries fornication and adultery in the real world, but the antics of lovers on the screen fascinate her. She will rarely miss an episode of her favorite soap opera and so Anna has asked Paula to tape the ones that aired while her mother was in the hospital.

"Only on TV." Anna hangs up her jacket in the closet. "How was your day?"

"Nothing to complain about," her mother says, and turns back to the TV.

"Did you have dinner?" Anna prepared the meal the night before and left it in the refrigerator.

"Yes," her mother says, her eyes still fixed on the TV. "Your father served me. And washed the dishes too!"

Her father is in the bedroom watching the news on the other TV as he does every evening. Without work to keep him busy, he is often morose. Anna suggested he write his memoir. It took him two days to jettison the idea. She proposed reading and gave him books she thought he would like, but he was restless. In his youth, and until almost the end of his seventies, he was an active man—but now he has little patience for the stillness writing and reading requires. He prefers walking around his fish pond, dropping dog nuggets into the water, and watching his fish zoom toward them. He likes swooping out frogs from the pond with a net and taking them to the river. He likes going on long walks down the streets in their neighborhood and chasing off the stray dogs that nip at his heels with the gnarled stick he carries; only in the evening is he ready to sit still.

His addiction to the news is not unlike her mother's addiction to the soaps. Her mother gets vicarious thrills from the scandalous antics of feisty women and he gets intellectual stimulation from finding faults in the arguments of pompous politicians, safe in front of the TV screen where he can rely on no one contradicting him as he sneers at their folly and criticizes their grand plans for improving the country. He used to love a good argument, winning, besting his opponent with his razor-sharp intellect. But his memory began to slip, and now he avoids conflicts that show him up, where he has little chance of winning. His pride is his worst enemy, her mother says. When he watches American TV, he tells Anna there is much he can advise the government on the fair treatment of workers, especially migrant workers. But he remains in awe of America's apparent disregard for the social status of people who break the law. The Watergate trials riveted him. He was astounded by the near indictment of a president and the imprisonment of cabinet officials. "That would never happen on our island," he said to Anna on one of her visits. "Here, *the wicked prize itself / Buys out the law*." He was not dissuaded when Anna remarked that most of the time the wicked prize has the same power and influence in America too.

When she knocks on the door he flicks off the TV and springs to his feet. "So how was it to be back at work?" He walks over to her.

"I got flowers," she says.

"From the office?" He kisses her on her forehead.

"No, from Paul."

His eyes crinkle to slits, his thin lips spread. "Paul's a good man like his father. No one could buy Henry Bishop. He was a union man, but above all a principled man. I think your Paul is just like him."

In the morning, before she walked into her office, she would have stopped him when he said *your* Paul. She would have objected, not because she did not want Paul Bishop to be *her* Paul, but because she had learned to be careful. Divorce made her careful. Tony was *her* Tony and she was caught defenseless when he was no longer hers. But now there are tulips on her desk and a card with a message that promises so much that she pressed it to her heart.

"I like him too."

"Carpe diem," her father says and winks at her.

Later at night she calls Paul. "How did you know I like tulips?" she asks him.

He laughs. "I know more about you than you think."

The warm glow that spread across her body when she opened his card returns. She does not want to spoil this feeling with talk of work. She was angry with Tim Greene, with his patronizing air. *Take that frown off your face.* Of course she was frowning; she was burning up. He was standing there cool as a cucumber. And why wouldn't he be? He had the upper hand. He'd had the upper hand all along, believing he could trick her into submission with his sycophantic deference to her supposed position as his boss. How he and Tanya must have laughed at her behind her back! Tanya was humoring her when she asked for her opinion about the jacket for Bess Milford's novel. Tim Greene must have been sure of himself at that meeting with the sales department, leaning back in his chair and speaking to her in that patronizing tone. *It's just a poster, Anna.*

They had humiliated her. Perhaps she was wanting in her enthusiasm for the books that were the most profitable for the company, but she never rejected them outright. She still approved their publication. What she wanted was balance, balance between books published strictly for their commercial value and books one could appreciate for their aesthetic and intellectual merits. She believed that was why she was hired, why Tanya allowed her to publish two books of literary fiction every year. But two books have proved too many with the allure of dollars. The company needs a businessman. Tim Greene is the man they want.

Anna forces herself to push these thoughts to the back on her mind. She is on the phone with Paul, Paul who wrote to her that she remains in his heart.

"What do you know about me?" she says, aware she is asking for a compliment, for reassurance that her impulse was right: he is the man who could make her happy, the man she could spend the rest of her life with.

"Did you like the photograph?" he asks.

"Every time I return home, I go there," she says. "It's not the best beach for swimming; the water is too rough. But I like watching the waves. I like being so close to the Atlantic, knowing I am at one end of an ocean that links me to where I now live and to where I was born."

"And which we crossed, chained in the holds of slave ships."

She is momentarily taken aback.

"Oh, I don't get depressed about it," he says, when he notices her silence. "It's just that you can't look at the Atlantic from our side of the world without thinking about how we got there. We are like the coconut trees in the photograph."

She knows the story about the coconut trees, though

she had not learned it in school. The British were educating girls and boys to serve them; the history of the Caribbean was irrelevant to them. How else would an island empire thousands of miles away from the countries it colonized keep the inhabitants from revolting? There had to be a front guard loyal to the Crown that would hold the natives in check. Slavemasters in America were torturing the Africans they enslaved for reading, but the British had discovered the hard way the truth of the maxim, *Nature abhors a vacuum. Fill their minds with your stories and they will adore you; leave their minds free to roam and they will hatch plans to destroy you.*

Anna found out about the coconut trees purely by chance. Once, on a visit to her parents, passing by a bookstore at the airport, a coffee-table volume about the history of the island caught her eye. It was in that book she learned that coconuts were not indigenous to the island. Their presence there was accidental. Over two hundred years ago, a ship loaded with coconuts on its way out of the Orinoco River had almost capsized in the waters near her island. It righted itself but lost most of its cargo. Strong currents swept the coconuts to the shore; within months they were sprouting leaves.

"They remind me of us," Paul says. "We are transplants too."

"But the coconuts took root on the island."

"Except, of course, we have voluntarily transplanted ourselves again."

"This time without our roots," she says quietly.

"Now you understand why I know so much about you. We're the same."

He means their history is the same. It is not what she hoped to hear. She had hoped for something more romantic. She had hoped he would say he felt the same way she felt.

* * *

All is quiet in the office when Anna comes to work the next morning. The receptionist says a perfunctory hello and swiftly casts her eyes back down on her desk. She shuffles through a stack of papers, flips one over, and studies it as if she has some pressing task she cannot interrupt with paying one more second of attention to Anna. Down the corridor, past rows of cubicles to her office, Anna can see bodies bent forward, eyes fixed on computer screens. No one looks up except two women who glance at her briefly, smile, and then abruptly turn away. Tim Greene is nowhere in sight.

Anna returns to the receptionist and asks if she knows when Tim is expected in the office. "He's at a meeting," the receptionist says.

Another meeting. There was one the day before too.

"Having breakfast with Ms. Foster, of course," the receptionist explains, responding to Anna's query whether the meeting is in the conference room or in another building. The whiff of impatience in her voice borders disrespect.

"Do you know when he'll be back?"

"They have to clear an office for him." The receptionist continues to flip through the stack of papers. "Ms. Foster's office."

Anna returns to her desk. In the absence of the usual office conversations, the clatter of computer keys is magnified. The phone startles her when it rings. There's an insistent buzzing in the air, not of machines nor of voices; it is the kind of vibration one feels when wires are pulled taut between rigid poles. It is invisible, soundless, but palpable. They know, all of them, Anna thinks. They are awaiting their fate; they are awaiting *her* fate, staying on the periphery until they find out where the axe will fall.

Fifteen minutes later, Rita knocks on her door—Rita, the butt of jokes among the men at the watercooler. She always wants to please, always has a kind word for everyone. "Loved the novel," she had said to Anna, as if to deflect the blow she knew was coming from the boys in the art department who'd already decided what was to happen to Bess Milford's cover. Anna wishes she could tell her that the tight pencil skirts she wears do not flatter her figure. Only the superskinny girls look alluring in those tight skirts. Rita's hips are too wide, her legs too thick. She would look better in the sort of pantsuits Hillary Clinton wears no matter the occasion.

Rita has brought her a cup of tea. She has prepared it the way Anna likes, with milk, no sugar. "I don't think things are as bad as they may seem," she says, handing Anna the tea. "I think we're going to be okay. I think things will be just fine."

Anna is glad to see her. The silence in the office is unnerving. She is glad for this chance to bring everything in the open, to put an end to the tension she can feel rumbling down the corridor toward her like a stream gathering speed over loose pebbles. "I suppose you already know Tim's going to be our new boss," she says.

"Change is not always bad. Change can be good." Rita recites these words like a robot on autopilot. She does not like conflict, head-on conflict especially. She wants to be liked. Anna has no doubt she agreed with the choice of cover for Bess Milford's novel, perhaps even recommended it, but she left the heavy lifting for Tanya.

"Don't worry about me," Anna says. "I'm fine."

Rita frowns and twists her mouth from side to side, and it occurs to Anna that though her colleague has come ostensibly to cheer her up, perhaps she has also come to be cheered up. Perhaps it is her own job she is worried about.

"Is the change going to affect you?" Anna asks.

"Oh, no! Tim has assured me . . ." She brings fingers to her mouth and presses them to her closed lips. Her eyes skim the floor.

Of course, Tim has assured her. Tim is the new boss. Anna points to a chair in her room. "Sit, sit," she says. "I'm glad to hear it. I'm glad you're okay."

"And you're going to be okay too. I came to tell you that. I know it here." Rita taps her chest where her heart beats.

"Know?"

"There's no one who has finer taste. I loved all the books you picked." She eases herself into the chair Anna offered.

"Finer taste is not in question here." Anna surprises herself by the sudden bitterness in her tone.

"Even Tim said so." A forced smile brightens Rita's face. "He said the company was lucky to have you. There is no better editor around."

So he has established her title: she is an editor. She is fully aware that this is her role, but she is also a manager, the head of Equiano. Anna does not know what angers her more: that he should so casually define her role publicly without giving her the courtesy of notifying the staff herself, or that he has so rapidly assumed his position as her boss when only days ago he was working for her and not the other way around. "It's nice to know he has a high opinion of me," she says evenly.

Rita sits forward in her chair. "You have nothing to worry about, Anna. You and Tim will work out just fine. Just fine. He admires you."

"Admires me?" Anna's temples twitch. "Don't you think

it was a little underhanded the way he came in the office?"

"Through the back door, you mean? That's the way business is done here, Anna. They wanted him to see the lay of the land, to see if he fit, before they made the big announcement."

"They had already decided he fit. They had decided that before he put a foot in the door," Anna says drily.

"What if there's a pay raise in this for you? Don't count that out, Anna."

Rita's Pollyanna cheeriness begins to get under Anna's skin, but she resists the temptation to direct her anger toward the woman. Rita is well intentioned, she wants to be helpful; she wants to prepare her for the changes to come. It makes no sense to lash out at her. Anna presses her hand. "Rita, you are one of the kindest people I've met here."

Rita blushes.

Paula is not so sanguine. Anna has invited her to lunch. She has chosen a table in the back of the restaurant where their conversation will not be overheard. If anyone can help her come to terms with the trick Tim Greene has played on her, it would be Paula. But Paula has news of her own that won't wait for Anna to unburden herself. She sails toward Anna, waving gaily, calling out her name, her face lit by the midmorning sun usually obscured by towering buildings but today pouring down from a clear blue fall sky. The air is crisp, the humidity of summer evaporated. Generally circumspect, though always ready to assist if asked, Manhattanites are greeting each with unusual exuberance, with an openness rare in a city that has learned to be guarded. Paula is wearing a soft tan pantsuit and over it a raspberry-red cape draped fashionably across her chest. One end flutters over her shoulder, the other flows past her waist, bouncing with her stride. For an ample woman in times when ample

186 ❖ Elizabeth Nunez

women are ignored, if not criticized, for being overweight, she exudes a sexiness that turns more than one head as she approaches. She kisses Anna on both cheeks. "It's days like this when I love New York. Everybody seems to come alive as if from the dead."

And when they sit down to lunch, she tells Anna her tale of a young male student, Roy, she has helped rise from the dead. He is the son of a single mother who became embittered when Roy's father left her. Roy was withdrawn in class, unapproachable, Paula says. But this summer she managed to convince a young black lawyer in her building to take an interest in him. "He's become a surrogate father to Roy, and all I hear from his teachers now is how well he is doing in his classes. It makes it all worthwhile, teaching. One student turning his life around and I know my time here is not wasted."

Anna is happy for her, happy to wait until Paula winds down. Paula told her once that she had given up hope for a meaningful career in an educational system where her job seems to be policing the students rather than teaching them. It does Anna's heart good to know she has not despaired.

"So tell me," Paula says when the waitress finally brings their meals, "how are things going with you and Paul?"

Anna tells her about the flowers Paul has sent her and the card. Her spirits still high, Paula claps her hands. "I told you," she says. "It means he loves you. A man doesn't send flowers and cards to just any woman."

"He has given me flowers before," Anna replies curtly. "And we had just met."

"What kind of flowers?"

"Daisies."

"And this time?"

"Tulips. Orange ones."

Paula strains her head forward. "Did you tell him you like tulips and that orange ones are your favorite?"

"Everyone likes tulips," Anna says.

Paula brushes away Anna's cynicism. "It's a sign, Anna. You two are a perfect match. I hear wedding bells."

In Paula's mouth that assertion sounds downright silly and Anna is struck by how easily she had succumbed to a childish fantasy, as if the tulips were a magic wand she could wave in a fairy tale and make her dreams come true. She thought she was more sensible than her mother who believed that all it took for a woman to be happy was marriage. She had gone to graduate school, she had pursued a career, she was a professional, and yet that small token of Paul's concern for her had set her heart beating wildly. As if to reprimand herself, she announces to Paula, "I've been demoted."

The contours of Paula's face change. She has been teasing Anna, halfway joking but halfway serious too, pausing only between mouthfuls of chicken to prod Anna into admitting that her relationship with Paul has become serious. Now she sets down her fork and leans across the table. The smile is gone, her lips are drawn tight, furrows gather on her forehead. "I warned you, Anna," she says.

"Well, not demoted. I have my job, but the company is being reorganized. Tim Greene is going to be the new boss." Anna gives her the details of the changes in the office.

Paula does not seem to be surprised. "And what did Tanya Foster say about that?"

"She hired Tim Greene for the job. She pretended he was to be my assistant, but it's clear it was always her intention that he would be my boss."

"We build; they rule," Paula says flatly. "There should be a sign at the entrance of JFK, *You build; we rule*, not that promise at the foot of the Statue of Liberty about giving me your tired and your poor. Your poor, yes. They'll take the poor, but they won't take the tired. They expect us to work. That's our job. That was your job, Anna. Your job was to build Equiano. They wanted to see if it would succeed before they moved to the next phase. They were already thinking of merging with McDuffy when they put you in charge of Equiano. It was their plan. If you made Equiano profitable, they would expand. But, of course, they can't let you rule. They rule."

They. Paula conflates Tanya Foster and Tim Greene with all the theys in America. "That's the bargain they make with us," she says.

"That was not my bargain."

"I keep reminding you, you are not them." Paula shakes her head. "Suppose two people were vying for the same job, both equally qualified, one an immigrant, the other a born American, who do you think will get it?"

Anna focuses on her salad.

"Who, Anna?"

"Where a person was born should have nothing to do with whether or not she would do a good job," Anna says, gritting her teeth.

"But who *should* get the job? Let's say on your island back home, would you think it was fair if the immigrant got the job?"

"The English always did," Anna says.

"You're talking about colonial times. Would you think so now?"

"I worked hard." Anna's voice is barely above a whisper.

"That's not an answer. What would you do?"

Anna butters the bread roll next to her plate. She does not respond.

"I'm not saying it's right, or it's fair. It's just the way things are," Paula says. "I'm sorry to hear this is happening to you, but you should have been prepared."

"Don't, Paula." Anna tries hard to keep her voice even. "I need you on my side."

"I am on your side, but you insist on believing in all that stuff about assimilation. The ancestors of all Americans may have been born in another country—except, of course, the Native Americans—but they all suffer from collective amnesia. Well, assimilation is for the next generation, not for us." Paula grimaces. "And even the next generation gets amnesia in a heartbeat. Soon they too expect the new crop of immigrants to work while they rule, because now they are speaking with American accents, now they have American birth certificates. Do you remember when I taught part-time at that college in Brooklyn? There it was in the heart of the Caribbean community, but the feudal system was alive and well. Everywhere you went in that college you'd hear thick Caribbean accents, and you'd think: *Wow! Things are different here*. But they are not. Yes, the majority of the people at the college are Caribbean immigrants, but they are the workers, the serfs at the bottom of the feudal pyramid, the laborers, the janitors, the people who clean and repair the buildings, throw out the trash. Then higher up the pyramid are the security guards, then comes the clerical staff, almost all of them speaking with Caribbean accents. Of course, there are the students and the faculty, but among the tenured faculty the accents become American. When you reach the top of the pyramid where the administrators sit, there is hardly a Caribbean accent to be heard—and yet I've never taught a class where at least 70 to 80 percent of the students weren't speaking with thick Caribbean accents. You choose to live outside of the Caribbean immigrant community, Anna. If not for me, you wouldn't know where to shop for West Indian food."

She has stirred up Paula. She has invited her to lunch expecting sympathy, but all she has managed to do is bring up an old quarrel they have never settled. It isn't that she has not had regrets, that in the cold, dark, drab, leafless winter months she has not berated herself for turning her back on blue skies, turquoise waters, sun-filled days, and green-leaved trees. She sometimes wonders if she had been foolhardy to sever herself from the comfort of people with whom she shares history, culture, myths. What or who she would have been had she never emigrated is a question that keeps immigrants tossing and turning in their beds at night.

"It's not fair what Tanya Foster did to you," Paula says, her voice calmer now. "It's not right, but without a ghetto—"

Anna cringes. She does not want to live in a country within a country; she does not want to be limited to a ghetto. "Let's not start that again," she admonishes her.

Paula rephrases the sentence Anna has not allowed her to finish. She chooses a more anodyne word. "Okay, not ghetto. A community, Anna. Without a community to fight for you, you're going to be exploited. You need to understand that."

"I don't think everything has to be about politics," Anna says.

"Everything *is* about politics. That's the way of the world. Even in that college with its feudal system, immigrants serve a political purpose. We swell the ranks of black people. We make up the numbers when a case has to be made for more support for black people. We are black people then, but after the prize is won, we become Caribbean immigrants again. We are not allowed to be ambitious. You, my dear Anna." She points her fork at her. "You are not allowed to be ambitious."

Anna does not remind her that she predicted she would be a vice president. She does not say, *Where is your prediction now?* Paula is her friend. She will not chastise her with recriminations Paula cannot be responsible for. How was Paula to know that Tanya had no plans for her to be vice president, that her position as head of Equiano would be under the supervision of a man who was once her subordinate?

But Paula notices Anna's frustration. "When you told me that Tim Greene was to be your assistant editor, not your office assistant, I had my suspicions, but I still thought they had big plans for you. I see now I was wrong. You may deserve to head Coffee Press—"

"TeaHouse Press," Anna corrects her.

"You may deserve to be the head of TeaHouse Press, but you don't have a voting block behind you. You don't have the political power Tim Greene has. They'll give the position to a Tim Greene."

"A Tim Greene?"

"An African American." Paula puts down her fork. "Don't ever forget that here you're a Caribbean immigrant. Stick to your own people. You can rely on them."

FIFTEEN

S*tick to your own people. You can rely on them.* Alice cured
her of that romantic conviction grounded more in
nostalgia, a longing for home, than in reality. They
will promise you anything so long as your need is remote,
says Machiavelli, the ultimate pragmatist. How many immigrants discover too late they should have heeded that
warning!

Anna believed Alice. Was she grasping at straws? She
didn't think so at the time, though she had felt she was
drowning, swept deeper and deeper to the bottom of the
ocean by currents she thought had long subsided. England
still ruled. Little had changed since the island won its independence. But such was England's power that even today, in the most powerful country in the world, the clipped
cadences of the Queen's English opens doors and is often
enough to admit one to the most exclusive echelons of society, or at least give one an advantage as a newscaster or
host of a TV show.

She thinks back now and realizes she had been depressed, her confidence stripped, when she ran into Alice
outside a store on a busy street back home on the island.
She couldn't find a teaching job, not one that recognized
her American degree. Alice held out a lifeline to her. "Come
to New York," she had said. "You can stay in my apartment
in Manhattan."

It was not Anna's intention to stay permanently. Her

plan was to find a job and in a few weeks move to her own apartment.

Weeks! Alice would not hear of it when Anna told her of her intentions. It would take months, she said, to find your footing in Manhattan. Anna was welcome to stay with her for as long as she needed. She could stay for months. A year if necessary. She would love her to stay for a year. She could show her around. "You can get in a lot of trouble if you make the mistake of believing all you see in the movies," Alice warned. "In America everybody is nice, but only if you pay. I have seen a lot of West Indians fall into the trap of believing that every time someone says *Have a nice day* or *Thank you* or *Come again* they mean it. Then they get confused and upset when all the smiles are gone if they don't tip the waiter, or the taxi driver, or the man in the airport who helps them with their bags. It's not a bribe, but without greasing palms, you don't get anywhere in America. Pay and doors open for you. Don't pay and you could be bleeding and the hospital will turn you away if you don't have insurance."

Alice promised to help Anna avoid the pitfalls. Anna had been sheltered in that Midwestern small town where she went to college. New York is the big time, the real place. It would be a pleasure to be Anna's guide when she comes to New York, Alice said. Anna was the only one who had made life tolerable for her in that awful secondary school they attended. Anna was her only friend, the only one who helped with her homework, who sat next to her in the cafeteria. It would be the least she could do to pay Anna back for her kindness.

When Anna demurred, Alice became more insistent. Life would have been hell for her if Anna had not come to her rescue, she said. "You'll be doing me a favor, giving me a chance to repay a debt." Anna reminded her that she too had few friends in school, and was indebted to Alice for her friendship. They went back and forth, each one insisting that the other had done more for her, until Alice was practically begging Anna to move in with her whenever she decided to come to New York. "I get lonely sometimes for a friendly face," she confessed, "someone from back home who understands our culture. It would be a privilege and a joy to have you stay with me."

Anna was reassured. Yet if she were not so desperate, so anxious to escape the claustrophobia of the island, she would have recognized the clues Alice left for her and would have known that the invitation rested on the assumption that it would take years for her to be granted a green card. Quotas for their part of the world, developing countries dismissed as the third world, were small, the backlog of hopefuls waiting to immigrate to the U.S. in the thousands. Alice could risk making extravagant promises, impressing Anna with her generosity, because it was safe for her to do so. The chances that she would have to make good on her offer were slim to none.

First, there were the unanswered letters Anna sent to Alice, three of them. In the first one Anna wrote excitedly about the miracle that had happened to her. She had been scheduled for an appointment at the U.S. embassy with an immigration officer. It was too soon to hope she would get a green card, but at least the process had begun. In her next letter, Anna gave Alice the news of the second miracle: she had indeed been approved for a green card. She had fifty days to leave the island and come to New York. Fifty days to pack her things. What should she bring? Would she need warm clothes? It was June, but she knew spring could still be chilly. Would she need a coat, sweaters? Would Alice want her to bring anything for her? Tamarind balls, mango chutney, roti skins? Alice did not respond. Anna sent a third letter, this time making excuses for Alice. Was Alice away? Had she not received her letters? The postal system on the island was not reliable. Sometimes letters get lost. She recalled all she had written in her first two letters, adding that she had booked her flight to New York. She would there by the end of the month. She would call but she did not have Alice's phone number. She asked Alice to call her collect. Two weeks later Alice did so. Her apology was hollow. She meant to write, but things got busy at work. She repeated what she had said to Anna when they met on the island. The invitation stood. She was looking forward to seeing Anna. But there was little enthusiasm in her voice. The words were spoken as if rehearsed. They came out detached, without emotion, as if she were closing on a contract that had already been negotiated. Anna had no choice but to be optimistic. There was no turning back. She had to stifle her doubts.

The day before Anna left for New York, Alice collect called again. She said something had come up and she couldn't greet Anna at the airport. *Something.* She seemed to think that was sufficient explanation. Anna must take a cab to the apartment. Alice gave her the address. Another clue, if Anna had had the courage to face such clues.

On the first night, Alice set down the rules. There was one bedroom in the apartment and it would be off-limits to Anna. She could sleep on the couch in the living room and use the bathroom early in the morning before Alice woke up. There was no space in the closet so Anna would have to store her clothes in her suitcase. She was welcome to use the iron and the ironing board if she needed to. Then there was the question of bills. Anna would have to pay half the

rent and half the utility bills. It would be better if she paid
weekly, the first payment due in advance. She knew of an
employment agency where Anna could get a temporary job
immediately. She would introduce Anna to the manager.
She was doing all this for Anna's own good, so that Anna
would be prepared to cope with life here. "It's pay as you
go in New York," Alice said.

But it was a New Yorker who saved Anna, a young
woman in the secretarial pool at the temp agency who
caught her wiping away tears and took pity on her.

For days Anna had forbidden herself to feel the slightest glimmer of self-pity. Immigrating to America was a
choice she had made. No one had held a gun to her head. It
was she alone, without prompting from anyone, who had
decided to leave her homeland. Alice was trying to help. If
not for Alice she would have nowhere to stay. She should
be grateful. Yet each day became harder and harder for her
to endure. Alice rarely spoke to her beyond the formalities
of *Good morning* and *Good evening*. When Alice came home
from work at night, she would complain about the heat,
about the dust, about the grime of the city. About the hundreds of sweaty bodies pressed together in the subway.
About the noise. She wanted to be alone, in the peace and
quiet of her bedroom. She shut the door and ate her dinner propped up in her bed in front of the TV. Any attempt
Anna made to start a conversation with her was met with a
sigh and a wave of dismissal. "Not now, Anna. I'm tired."

Anna grew more and more depressed. She felt impris-
oned in the tiny apartment but she was afraid to go outside. She did not know the city and Alice had filled her
head with stories of the terrible things that happened to
strangers, especially to young women. "New York City is
not like your small island town where everybody knows

everybody," Alice said. "There's nobody to help you if some man pulls you in his car or behind a building and rapes you." Anna had nightmares that such a thing could happen to her.

She had not realized that tears were streaming down her cheeks until she tasted salt at the corners of her mouth. The pretty young blond girl who sat at the computer terminal next to her reached over and touched her arm. "It'll get better, you'll see." Her name was Lisa. Once Anna told her she was from the Caribbean, she wanted to know more about her island. "If I were you, I would never have left," Lisa said. "I'd be on the beach right now, soaking up the sun."

Lisa was in her last year of college. She was working at the temp agency to save for a trip to Grenada. Her mother was going to teach at the university there in the fall and she planned to go with her. She said she wanted to see what Reagan had done when he sent the troops to wage war on the island. She was expecting to find a wasteland. Anna did not have the heart to disappoint her, to tell her Grenada was anything but a wasteland. Hotels had sprouted up overnight and even in the countryside graffiti scrawled across concrete walls welcomed Americans. *God Bless the Yankees*, the signs said. The gratitude was everywhere, on the sides of old wood shacks, in front of rum shops, all along the roadside. *We glad you come.* Tourists sunbathed without the least apprehension on the brown-speckled sand at Grand Anse Beach that skirted the shimmering, impossibly blue water. Americans had saved the island for them!

Lisa was a political science major; her mother was an active feminist. Her grandfather marched with Martin Luther King Jr. "Not all the people who fought for civil rights were black," Lisa said to Anna. She was white, blond haired, blue eyed, so was her mother and her grandparents. They were ashamed of their country's history of slavery. They wanted to do their part to make amends.

"Come stay with my mother and me," Lisa said. "We have a house in Brooklyn."

So Paula was wrong. She had stuck with her own kind and her own kind was not good to her. Lisa, far removed from her own kind, had been good to her. Lisa's mother made her feel at home. She refused Anna's offer to pay for her room; neither would she take money for the meals she provided for her. Anna stayed with them for two months until they both left for Grenada, Lisa pursuing her dream to spend her days on the beach soaking up the sun, though filled with righteous indignation for what Reagan had done.

The following week, Anna landed a job in the slush pile at Windsor.

SIXTEEN

Her mother is serving pelau for dinner. She did not make it herself; it is her husband who has done the cooking under her direction, but when Anna comes home, her father declares proudly, "Your mother made pelau. Isn't that great?"

Anna would not have believed her father had cooked if it were not obvious that with her left arm in a sling and the muscles in her chest weakened and more than likely causing her pain, her mother would not have been able to slice the onions and garlic, season the chicken with thyme, salt, and pepper, and caramelize it with brown sugar sizzling in hot oil. Her father brews tea for her mother, but he does nothing more in the kitchen. It is a standing joke that if his wife were not at home on Lydia's day off, her father would starve. Her mother claims he does not know where the pots are and could not even boil rice if he found one. But he has cooked dinner, adding pigeon peas and rice to the chicken and just enough water that when Anna opens the pot she sees that the pelau is not sticky but grainy the way she likes it.

"Your father is quick learner," her mother says. "Of course, he had to brown the chicken twice. The first time he let the sugar stay too long in the oil and it beaded up like hard little globs of tar."

"The second time wasn't much better," her father says, ready to accept blame, though Anna can tell he is pretending by the glitter in his eyes. "I thought the fire alarm in the kitchen would go off. There was so much smoke when I dumped the cold chicken in the hot oil."

Her mother shakes her head. "He wanted to call the fire brigade! I had to calm him down and reassure him that this happens all the time. But what does he know about the kitchen? All you had to do was to stir it, John," she berates him playfully. "Then it gets nice and brown."

They are in a good mood. Anna wants them to stay that way. Her mother does not like bad news. Anna will not spoil her day with the bad news from her office. It had only taken her first failed book for Anna to realize that the reading public is no different from her mother. Readers too, at least most readers of fiction, do not like bad news. They will reject a novel that is too grim. They want a happy ending, redemption for the sinner, and if not redemption, punishment. The good guys must be rewarded; the future must promise them a life of bliss and contentment.

Anna thinks these readers would rather live in a fantasy world, with their illusions, than face the social ills that make life difficult for so many. But how to correct these social ills, which Anna believes are correctable, without admitting them, confronting them? An impossible feat, Anna thinks.

Her father spent years in the outside world. He knows of the petty quarrels, the jealousies, the back-biting, the resentments, the power struggles. A day at work is not always a good-news day. He would listen, he would empathize, if she told him what has happened to her at work. But he is happy now, laughing with her mother. He does not need to hear her bad news.

At dinner her parents tease each other, her father still pretending to be chastised as her mother regales him with the mistakes he made cutting and chopping the season-ings, browning the chicken, measuring the rice, the wa-ter, the pigeon peas. Color rises to her mother's face, her cheeks glow, laughter rumbles up her throat at her hus-band's silly jokes.

She would not be able to recover so quickly if it hap-pened to her, Anna is certain. If she were the one who had breast cancer, she would not be able to laugh, to chat gaily at dinner as her mother is doing now. She would wallow in self-pity; she would want someone to hold her hand, to comfort her, to reassure her. She would be stretched out on her bed, expecting to be served, pampered. She would not be sitting at the table having dinner as if her life had not been seriously threatened. Could still be threatened.

Perhaps it is her mother's philosophy that saves her now. Her mother believes in the palliative power of forget-ting. *Black Orpheus* is her favorite movie, and not because the characters are black or because they are not bug-eyed buffoons or servile maids in a white woman's kitchen, or because she loves the Brazilian samba, but because the movie reaffirms her conviction that the past cannot be recaptured, that our survival depends on forgetting the things we cannot have again, the things that are too pain-ful to remember. If Orpheus had not looked back, she has often said to Anna, he would have had his Eurydice.

Only once had her mother unlocked the vault where she sealed her painful past: a mother who was restrained, who did not hug and kiss her. By midafternoon she was closed-lipped again. It is the present that counts for her, the present she chooses now. She has had her miracle. The tumors are gone. She does not think of a future beyond this.

Later at night Anna settles down on the couch with one of the manuscripts that have piled up on her desk. It is almost eleven when she finally puts down her blue pencil. She is about to get up when she hears the bedroom door creak open. It is her father. He is in his robe; the belt, untied, hangs loosely at the sides and his pajamas flap through the opening. He reaches for the belt as he approaches her, but it slips from his fingers. "Your mother is fast asleep," he says.

"You couldn't sleep?" Anna pats the cushion next to her on the couch. "Come, sit with me."

"The minute your mother put her head on the pillow, she was out."

"I don't know how she does it," Anna says.

"Your mother is resilient." He's still standing. His arms are wrapped across his robe, hugging it to his body.

Anna gets up. "Can I make you tea?"

"I'd like that," he says and follows her to the kitchen.

"I'll have tea too." She reaches for the canister with the tea bags and takes out three, two for him, one for her.

He is standing behind her. He coughs, swallows, coughs again.

"Can I get you some water?" Anna turns around.

He shakes his head. "She's had miscarriages, you know."

Frost encircles Anna's heart. She screws the cover on the canister so tightly the tips of her fingers turn white when she presses them against the metal. "She?"

"Your mother. Two years before you were born."

"How many?"

"Four."

The frost in her chest has turned to icicles. She empties her mind. She throws out everything—fear, hope—everything except what she is doing at that very moment. She concentrates on filling the kettle with water. She brings it to the stove, she lights the stove, she takes the two mugs to the coffee table.

"And then she had you." Her father walks back with her to the living room.

They kept the secret of the tumor blooming in her mother's breast hidden for years. Why shouldn't they have kept this one? "Four before me?"

"Four in less than two years."

"In less . . ." Anna trails off.

"That's why she loved you so much. You survived. You made it. She says you are a fighter. You're her fighter daughter."

Air rushes through Anna's nostrils. It fills her lungs until her chest hurts and she is forced to release it. *Loved you so much?*

"She almost died with the last one." Her father is sitting on the armchair facing the couch.

"The last one?"

"Before you. She lost a lot of blood. I had to give her some of mine." He chuckles, a grim sound that ends with a sigh. "I didn't want her to try again."

She is prepared for secrets but not this one. "You didn't want me?" Her voice is strained.

He does not hear her. "She wanted to try again," he says. "She wanted you. I couldn't stop her."

"But me?" It was *he* who saved her, giving her hugs and kisses when she was a child, telling her she was beautiful even when she was scrawny and unattractive, when her body refused to blossom with the curves that rounded the breasts and hips of her teenage schoolmates. "You didn't want me?"

He hears her now. "Oh no," he says. "I wanted you the minute you were born. You were a beautiful baby."

204 ❖ Elizabeth Nunez

"And before that?"

"I was afraid she would die."

Anna has taken three tea bags from the canister, but she puts only one in each of the mugs. She lifts the kettle from the stove and fills the mugs with hot water. She hands one of them to her father. The water in it has turned light brown, not dark, the tea not as strong he would want it.

"How much sugar?" she asks. He wants two teaspoons. She puts one in his mug. "And milk?" He says he has opened a can of evaporated milk. It is in the refrigerator. She takes out the carton of milk she uses with her cereal and pours some into his mug.

Her father sips the tea she has given him. He does not say a word. She knows he has noticed the difference in the taste, but he continues to drink the tea as if it is to his liking. These are the courtesies she has been taught at home: You do not offend the host. The host has gone through a lot of trouble to please you. But she has not gone through a lot of trouble to please her father. She has been spiteful, petty, childish. *He did not want her.*

"Your mother is a good Catholic. She follows the rules." Her father stirs his tea. He does not like it, but he does not complain. "To the letter," he adds and looks up at her.

In the Catholic high school she attended on the island, abandoned to the convent by parents who could not feed them, Irish nuns had taught her mother that the doctor must save the unborn child. The mother is God's instrument, His way of giving human life to the soul. The mother's life does not count when she is giving birth to the soul. She is merely the vehicle.

"I am a convert." He has stopped stirring his tea. "I did not grow up in the religion the way your mother did. I don't agree with all the rules. Your mother said the pope was infallible. On matters like this, he knew best, she said. But I wanted my wife. I didn't want her to die."

"So you didn't want her to try again?"

"She lived. You lived. That's all that mattered." He sips the tea, grimaces, and puts the mug down. "After that, she was careful with you. She wanted you to be strong. Like her." His eyes soften and he smiles at her. "A mother bird knows she has done her job well when her babies fly out of the nest on their own. We are proud of you, Anna. You have made a life for yourself. You are a fighter."

SEVENTEEN

A fighter? She barely raised a murmur of protest when Tanya Foster announced that she would be working for Tim Greene, a man who just days ago was her assistant. Did she fight back? Did she shout out angry words at her? *Where will that leave me?* That was all she said, her voice like a child's begging for fairness on the playground. But the strong always win. Even the child in the playground knows that. Either he caves in or he learns to fight.

Paula blames her for distancing herself from the Caribbean immigrant community. There is strength in numbers, she tells her. It is easy to kill the lone wolf, harder when he's with his pack. Perhaps she should have sought ties with the Caribbean immigrant community. She should have become involved in their clubs, in their political organizations. Then she would not have been alone. It would not have been so easy for Tanya Foster to dismiss her, to push her aside. African Americans have their clubs, their political organizations. They come out in numbers to fight for one of their own. But she is not one of their own. Tim Greene is one of their own.

It is too late now to ask for help, to go to the politician in her neighborhood, the one with Caribbean roots. It is too late to say to him: I need your help. I've been pushed aside. I've been passed over for someone who has less credentials than I have, who has not worked as hard as I have for the company. Equiano profited from my hard work; they made money because of me. But even if it were not too late, even if it were not after the fact, after Tim Greene has been given the position that should have been hers, Anna knows that she still would not seek the help of a politician nor would she use her affiliation with a club or an organization in the community to secure her job. Her father's repugnance for the slightest whiff of cronyism or nepotism has been drummed into her head. *Earn your way through your own merit.* That is his unshakeable conviction which he has passed on to her. There is dignity, he says, in achieving success because of your hard work, not because some big shot opened the door for you.

And there is no free lunch. At some point the politician or the person you assumed to be your altruistic benefactor will present a bill. You'll have to pay. The piper always gets paid. Now or later. Later, you'll have no choice. The price could determine your very survival.

America is a bowl of salad, Paula has said to her. The ingredients brush against each other, but they are self-contained, each an individual unit. "To which unit do you belong?" Paula asked her.

When Paula prodded, she answered: "I belong to the human family. It does not matter the human's shape, size, or color, I am part of his club, his organization. That is the group to which I belong."

And to this Paula responded: "The family you belong to sees your shape, your size, and your color, and makes the distinction. Whether you want to or not, you are seen as a black woman in America, and when it suits America, you are a black Caribbean woman immigrant."

Her mother seems to know this. In spite of the praise she heaps on the nurses and doctors who treated her in the hospital in New Jersey, she declares she wants to go home. This time she means back to her island, to her own people, her own doctors in her own country.

They are having breakfast the next morning when she makes this announcement. "Your father and I have decided to leave by the weekend," she says.

Anna immediately thinks she is the cause. Perhaps she has not made them comfortable enough. Perhaps she should invite Paula to dinner to keep them company. She could come home early and take them to the park. On the weekend they could go to a museum, or to a concert.

"That isn't it," her mother says. "We . . . I want to go home."

Home. She says the word with complete assurance. "We belong at home now," she says.

Belong, not merely to the human family but to a specific community, a specific place. She longs to be there. *Be*: it is the place where she locates her identity, where she is herself. *Long*: it is where she yearns to be.

Anna tries to convince her that she is not well enough to go home now.

"Your father will be with me," her mother responds.

Anna reminds her that she will need another round of chemotherapy and radiation.

"I have an oncologist back home. Dr. Ramdoolal will take care of me."

"I don't think this is wise," Anna says. "Don't you think you should finish your treatment here?"

"That's not what your mother wants." Her father puts an end to any possibility of compromise.

Anna calls Paul Bishop. He is not surprised. In fact, he approves. Anna is appalled. Her mother cannot be well enough to travel. Paul Bishop tells her that medicine may be a science but it is also an art. Your mother knows the secret of the art, he explains. He has done all he can. "Your mother knows better than I do how to heal herself," he says. When Anna protests again, he tells her he will drop by to talk to her mother later in the evening. Then he lowers his voice. "I want to see you, Anna. I miss you."

The same deathly silence greets Anna when she arrives at work. The buzz of office chatter comes to an abrupt end and the clatter of computer keys echoes off the walls. Everyone is suddenly busy, occupied with some urgent task. Anna opens her office door. Immediately her eyes zoom to the gaping absence on her desk. All the manuscripts are gone, the ones she plans to read that she had placed in a pile next to her phone, the ones on the other side of her desk, in front of her pencil holder, that she has already edited. She spins around. The ones on her shelves are gone too. Those are the manuscripts she has rejected but has yet to send letters to the writers.

Tim Greene! He is the one who has removed them. She is certain of this. She drops her briefcase on the floor; she does not stop to take off her coat. She bolts through the door and collides with Rita.

"Where is he? I need to speak to him. Now!"

Rita places her hand on Anna's elbow. "He's not here. Come." She leads Anna back into her office and shuts the door. "Cool down. Think about what you want to say before you speak to him."

Anna paces the floor. "How dare he! How dare he!"

"Sit," Rita tries to coax her into a chair, but Anna refuses. "He took my manuscripts. Who gave him permission to take my manuscripts?" The words whistle through her clenched teeth.

"He's the boss now, Anna," Rita says. "He wanted to read the books on our list."

"They are on *my* list. I acquired those books. They are mine to edit."

"But he is responsible."

Anna stops pacing. "Responsible for what? I am responsible for my books, for making sure they are well written."

"And Tim is responsible for making sure they sell well," Rita replies quietly.

Anna walks over to her desk and slumps down on the chair. Slowly, her energy begins to drain down her neck and out of her arms and legs. It is not despair she feels, though it is something akin to despair; it is the futility of arguing. She has already lost the battle. Her vision for the company, for the purpose of publishing stories, is not the same as Tanya's; it's not the same as Tim Greene's. If she is to stay with the company she has to yield to their vision, she has to do as they say.

"Everything will work out fine," Rita coos. "You'll see. Tim called this morning. He wants to meet with you."

"When?"

"At ten."

"That's half an hour from now."

"I am to call you when he arrives. He wants you to come to his office."

"His office?"

"Tanya's old office." Rita rubs Anna's neck. "Your shoulders are stiff. You're too tense. Relax, Anna. Don't worry so much. Tim needs you."

Tim Greene is gracious. He leaves his desk and comes to the door when she knocks. He is decked out in sartorial splendor—Brooks Brothers pinstriped navy suit, crisp white shirt, and delicately patterned silk blue tie. When he feigned assistant to her, he took off his jacket. He keeps it on now. He is the boss and his manner of dress declares his status, but like the rich and powerful he adopts an air of informality when he greets her, knowing full well that she is aware of his position and his power over her, over everyone in the company. "How good to see you, Anna." He holds out his hand.

Anna. She is Anna now, not boss, not Ms. Sinclair. "Good to see you too, Tim."

He shakes her hand vigorously. "Come, sit with me." He gestures to an armchair next to a couch. The office looks different. It is not the same as when Tanya Foster occupied it. "I made some changes, as you can tell," he says, following her widening eyes.

He has kept the large mahogany desk and Tanya's Herman Miller Aeron desk chair. If Anna had the slightest doubt, the chair is proof enough that he and Tanya are friends, and probably because they are friends he was hired by the company. Tanya had had the chair adjusted to the right angles to suit her height, the curve of her back, and the length of her thighs and arms. She boasted she could sit in that chair for hours and not feel the slightest cramp in her muscles.

"I had a hard time persuading Tanya to give it to me." Tim Greene taps the back of the chair.

"I didn't think she would part with it."

"She had it adjusted for me."

It is a fashionable desk chair, a favorite of fashionable heads of companies, and Tim Greene is a fashionable man. Instead of the round conference table with four chairs where Tanya held meetings with her immediate staff, he has created the sort of sitting-room atmosphere one would find in an exclusive men's club in Manhattan. The couch and two armchairs are covered in dark brown leather and studded to the polished wood frames with round shiny brass nails. The chairs and couch are arranged tastefully around a mahogany coffee table placed on top of what looks like an antique Oriental rug. "Persian," Tim Greene says when he catches Anna admiring it. "Got it at an estate auction in Long Island."

On the table is a red leather-bound copy of Ralph Ellison's *Invisible Man*, and next to it, a black plaster cast of Rodin's *The Thinker*. It would be easy to assume this is the office of man who has fine taste in literature and the arts, and not a man who purchases books as he would any other commodity, buying and selling them with only one purpose in mind: money he can make for the company.

"Well, what do you think?" he asks, taking the armchair opposite hers.

"It's different," she mumbles.

"Different good or different bad?"

It is clear he expects a compliment. "Of course, good. Different good."

"I want people to be comfortable when they come to my office. We are one big family. That's the way I want to run this company. Families may have their internal quarrels, but they present one united face to the world. You know what I mean?" He bends toward her and extends his hand forward as if he is about to touch her, but that is not what he intends to do at all. What he does is let his hand drop to his knee, the palm spread wide, clutching it. He smiles. It is a smile Anna believes is meant to put her at ease, to soothe her, to make her forget how he had deliberately set out to deceive her, as he probably thinks he can do again.

She is glad she chose a black pantsuit to wear to work and not a dress, that she is dressed for business, as the professional she is. "Yes," she says, buttoning her jacket, "*happy* families stick together."

He does not miss her emphasis. He raises his eyebrows. "Happy?"

"Not all families are happy."

"Surely you don't—" He stops in midsentence and bites his lip. When he resumes, his tone has changed. His voice is weighted with concern. "Speaking of families," he says, "how is your mother?"

"She's recovering well and quickly, thank you."

"They don't make them like they used to."

"My mother is a strong woman." She is about to elaborate, to say that her mother is doing so well she's decided to return home to the Caribbean, when he declares that his mother also had a big scare.

"They had to do a biopsy. Turned out to be nothing. Calcifications. But we were all worried."

Anna does not say the obvious: that for her mother it was not a big scare; it was the real thing. "You must have been relieved," she says.

"My mother too. I have to give it to you, Anna. I don't think I'd have been able to concentrate if the diagnosis was different."

Does he mean to praise her, or is he suggesting she hasn't been able to focus on her work? "It wasn't . . . It isn't easy for me," she says.

"But you managed. All those e-mails. I didn't answer them all, as you must have noticed."

"I noticed."

"About Raine . . . Well, as you know now, there was no need—"

"To answer my questions?"

"I was not at liberty, Anna. You have to understand that. The merger had not taken place."

"But you knew there was to be a merger."

"Until the ink had dried, there was nothing to tell."

"You could have warned me."

"I did." He crosses and uncrosses his legs.

Was it hubris, overconfidence in her value to Windsor, that had blinded her? Or was it plain stupidity that had allowed her to be lulled into the false hope that when Tanya left she would take Tim Greene with her? Anna rubs the space between her eyebrows. "You lied to me," she says. A sudden pain shoots up the back of her neck.

Tim Greene stands up. "Those are strong words, Anna. I'm trying to make this as easy as possible for the two of us."

"I saved the e-mail you sent me." The pain in her neck has not subsided but she resists the urge to massage the throbbing muscle. She must remain focused. She cannot allow him to think he has defeated her. "*You are my boss*, you wrote. You knew that was a lie when you wrote it."

Tim Greene walks over to his desk and comes back with a piece of paper. "I had hoped this would be easy, Anna, but I see it's not going to be." He waves the paper at her. "Bess Milford is threatening to sue us. She doesn't have a chance, of course. She knows as well as I do that when she signed her contract she gave us the right to market her book the way we thought would make it most attractive to buyers."

"So long as what you did was tasteful," Anna says.

"So long as it was not offensive," Tim Greene responds.

"Bess Milford thinks it's offensive."

"And what about you, Anna? What do you think?"

"You know what I think about that explicitly crude and

erotic cover. It has nothing to do with the story Bess Milford wrote."

"You work for the company, Anna. You are part of our family. You can't fight with outsiders against the family." He sits down and folds the paper carefully, sliding his nails along the creases.

"This is not a family. This is a business," Anna replies tersely.

"I'm sorry you think this way because Tanya cares about you."

"Cares so much she gives you my job."

"She didn't give me your job, Anna. TeaHouse Press is a new company. You were not the head of TeaHouse Press."

"A matter of semantics," she says.

"Look, Anna. I asked to meet with you because I wanted to talk about your role in the new company."

"Tanya said I'll still be in charge of Equiano."

Tim Greene emits a low guttural sound, a growl it seems to Anna, but his lips are smiling. "Tanya, Tanya," he coos.

"She said my position will not change."

"She is too nice."

"You said that too. I remember your exact words. You said, *You are still the boss of Equiano.* That's what you said to me." *Still.* Suddenly the word stands out from the rest. *Still,* as in the past, as in the present, at that moment—not meaning in the future.

He straightens up. His back is as rigid as an iron pole. "But you must have known better, Anna."

"Better than what?"

"Come on, Anna. You must have read between the lines. Tanya was trying to let you down slowly."

The tea leaves. Tanya expected her to read the tea leaves.

"And what about you? Did you expect me to read between the lines too?"

"I thought it would be obvious to you. With TeaHouse Press there will be no need for Equiano."

We believe what we need to believe, what we need to believe to stave off despair, to keep on functioning. The moment Tanya told her about the merger and that the new TeaHouse Press would acquire all McDuffy's titles by writers of color, she should have figured out that Equiano would be shut down. She had fallen for the old ruse the British had perfected in their colonies. Give them half a loaf and they won't resist. Give them schools, lower-level jobs in the civil service, keep them hoping for advancement that will never materialize. They won't risk losing the crumbs they have. A bird in hand is worth two in the bush. Still, she is surprised that Tim Greene would use the same strategy. But human nature is human nature, no matter the physical trappings. She is a woman; men have pacified women for years with their baseless promises.

"And if there is no Equiano, what happens to me?" she asks.

"First, let me say, Tanya is not to blame. The new configuration for the company is my idea. I am sure you can see it makes no sense to have an imprint for writers of color in a company that publishes writers of color. It'll be redundant."

"Am I to be redundant?"

"You're valuable to us, Anna. We want to keep you here as an editor, a senior editor. But I need someone working close to me who shares my vision. I want to form the Greene team."

"The Greene team?"

"I need a managing editor, someone I can rely on, who can help me put this company in the black."

"Equiano is in the black," Anna says.

"We can do better. Conrad Hilton can help us do better."

"Conrad Hilton? The owner of the chain of Hilton hotels?" She means to be sarcastic, but there is no edge in her tone.

Tim Greene reaches over to the coffee table and picks up the red leather-bound copy of *Invisible Man* lying there. "I think the problem with you, Anna, is you don't have a feel for our readers. I can't blame you. Sometimes I don't understand my people myself." He chuckles. "This man . . ." He holds up the book. "This man, he understood. He felt the pain of being invisible in America. What I want to do here with this company is to make us visible."

"With chick lit and ghetto lit?" Anna does not withhold her alarm.

Tim Greene sighs. "What you interpret as chick lit and ghetto lit," he says with exaggerated patience, "I see as stories about my people."

My people. He has said it, made it plain to her. No more guessing, beating around the bush: he has excluded her. She is not included in *my*; she is alien to *my*, an alien in America, though with the legal right to live and work in America. On her U.S. passport she is defined as a naturalized citizen, a distinction that never misses the immigration officers whenever she reenters the country. *Naturalized: not born here. Not the real thing. Not the real American.* Fingers tap on the computer keys, eyes glance over her and back to the screen. Seconds pass. Finally her passport is stamped. Welcome to the U.S.!

For Tim Greene, chick lit and ghetto lit are stories about his people. It wouldn't matter if she told him about the mirror and the lamp. It wouldn't matter if she said to him that she agrees that fiction should mirror life, but that the lives these books mirror are a tiny fraction of the lives his people really live. That he is perpetuating a pernicious stereotype by promoting these books as if they reflect the lives of the majority of his people. It wouldn't matter either to argue that books have the power to give us insights into the past, the present, the future. To give us something to reach for. That books can inspire us to be more than what we are. If she should say these things to him, he would respond that he is working for a company that does business for profit. Neither Windsor nor the new TeaHouse Press is a philanthropic organization. Neither is in the charity business. His job is to keep his eyes on the bottom line.

As if he has read her thoughts, he says, "It's not just about the money, Anna. It's about literacy too."

She stares at him in disbelief.

"Young people like these books," he says. "At least these books get them reading."

She has heard the argument many times before—though it still shocks her that intelligent people, people in positions of leadership, with the responsibility of guiding the young, still promote such drivel. *At least these books get them reading.* It is an expression of despair, of the failure of schools to educate the young. Test results of black children in the inner-city are dismal and blame is cast on the powerful, seductive force of the visual media. Educators throw up their hands and surrender. The battle against the lure of cable TV and video games is one they cannot win. *At least these books get them reading.* But reading what? Young people, like young people throughout the ages, get pleasure from the stimulation of their imagination, and Anna is convinced that no other medium stimulates the imagination more than reading. For the reader must transform black-

and-white symbols into colorful pictures in his mind. He must bond with people he has not met in the flesh or seen on the screen. He becomes judge and jury in battles between good and evil. If all we can say is *at least they are reading*, we have failed to pass on to the next generation the pleasures that come from good books that challenge us to imagine lives we have not lived, to empathize with those we do not know.

Books, Anna believes, are our defense against those who would lead us like lambs to the slaughterhouse. Books teach us to think, to use our intelligence to sort out right from wrong, good from bad, the beautiful from the ugly, to make decisions based on what we know is right and just, not on what we have been told to do or think by powerful people concerned with their welfare instead of our own. Books can prevent wars, keep us from destroying ourselves and our planet. Why else do dictators and warmongers burn books in the public square? Why else was a fatwa declared against a novelist, calling for his execution?

"And is it enough that these are the only types of books they read?" Anna asks.

"It's a good beginning," Tim Greene answers. "These books open up the world of reading to them. They get to find out there's fun in reading, and who knows?" He smiles brightly at her. "They may get to like the books you read, Anna."

She does not think that reading poorly written, exclusively plot-driven books will lead a young person to seek out more challenging ones. She believes children have to be taught. She believes teachers must do the hard work of giving children the tools to decode words on the printed page, to appreciate the beauty of a well-turned phrase, to ponder the validity of ideas they have not considered before. She believes a society is in danger when good books are neither written nor read.

Was it reading the kind of books he wants to publish that turned him on to Ellison? Anna seriously doubts that. He went to good schools; he studied at Cornell. His teachers did not experiment with him; they did not ease him into appreciating Ellison by having him read novels by the likes of Raine and Benton. He and too many like him seem to lack faith in the possibility of remedying an inferior education, of resetting the clock for young men and women whose deficiencies in reading and writing have accumulated after years of neglect. Yet these are the vulnerable young minds most in need of inspiration and hope; these are the underprivileged youth whose notion of the good life will remain limited unless expanded by good books that could open the way for them to the beauties of the world.

"I don't think that someone who reads *Ghetto Wife* will graduate to reading *Invisible Man*," Anna says.

Tim Greene is still holding Ralph Ellison's novel in his hand. Slowly and carefully he places it on the coffee table. Ridges form on the sides of his face. They contract and loosen, making tiny waves along his temples. Anna can tell he is trying to suppress his anger. *Ghetto Wife* is the title of Raine's new novel, the book he most likely intends to promote at the top of his list for the new TeaHouse Press. "I need Conrad Hilton to start soon," he says abruptly. He does not look at Anna. He clutches the sides of the book with the tips of his fingers and slides it back and forth on the table.

"And when would that be?"

"As soon as possible."

"When?"

"Tomorrow." He is no longer sliding the book. He gives

it a final pat and puts it next to the plaster cast of Rodin's sculpture. "If you could clear out your office by this afternoon, I'd appreciate it." He sits back on his chair.

"And the manuscripts you have taken from my office?" Anna hears her voice but she is not conscious that it is she who has spoken. A dark haze takes over the room and Tim Greene merges into it.

"They will be Conrad's responsibility now."

Conrad. Through the haze, a face shimmers before her. She has seen it before; it is the face of the man in the café sitting with Tim Greene, both of them huddled over a stack of papers. She had guessed correctly. It was a manuscript, not just any stack of papers. Perhaps Raine's, perhaps Benton's manuscript, perhaps the latest chick lit Tim planned to acquire. His plan was already in place while she was naïvely thinking that she was the head of Equiano and he was an assistant editor, and her only problem was to make sure he did not edit the literary novels she had acquired.

"I've seen you with him," she says.

"With whom?"

"Conrad Hilton. At the corner restaurant having lunch. I saw you twice. You were so deep in conversation plotting my demise, you didn't see me even when I waved at you. You must have been cooking up this plan a long time ago. What a big laugh you must have had at my stupidity."

"Anna . . . Ms. Sinclair." All talk of family has ended. Informalities end too. "This is not about you. Mr. Hilton and I weren't plotting your demise."

"You were plotting to close down Equiano."

"To organize TeaHouse Press."

"It's the same to me."

Tim Greene stands up. "Mr. Hilton will need your list of writers," he says.

"Are you firing me?"

"Not unless you want to go."

She needs her job. She has a mortgage to pay, bills that accumulate. She clamps her lips shut.

"There's still a place for you here as an editor." He walks around his desk toward her. He wants her to leave. He does not have to say so. He is standing above her, his hands arched together, locking and unlocking his fingers.

She gets up. "To correct syntax and spelling, is that it?"

He neither affirms nor denies her assumption. "Mr. Hilton will do the job of acquiring books for the company. Of course, you can propose titles."

"And my salary?"

"We have a limited budget. Until the company makes more money through the sales of . . ." He pauses, waiting for her to absorb the full impact of her folly. "You know, the books that bring in the money, the books you don't like."

She is in his power. She will be expected to support the books she does not like.

"Until then," he says, his eyes hardened now, "you'll have to take a 20 percent cut."

Rita comes to help her clear her office. "Don't take it so hard, Anna," she says.

Anna is furiously ripping up sheets of paper.

"You don't have to do that." Rita places her hand gently over Anna's wrist. "We have a shredder in the office."

Anna shrugs off Rita's hand. "I don't trust the shredder. I don't trust anything or anyone here anymore."

"You don't mean that, Anna. You can trust me."

"Calling me boss while knowing all the time that he was going to take my job. That he was going to be *my* boss."

"Did he fire you?"

"Oh, he said I was valuable." Anna throws a letter she has just torn in half into the wastebasket.

"See, just as I told you. He knows how good you are."

"At first he said I could remain as a senior editor. By the time we parted, he was talking about a cut in salary."

Rita says nothing.

"There's so much here." Anna pulls open the drawer at the side of her desk. Her eyes travel aimlessly across the stacks of notes in the drawer. She does not touch them. "So much of my time and energy."

"None of it wasted," Rita says with exaggerated gaiety.

Anna shuts the drawer. "You know what he said to me, Rita?" She doesn't wait for her response. "He said I don't have a feel for our readers. A feel? What does that mean? What he really wants to say is that I am not an African American. Conrad Hilton is an African American, and so it stands by reason of his birth that Mr. Hilton has a feel for the readers."

"It's not about that," Rita says. "It's about gender politics. Sexism." The word sounds odd in Rita's mouth and Anna's frown deepens. "This is still a man's world. Tim wants a man as his right-hand man. He doesn't think a woman is good enough."

"Is that how things are for you here?" Anna asks. Rita seemed so passive to her, so submissive, so willing to stand in the shadows.

"I play the game, but I know the real score."

"But isn't that hard, pretending?"

"Women have pretended for years. It's a way to survive."

"There are other ways."

"This way has worked for me. I've survived other mergers."

And didn't Anna pretend when she allowed Tim to comfort her with his lie? *Everything will work out all right. We'll talk. You'll see.* But she does not believe sexism is his motive. "Tribalism," she says to Rita. "That's his motive."

Rita does not understand.

"We have the same skin color but we belong to different tribes."

"Tribes?'

"Cultures," Anna clarifies. "Our cultures are not the same. I'm not African American."

Rita sighs. "Tim Greene is a complicated man. You talk about trust. I think Tim is the one who has problems trusting people he doesn't know well."

"People who are not African American, you mean."

"It's not as simple as that. He's had a hard life."

"He went to Cornell."

"The story is that his mother's boyfriend paid his way to Cornell. He was a white man. Married."

A sort of scholarship, Tanya had said when Anna ventured that Tim Greene had financial support.

"They say he never liked his mother's boyfriend," Rita adds.

"Because he was white or because he was married?"

"Both, I suppose. His father was never in the picture. I suppose Tim resented having him replaced by a white man, and a married man at that, who had his own family and had no intention of marrying his mother. But his mother's boyfriend paid for him to go to private schools and to Cornell."

"He didn't have to go to Cornell," Anna says bitterly. "He could have gone to a state university or a city college. He could have worked and paid his way. Many people do."

"His mother wanted him to go to Cornell. Her boyfriend went to Cornell. She wanted to prove to her boy-friend that her son was just as smart as him. I think Tim Greene has a lot of anger in him. He doesn't show it, but—"

"So he takes it out on people like me."

"You're taking this too personally," Rita says. "It's business. A new boss comes in, he wants his own people. Look at it this way: you still have a job."

"*If it be, why seems it so particular with thee?*"

Rita stretches open her eyes. "With thee?"

"*Hamlet*," Anna says. "Hamlet's mother and her new husband try to convince Hamlet that death is common, but it is *his* father who died. It is particular with him because what has happened affects him personally. It is particular with me because what has happened affects me personally. It is not business to me."

EIGHTEEN

When Rita leaves, Anna stands forlornly in front of her bookshelf scanning the titles she acquired and those she agreed to publish only because Tanya Foster had insisted. *You still have a job.* This is the consolation Rita has offered her and perhaps she should be consoled. The publishing industry is not the same as when she first began at Windsor. Small presses are struggling to stay afloat and large publishing houses are consolidating. It shouldn't be surprising that Windsor would be merged with McDuffy or that Equiano would be subsumed under TeaHouse Press. Print media is in trouble. All over the country newspapers are folding, the dailies in small towns a luxury of the past. Even in big cities like New York and Chicago cable news and the Internet are threatening sales. She has heard of layoffs at the *New York Times* and the *Chicago Tribune*. The prediction is that soon we will read many of our books on electronic tablets, e-books available at a lower cost than printed books. She is aware there are editors who have already lost their jobs. She should be grateful she still has hers. A 20 percent cut in salary will require belt-tightening, but she can manage. She has savings. And her cut may not be permanent; Tim Greene has implied as much.

What a hypocrite she is! How desperate she has become, hanging her hopes on Raine and B. Benton, her future in the company anchored on the expectation that their novels will become best sellers! For if her salary is to be restored, if she is to regain the 20 percent cut, it will be because of sales of the very kind of books she has decried.

Someone knocks on her door and, flushed with shame, Anna rushes to open it, grasping at the chance for relief from the mortifying thoughts that have overtaken her. It is the secretary. She brings a message from Tim Greene. Anna is to put on the desk any items she wishes the maintenance staff to move to the cubicle Tim Greene has assigned to her. The secretary throws her a pained smile in sympathy.

What is perfectly clear to Anna now is that she has a job, a source of income, nothing more. She will no longer acquire books for the company or be part of the team that will decide which books to promote and how. Her opinion will not count. She will be expected to follow orders, correct grammar and spelling, check facts, tasks that programs on the computer do more efficiently than humans. She will be . . . She searches for the word and remembers the one Tim Greene used when they spoke: *redundant*. She will be redundant, her talents not required, her experience irrelevant. Yet what pains her most is not the money, nor is it the humiliation she has had to endure with Tim Greene asserting himself as her boss. It is the end of a dream, the vision she had for Equiano. But she will not be lured again by the rope Tim throws out to her with every intent of cutting it the moment she tries to grab ahold. *Of course, you can propose titles*. It is obvious to her now he does not mean a word of that promise.

It angers her that she should be dismissed so lightly, her years in the company so easily disregarded. She has worked her way up from the slush pile at Windsor, getting pennies for her labor, straining her eyes reading hundreds of manuscripts until she found the one that got her noticed. She earned her place at the head of Equiano not because someone liked her, but because she had acquired best sellers for Windsor. Perhaps she did not do the same for Equiano, but even the books she did not like she had made readable. Tanya Foster depended on her editorial eye to fix inconsistencies, to make narratives coherent, to give plausibility to characters. What has Conrad Hilton done? Tim Greene did not find it necessary to tell her. He is Tim Greene's friend. They know each other; Tim feels comfortable with him. These are the only qualifications necessary to put Conrad Hilton on the Greene team.

Cronyism. The word pulsates in her temples. When her father was in a position of power at the largest oil company on the island, he was pestered by friends and even by relatives for tips on when to buy and sell oil shares. He refused them all. He even refused to write letters of recommendation for friends who sought jobs in the company. He would not be a barrier to a friend, but neither would he use his position to give a friend an advantage. On these matters he was unbending. One must have the qualifications for the job. Friendship was not a qualification. His insistence almost cost him his relationship with Neil Lee Pak, his closest friend.

Neil Lee Pak is the Sinclairs' family doctor, though not the doctor who found the tumor in Beatrice Sinclair's breast. Beatrice had strict rules regarding the extent to which a doctor was allowed to examine her. Anywhere, she said, except her private parts. Her breasts and the triangle between her thighs were private, off-limits to Neil Lee Pak. When the size of her tumor finally terrified her into reaching out for help, Neil Lee Pak was the one who referred the Sinclairs to Dr. Ramdoolal, the best oncologist on the island. This was the role Dr. Lee Pak played in the lives of the Sinclairs: he was first their friend and confidant, and then their consultant on medical matters. He was also John Sinclair's fiercest opponent at chess, which they played religiously every Wednesday night. John looked forward to these evenings and would begin preparing for them days in advance, studying the chessboard and reading whatever he could find to gain mastery of the game. "Get ready for a beating," he would inevitably say to Neil Lee Pak when he arrived at his home.

Neil would grin from ear to ear and reply coolly, "In your dreams." Then the day came when Neil Lee Pak asked John Sinclair for a job.

The oil company kept a medical team on staff for their employees, and the doctor in charge was retiring. The job paid handsomely and the responsibilities were not demanding. The role was mostly an administrative one: to ensure that all employees passed the required medical tests and to refer difficult cases to the appropriate physicians on the island. Neil Lee Pak believed he should get the job when the doctor in charge retired. After all, he was a physician, and at the time John Sinclair was the personnel manager of the company, in an influential position to secure his appointment. And they were good friends. But John did not think Neil was the right person for the job. He liked the man. Beyond their Wednesday night chess games, Neil Lee Pak was a welcome guest at his home for dinner or simply for drinks and casual conversation, but he secretly disapproved of Neil's easy acquiescence to his wife's scruples. Neil was a doctor, and as a doctor he was responsible for his patients' health and should have found a way to persuade Beatrice to submit to a full medical examination. But most of all, he could not, and did not, recommend Neil Lee Pak for the position because there was another doctor, a brilliant man, eminently qualified, who had worked with the doctor who was retiring and had served the company loyally for years.

For many months, Beatrice went out of her way to arrange intimate dinner parties at her home with friends she knew Neil liked, but beyond the general courtesies expected of civilized adults, John Sinclair and Neil Lee Pak barely said a word to each other. Yet the coldness between them could not last; a détente was inevitable. Both men sorely missed their chess games (*tournaments*, Neil referred to them), and it took only a rumor that his doctor friend, or doctor ex-friend, was boasting that he could beat any man on the island for John Sinclair to issue a challenge. "Come to the house Wednesday night and we'll see who's the real champion," he said over the telephone. The match lasted beyond midnight and ended in a draw that required a rematch the following Wednesday. By then both men decided to let bygones be bygones and no mention was ever made of the incident that caused the break in their friendship. No blame passed John's lips either when years later Dr. Ramdoolal informed him that his wife had a tumor that had been growing in her breast for more than two years.

Given her father's willingness to risk a valued friendship for his principles, Anna is certain he will not agree with Rita that she should have assumed that Tim Greene, like any new boss, has the right to remove the old staff no matter how accomplished, no matter how their dismissal might affect them, no matter that plans worked on for weeks, months, would be squished like so much air from a balloon. The new boss is free to appoint a new team with people he knows, cronies, friends. This is Rita's opinion. It happens frequently, she said, but Anna is confident her father will not approve. Only once that she knows of had he broken his rule, bent it really, when he offered to speak to a friend on her behalf. But the job she was seeking was not in the oil company where he worked. She wanted to teach; she had the credentials to teach; expatriates had been favored above her. Her father could not be witness to his daughter's growing depression and do nothing.

Her parents are glad to see her. They have made dinner, or her father has cooked again, guided by his wife's directions. Anna smells the pungent odor of curry wafting through the corridor as she approaches her apartment. It's been a year since she has cooked curry and she did so only because it was Paula's birthday and she wanted a home-cooked Caribbean meal. The next day there was a note in her mailbox:

> *Have some consideration for your neighbors, Ms. Sinclair.*
> *You're in America now. Eat American food. It does not smell.*

"We wanted you have some island cooking before we left," her mother says when Anna opens the door. She is sitting on the couch in the living room. She does not get up.

Anna walks over to her and offers her cheek. "So you *are* serious," she says. "You intend to leave."

Her mother presses her cheek against Anna's. "This weekend."

"If Paul Bishop gives her permission." Her father, who stood up when Anna came into the apartment, kisses her, his lips brushing her cheek.

Her mother glances at them, narrows her eyes, and then looks away. "Of course he'll give permission. I feel fine."

"We'll see. Paul called. He said he'll come by this evening. But I suppose you already know that, Anna."

"Yes," Anna says. She goes to the kitchen and switches on the exhaust fan above the stove.

"I didn't know where it was," her father admits sheepishly.

"That's why I miss home so much," her mother says. "Back home, all the windows and doors are open. You don't smell the curry."

"We boil vinegar in water and light candles here," Anna explains.

Her mother wrinkles her nose. "All that to cook curry!"

"To absorb the scent." Anna puts a pot of water on the stove and pours a cup of vinegar into it. "With the fan and this, the scent won't be as strong." She lights a perfumed candle.

Her mother shakes her head. "That's why I miss home," she says again.

"When Paul comes, he'll give us his recommendation." John Sinclair sits down on the couch next to his wife.

"Recommendation or not," Beatrice says irritably, "I want to go home."

John Sinclair sighs. The rush of breath expelled from his throat is all it takes for his wife to understand he is displeased with her petulance.

"Not that you haven't made us most comfortable here," she says to Anna. "You're a good daughter. I couldn't want more than you have already done for me, for us. It's just that I miss my garden. Who knows what Singh has done to my orchids? And if he doesn't move the pots of red impatiens in the shade by midday, they'll shrivel and burn to a crisp in the hot sun."

"Oh, Beatrice," John Sinclair says, barely masking his impatience. "Singh takes good care of your garden."

"When I supervise him."

"Singh does not need supervision. He's a master gardener."

"And I am not?"

Her husband has entered dangerous waters and so now he does his best to pull himself out. "Of course you are," he says, patting her knee. "If not for you—"

"And your fish. I'm sure you're worried about your fish."

"I hope Lydia's fed them," John Sinclair says. "Most of the time she overfeeds them and my fish pond gets all clogged up."

"With dog food," Beatrice explains to Anna, but she knows this already. Her father has had to give up his dogs and though he has a fish pond now, fish food is scarce. Dogs, not fish, can protect you from the vicious crimes drug dealers have unleashed on the island now that NAFTA has made growing bananas and sugarcane in the Caribbean no longer profitable, and fishermen can quadruple their income ferrying drugs in their pirogues.

"I can't seem to get Lydia to understand that she should sprinkle the nuggets in the water," John Sinclair says. "She fills up the bowl as if she's feeding a dog, not fish."

"So there," Beatrice says. "You worry about your fish and I worry about my garden."

John scratches his head. His eyes are glazed. He seems deep in thought, worried.

Now that she has managed to redirect his attention, Beatrice returns to her complaint: she wants to go home, and as early as possible. "I miss church."

"I can take you," Anna says. "There's a Catholic church not far from here."

"It's not the same. We have friends in the church. After Mass, your father and I get to catch up on the news with them. We have steel-pan music in church. Do you know that, Anna?"

Anna does not know that.

"And sometimes after church, your father and I go to the botanic gardens."

"We have a botanic garden here in Brooklyn," Anna says.

"I suppose." Her mother adjusts the folds of her skirt around her legs. "But the anthuriums under the bamboo shed! You should see them, Anna."

She cannot offer her steel-pan music in church or anthuriums under the bamboo shed in the botanic garden in Brooklyn. There is a greenhouse there, but the flowers are not as vibrant, the pink, red, and white anthuriums not as bright as the ones that grow under the tropical sun, seeping through spaces in the flowering vines that loop around bamboo slats. And if she took them to the Catholic church not far from her apartment, there would be no one there they know, no one to talk to about daughters and sons who have made it big in the big countries. No one to tell that their Anna is the head of a publishing house in big New York. The parents of children who have emigrated keep the fairy tale alive. The roads are paved with gold in the big countries across the ocean.

"Well, Paul Bishop will settle the matter when he comes," John Sinclair says. "He'll let us know if we can leave by the weekend."

"Did you invite him for dinner?" Anna frames the question as though she has no stake in the answer.

"Oh, we couldn't have him here without inviting him to dine with us," her mother says.

"Of course." Anna looks away from her, but her mother is quick to notice her agitation.

"Not to worry, we don't plan to keep you. Your father and I intend to turn in early. You and Paul probably have things to talk about. Don't look so disappointed."

But Anna is not disappointed because she will have less time with Paul; she is disappointed because she wants more time with her father before Paul arrives. She wants to tell him about Tim Greene. She knows he will agree with her and she wants the reinforcement she is certain he will give her when he confirms that her anger is justified.

Anna does not respond to her mother. Instead, she turns to her father and relates to him all that has happened to her at work. He listens and does not interrupt. He waits in silence until she comes to the end of her tale, until she flops down on the armchair facing the couch where he and his wife are sitting, and says, her voice rising to a whine, "Conrad Hilton may have the qualifications, but the only one that Tim found necessary to have me know is that he's his friend."

"An African American?" These are her father's first words.

"Of course," Anna says, stretching out her legs.

"Then that's different."

"And how so?" Anna sits up.

"You shouldn't fight this, Anna. Accept it."

"Why should she accept it?" They turn in unison toward Beatrice, surprised to hear her voice, for Anna has been speaking directly to her father. Not once has she even glanced at her mother. She was talking about work, what had happened to her at work. Her mother is a housewife; she knows nothing about the world of work; she cannot advise her. "Why?" her mother asks again.

"Because she should," John Sinclair answers.

"You never did." Beatrice shifts her body slightly away from her husband. The movement is barely perceptible, but Anna notices it.

"I don't know what you're talking about, Beatrice."

"Neil. I'm talking about Neil."

"Neil has forgotten that whole business a long time ago."

"I pleaded with him, Anna, to put in a word for his friend, but he refused."

"That's done and finished, Beatrice."

"Just a word, John. I didn't ask you to demand that your boss hire him."

"The other doctor was better than Neil," John murmurs.

"And are you saying this . . . What's his name, Anna?"

Anna is too dumbfounded to speak. *After all these years, opposing her husband for her!*

"He was a hotel manager. Isn't that what you said, Anna?"

"Conrad Hilton," Anna says, finding her voice.

"The owner of the hotel?"

"This is not a time for joking, Beatrice." Her husband's tone is scathing. "He's African American. Anna already said so."

"I think he used to work for another publishing company," Anna says.

"It doesn't matter." Her mother waves her hand in the air dismissively. "He can't be more qualified than you, Anna. You have worked for Windsor for years. They owe you."

"It's not the same situation, Beatrice."

"I remember that was the argument you used when you refused to recommend Neil. You said the other doctor had worked for the company for years."

John shakes his head in frustration. "Anna." He addresses his daughter. "Anna, I think—"

Beatrice interrupts him. "I know how it feels." She is looking at Anna too.

"How what feels?" John turns to his wife.

"I know how I felt when I was forced to give up my job. I was good at it, as Anna is good at hers."

"Tim Greene didn't care how I felt." Anna is speaking to her mother, the woman who suffered through four miscarriages to give birth to her.

"I felt like some useless piece of garbage, as if my feelings did not count." Beatrice's eyes are still fixed on Anna.

"My feelings did not matter to him. He was thinking of himself and his friend. I was used, kicked to the curb when I had served my purpose. My job was to show Tim Greene the ropes. Those were the words Tanya used: the ropes. She hired him to work with me so I'd show him the ropes."

"My boss hired my replacement while I was still on the job. My job was to train my replacement to take my place."

"Now that Equiano is on its way to getting some measure of respectability, now that I have a chance to publish a Bess Milford, they take it away from me."

"It took me months to get over the rejection, the humiliation, the feelings of powerlessness. Someone was controlling my life and there was nothing I could do."

"What about me?" John Sinclair is now staring at his wife in disbelief. "What about our marriage? Wasn't our marriage enough for you?"

"You needed more than our marriage. You needed something to do." Beatrice meets his eyes, refusing to back down.

"I didn't have a choice." John lowers his voice. "I had to earn an income. Put a roof over our heads, food on the table."

"And was that all work meant to you?"

John's lips part in befuddlement. The folds in the space between his eyes contract. "Beatrice, please."

"I saw how excited you were every time you won a case and got both parties to agree to your terms. I lived with you. I saw how energized you were. I wanted that too."

"My job?"

"Something that excited me besides you."

"I wasn't enough for you?"

"There would have been more for us to talk about. I would have known you better if I knew what it felt like to be successful, to do a job that you were praised for, appreciated for. If I had experienced that feeling, I could have helped you."

"You did help me. You gave me a home to come back to."

"You could have had more of me. You could have known me better."

"But I know you, Beatrice."

The hurt in her husband's eyes is more than Beatrice can bear. She surrenders. "Yes," she says softly. "You know me as well as I know myself." She comes closer to him. "But I don't want Anna to give up like I gave up. We could have fought them."

"It was the law then, Beatrice," he responds quietly.

"It was the wrong law even then."

"This is a different matter."

"Anna was hurt in the same way," she says.

"I don't want her to be bitter. She has to live in America. She needs to understand. There is a history here we were not part of. Remember the story about my friend Ulrich Cross?"

"What story?" Anna asks.

John Sinclair looks at his wife. He is seeking her approval. She nods. "Go ahead. Tell her, John."

He slides to the edge of the couch. "Ulrich Cross was the senior navigator on his squadron of bomber fighters in World War II." He swivels back to his wife. She lays her hand lightly on his back. It is all the encouragement he needs. "He was a brilliant mathematician," he explains to Anna. "He told me he joined the RAF when Pope Pius XII gave his blessing to Mussolini to kill Africans in Ethiopia. He was burning up with anger, so were the 252 young men from our island who joined up too. It was only later, when America felt the blows on her shores at Pearl Harbor, that she entered the war. Like in the RAF, there were also black airmen in the air force, but the American squadrons were segregated. Not so the British air force. Even in war, America wanted to sustain the myth of white superiority. Ulrich said he would never forget the trip he took down south in the last year of the war. He was a squadron leader in the RAF, and as all British officers he sat in the dining car on the Pullman. Cold hard stares bored into his back, some pointed directly at his face. He didn't so much mind this. What he minded, what broke his heart, what almost brought him to tears, were the signs. At every station in Virginia, North Carolina, South Carolina, Georgia, Florida, Mississippi, Alabama, Louisiana, every state where the train stopped, the signs were the same: *Whites only. Coloreds.* Even on the water fountains. By the time he returned to Washington everyone was praising him for having survived eighty sorties. Eighty, imagine that! On seven of them he navigated bombs on a wooden, twin-engine Mosquito aircraft that had lost its wheels in battle."

John Sinclair pauses. His eyes are shining with pride, admiration for his friend's miraculous feat. He picks up where he left off before his mind skidded to the time when men like his friend helped win the war for England—even though their homelands had been colonized. "By the time he got to D.C., the heartbreak Ulrich felt had turned to anger that burned a hole in his chest. He had seen African American soldiers prepared to give their lives for their country, humiliated by the signs. They wore the uniform of the U.S. military, but they were treated as second-class citizens. That history is seared in the collective souls of African Americans. They paid a heavy price for the opportunities immigrants of color have today. Not only the humiliation but the killings, the hundreds of African Americans lynched just because of the color of their skin. If Tim Greene feels it's his turn and you must wait for your turn, you should yield to him, Anna."

NINETEEN

She should yield. That is what her father wants her to do. She should accept Tim Greene's decision. More than that, though he has not said it, the expression on his face makes it plain that he believes she owes it to him as his daughter to follow his advice. And her mother, who minutes before had taken her side, withdraws.

They say little to each other after her father ends his impassioned exhortation. Perhaps her mother shuts her eyes because she knows it is futile to argue with her husband. He had the reputation for being a tough labor negotiator. No amount of pressure from the powerful labor unions, none of the financial enticements companies eagerly offered him, swayed his opinions. Perhaps her mother is still on her side and those minutes when she felt closer to her than she had ever felt in her life will return. Her mother has surrendered but she has not agreed with her husband. When he offers her a cup of tea, she does not open her eyes, she does not respond. It occurs to Anna now that restraint can protect even though it excludes. She has the answer to her question: her mother is restrained but perhaps because she wants to protect her.

If John Sinclair has more advice to give to his daughter, he withholds it. He helps her set the table for dinner and talks nonstop of frivolous matters: about relatives Anna has not seen in years whose lives interest neither of them; about the hot dry season, the humid wet season, anything it seems that will reassure her that though he disagrees with her, he loves her, he would never do or say anything to hurt her. At last his babble is interrupted by the sound of the buzzer.

Beatrice, who until now has kept her eyes resolutely closed, sits up. Alert. "That must be Paul," she says.

Anna can buzz Paul in from upstairs, but she lifts the garbage bag out of its container and tells her father she'll put it in the incinerator and meet Paul at the entrance to the building.

He begins to object, but her mother calls out to him: "Let her, John."

She is not prepared when she opens the door and Paul walks in, beaming, his eyes dancing. He is holding a bunch of tulips in one hand and a box of chocolates in the other, but it is neither the tulips nor the chocolates that propel Anna into his widespread arms. It is his whole presence, comforting and reassuring: his smile, his dancing eyes, the sprinkling of gray in his hair, the soft paunch that droops slightly over his belted khaki pants, the blue shirt and navy sports jacket with brass buttons he must have chosen both in honor of her parents and to please her too, the natural odor of his body she breathes in reminding her of pleasurable sex, delicious sex, the sex that was so much better than any she has ever had. She buries her head in his chest and he wraps his arms around her, crossing them at his wrists, for he is still holding the tulips and the chocolates in his hands.

"What is it, love? What is the matter?" He kisses the top of her head and the delicate spot behind her earlobe.

Someone turns his key in the front door. They are in a public corridor. Anna raises her head and wriggles out of his arms. Her eyes are wet with tears.

Paul hands her the tulips, reaches into his pocket for his handkerchief, and wipes her eyes. "Do you want to go somewhere where we can talk?"

"They are waiting for you." She strokes the petals of the tulips.

"We could go to my car," he says.

"They made dinner."

"I wanted to take you out."

"They are good West Indians. You can't come to their home without having something to eat."

"Yes. I remember." He tickles the tip of her chin and her lips spread to a smile.

"The first time you met them on the island, you gave them less than an hour's notice and they had ham and pastels ready," she says.

"And rum punch. Don't forget the rum punch." He kisses her again, this time on her mouth. "It's good to see you smile. Why the tears?"

"Something at work," she says.

"With that writer you told me about?"

"Later, when we're alone, I'll tell you."

"I don't have surgery tomorrow. We can spend the night at my place."

"I can't leave them in the apartment alone," she says.

"It's hard for me to see you unhappy."

"I'm not unhappy now."

They are at the elevator. He bends down and whispers in her ear, "I couldn't wait to see you. I told your mother I'd come by, but it is you I wanted to see."

The chocolates are not for her; they are for her mother. Beatrice is thrilled. A girlish giggle ripples up her throat when Paul gives them to her. "Look what Paul has brought for us," she says to her husband, overtaken by a rush of emotion.

"For you," John Sinclair says.

"And tulips for Anna." Beatrice inclines her head toward her daughter.

"For two beautiful women," Paul Bishop says.

"The man has good taste." John puts his arm around his wife's shoulders. "Though without this beautiful woman," he says, tightening his arm, "there couldn't be a beautiful daughter."

"You say such nonsense, John." Beatrice taps him playfully on his arm.

Their quarrel is apparently over. Whatever happened in her absence when she was in the lobby with Paul, Anna is certain her mother and father have made up.

At the dinner table, John serves his wife first and then passes the dish of curry to Paul, who is the epitome of gallantry. He had planned to take Anna out to dinner, but he tells Beatrice that a home-cooked meal is just what he has been longing for.

"John made it," Beatrice says.

"Under military supervision!" John Sinclair winks at his wife and cuts the meat on her plate in small bits so that with one hand she can easily pick up the pieces with her fork.

Beatrice is watching Paul closely, waiting for his reaction as he puts a forkful of the curry in his mouth. "Hmm," he says, swallowing. "This is better curry than I've had in many a restaurant."

Beatrice's face lights up. "Anna's curry is even better," she says.

Anna has never cooked curry for her mother. Ordinarily she would have been angry at her for the transparent lie, but her mother's earlier defense of her makes her sympathetic. Beatrice likes Paul; she is pleased by the attention he pays to her daughter, by the courtesies he extends to her as the mother. So Anna restrains herself. Her mother wants to present her in a flattering light to a man she obviously thinks could be a potential husband, a man who would bring happiness to Anna after her unfortunate divorce. She can endure the embarrassment. Paul is not a teenager but a mature man; he can see through her mother's blatant ploy. Her mother's remark will not frighten him away, change his feelings toward her. Her faith in him gets confirmed when he reaches under the table and squeezes her knee. "I hope I can have the pleasure of tasting Anna's curry soon," he says.

"The sooner the better." Beatrice's head bobs up and down in her excitement. "Not so, Anna?"

It is too much for Anna. Her patience wears thin. "Don't you have a question for Paul, Mummy?"

Beatrice puts down her fork. The mischievous twinkle in her eyes disappears. She is all seriousness when she speaks. "We want to leave this weekend. Anna tells me you'll let us know if we can."

Paul turns to Anna. She knows he is hoping she will give him some sign of how he should respond, but she looks away. The decision is his and her mother's.

"There are some things, Mrs. Sinclair, that medicine cannot do," Paul begins cautiously. "We doctors have our limits."

"So it's not good news then." Beatrice straightens her back, bracing herself for disappointment. "Well, don't pretty it up for our sakes. We're ready."

We, she says. For whatever affects her, affects her husband. Anna fights against a growing feeling that is uncomfortably akin to envy. The commitment her parents have to each other is what she had hoped for. What she wanted when she married.

"Yes," John Sinclair says. "We know you've done your best and we are grateful."

"Oh, that's not what I mean. That's not it at all," Paul says. "I'm pleased, very pleased with your progress, Mrs. Sinclair. I've never had a patient recover so quickly after major surgery. I spoke to Dr. Ramdoolal about your wish to return home."

"He's not the best person to advise us," John says. "He was angry with my wife."

"He blamed her for not coming to him sooner," Anna explains. "He was angry with her for letting the tumors grow so big."

"And yet here she is," Paul says. "By all likelihood, Mrs. Sinclair, you will live a normal life. There was no indication of metastasis beyond the two tumors."

"The power of prayer," Beatrice says.

"I've seen evidence of that time and time again in my practice. My patients who have a strong religious faith have a higher rate of recovery and cure. I think you are one of those patients."

"Her faith, yes, but also her positive attitude, her determination to live. My wife is very strong-willed," John Sinclair says.

"The mind is a powerful instrument. People walk on fire and claim they don't feel a thing."

"My wife can walk on fire."

Beatrice glances sharply at him. "I don't know about that," she says.

"Metaphorically speaking, Beatrice," her husband replies soothingly. "Look what you've been through and not a complaint."

"I can handle pain, if that's what you meant."

"You have a strong mind, Mrs. Sinclair," Paul Bishop says.

"So can we leave?" Beatrice presses him.

"You'll need more chemo and radiation to be sure we got everything. Dr. Ramdoolal is prepared to give you both. He said you responded beautifully before. He's sure with your husband's help you will manage again."

"She'll manage. We'll manage," John Sinclair says.

"Then I have no objection."

After dinner, Paul and Anna help her father clear the dishes from the table. Beatrice relaxes on the couch. Anna cannot remember when she has seen her mother so happy. Her surgery has been successful; soon she will be back on her beloved island. She will have a long life.

And as if that isn't enough, her daughter has a boyfriend. "I think your beau is in love with you," she whispers in Anna's ear. John Sinclair is happy too, happy to see his wife happy; happy because he believes Paul Bishop is the right mate for his daughter. But Paul has not mentioned marriage either to Anna or the Sinclairs. He has made no announcement, no promises. Not that Beatrice does not attempt to exact one. When Anna brings her a cup of tea, she approaches the subject in her own inimitable way.

"You and Anna have a lot in common," she says to Paul from across the room where she is lying with her feet propped up on the couch. "You were born in the same place, immigrated to the same place, lived away from your birthplace almost the same number of years. You couldn't be more alike."

Paul grins. "I told Anna we're hyphenated people. We have a foot in both places."

"A toe. That's all I think you have in the Caribbean.

Not a foot," she says. "I don't think Anna can live there again."

"And why not?" Anna has a stack of plates in her hand. She puts them in the sink and faces her mother.

"Because you seem to fit in here, in America," Beatrice says.

"And I don't fit in there?"

"To me you seem more comfortable here than you were on the island when you visited me. You seem to have made a life here."

It is true. She has made a life for herself in America. She is comfortable here. Yet her mother's dismissal still hurts. She wants to belong there too. It is where she grew up, where she learned to speak, to read. Where as a little girl, and then a teenager, she went to school. Where her navel string is buried.

"Is that what you want, or is it what you see?" Habits die hard. As much as she tries, Anna cannot keep the hurt from breaking up her voice. Her words are unsteady when they leave her mouth.

"Oh, Anna. Not again," her mother whimpers. "Your father and I would be happy to have you home anytime you want to come back. I was just saying—"

Paul moves swiftly to Anna's side. "She was teasing you, weren't you, Anna?"

She is ashamed of herself. She needs to let go. She is too old to be holding on to childhood resentments. But she is an outsider in America. When disasters befall Americans, when they celebrate their victories, they close ranks. They fly the red, white, and blue from their porches and cars and she is left on the outside, a foreigner, an alien. To surrender her past, her beginnings, is to be set adrift with no moorings in sight. She has made a home for herself in

America, but she does not fit in. Tim Greene has made that plain to her. "You don't have a feel for our readers," he said. Tanya offered what she thought was a compliment, but she too opened a gully, Anna on one side, Americans on the other. "You're different from the average black reader," Tanya had said. Anna didn't need her to elaborate, to say that she didn't mean Anna's tastes are the same as the white reader's.

Paul draws her to him. "My parents tell me the same thing. They say I can come home anytime, but they know, and I know, I can't. It's too late for Anna and me. We've become hybrids. Caribbean-Americans. Isn't that so, Anna?"

Anna manages a weak smile.

"The mosquito knows," Paul says.

"The mosquito?" Beatrice raises her eyebrows and queries her husband, the laugh lines on her face spreading with her relief that Paul has broken the tension that was threatening to spoil the gay evening.

"We have yet to hear the mosquito speak," John says jokingly.

"It bites," Paul says.

"Only you," Beatrice chimes in. "Anna always complains when she comes home. We have to burn cockset for her." Cockset, the mosquito coils her mother burns to repel the insects. Anna remembers how her mother fusses whenever she has to bring them out of the closet for her. "Mosquitoes? What mosquitoes? I don't feel a thing. Do you, John?"

"Exactly," Paul says. "It smells our foreign blood."

It takes a second for his point to sink in and when it does, Beatrice shouts out, "You're a match!" Her face is glowing; she is beaming at Anna.

Her enthusiasm embarrasses her husband. He stands

in front of her and holds out his hand. "Shouldn't we be turning in, Beatrice?"

"The dishes," she says.

John Sinclair tightens his grip on her hand. "Come. Tonight we will leave the dishes in the sink."

TWENTY

The small French café near Anna's apartment where Paul and Anna have gone for dessert is sandwiched between a bodega and a three-story walk-up with a broken concrete front stoop. Outside, a cluster of teenagers, most of them black or Latino, two of them white, are trying out the latest hip-hop dance to music blaring out of a boom box. Inside, the pastry chef who greets Anna is a Frenchman, his wife an Algerian. A Chinese girl and a white male teenager, both with tattoos, hers on her right arm, his on both arms and another on one side of his neck, are waiting tables. Anna and Paul are the oldest customers but also the only exclusively black couple in the café. There are other black customers but none paired with another black person. A black man (he seems an African) sits opposite a white man, obviously his lover; a Latino girl is talking animatedly to a black man; a black girl is sharing a raspberry tart with her white boyfriend.

Paul looks around and observes to Anna that immigrants are changing the color of America. "Soon whites will be a minority. At least in Brooklyn."

"It's what Tim Greene fears," she says, opening the way to answering Paul's question when he dried her tears.

"Tim Greene is African American, isn't he?"

"Oh, Tim isn't worried about Americans becoming browner. He's afraid African Americans will be displaced by Caribbean immigrants. He seems to think we're taking advantage of the opportunities African Americans achieved with their blood, through years of slavery and lynchings." She tells him of Tim's promotion, about the merger, about the end of the Equiano imprint, about the new TeaHouse Press, about the appointment of Conrad Hilton, about her demotion. About the reason why she was removed from her position.

"Was that his explanation or yours?" Paul asks.

"He said I didn't have a feel for his people."

"Were those his exact words?"

"Pretty much."

Paul rubs his temples. His fingers make circular motions folding his skin over the corners of his eyes. "Did you discuss this with your father?" he asks. He releases his fingers and slides them down the sides of his face.

"Yes."

"And what did he say?"

"He said I should accept the changes. He said there is a history here, in America, that we weren't part of."

Paul presses his fingers against the tip of his chin. "Your father is a wise man."

"You can't be agreeing with him?" Anna says this so loudly she startles the young waitress who is about to fill their glasses. Water spills over the table. The waitress mops it up and after she leaves, Paul says quietly, "It doesn't make sense to spin your top in mud, Anna."

He means she has lost. He means she should accept her loss as her father has advised her to. But she cannot give up that easily. "I've put in time in the company," she says. "Windsor has made money from the books I found for them. Many were best sellers; they made millions for Windsor. What has Conrad Hilton, or Tim Greene for that matter, done for the company?"

"You're missing the point, Anna." Paul keeps his voice even, devoid almost of emotion.

"What point? Everyone wants to be appreciated. It doesn't matter if they are black or white, or what ethnic group they belong to. It's in our human DNA to want—no, to expect—reward for our hard labor."

"It's the price of the ticket, Anna," Paul says softly.

"What ticket?"

"For the green card. For being allowed citizenship."

The word *allowed* stops her. So that is it? She was in their power; she had no rights.

"They didn't have to give it to us." Paul reaches for her hand. She is still simmering with anger, but she does not pull away. "If it's in the universal DNA to expect reward," he says, "it's in our DNA, too, to expect gratitude." He reminds her of the connection between the Civil Rights Act of 1964 and the amendment to the Immigration Act that came one year later, in 1965, striking down country of origin as a criterion for immigrating to America. "The proximity of those dates is not accidental."

"Still," Anna murmurs, "it isn't fair." And suddenly she remembers a line from Toni Morrison's *Beloved*. *What's fair ain't necessarily right*. Beloved has returned from the dead to persecute her mother, Sethe, for taking her life. The community sides with Beloved, not Ella, the wise one, the leader of the community. Sethe is on her deathbed, her body reduced to a sack of bones; Beloved is plump, bursting with the food Sethe, tortured by guilt and love, has fed her. "What's fair ain't necessarily right," Ella says. She chases Sethe's tormentors out of the house.

"It may not be fair to you," Paul says, "but it's fair to Tim Greene. Look, Anna, I agree that in a just world, a fair world, you should keep the position you earned with your hard work. But this has not been a fair world or a just world for Tim Greene's relatives. Your father is right: we have not lived their history. They have had four hundred years of suffering and hardships."

"And we haven't? They picked cotton and we planted sugarcane. The lash on our backs was the same."

"This is their country, Anna. Their suffering happened here, in America. To Tim Greene it isn't right that his friend should have to be put at the end of the line again in his own country."

Rosa Parks refusing to sit at the back of the bus. The image looms before Anna and silences her.

"Tim Greene may have had to wait until whites got theirs, but he's not prepared to wait until immigrants get theirs too."

The waitress is back. She taps her pencil impatiently on her notepad, anxious to get their orders. Anna opens the menu. She is glad for this break, for this chance to cool down. She needs to be more sympathetic. Even Rita has pleaded with her to be more understanding. Tim Greene's life was not easy. Her father has always been in her life; his father abandoned him. It must have been painful for Tim to know that his mother was dependent on a man who had no intention of marrying her, who kept her in the dark, hidden away, while he romanced his wife in public. Hard for him, too, to be dependent on that man, even if he paid his way to Cornell.

She does not want to fight with Paul. Not now. She cringed when her mother attempted to show her off, as if she were a commodity up for sale. She is a decent cook, but not an excellent cook. Her taste for spicy Caribbean food has diminished. She rarely cooks curry. But deep down she was glad her mother made this clumsy attempt to push

Paul to declare his intentions. She is not young. She does not have the time this tattooed waitress has; she does not have years left to try out dates, this one and that one, to camouflage a tattoo on her arm if her new lover so desires. It would be good to know now, to know if they are to remain lovers, or if he intends a deeper commitment. Marriage. She would like marriage.

Their desserts arrive. Paul has ordered sweet potato pie; she, apple pie á la mode. He wants to share, but she says, "Not the ice cream." She is teasing him and they laugh over her secret passion that she claims she has inherited honestly from her mother, whose fattened hips are attributable to her craving for coconut ice cream and Julie mangoes. "But not *your* hips," Paul says. "They are just right."

They are still laughing when she inserts her knife into her pie to cut it in half. Paul reaches for her wrist and holds her hand still. "Anna," he begins. He is looking deeply into her eyes. Her heart skips a beat. "I didn't mean to say I don't feel for you."

She does not want to go back. Tim Greene has won. She will accept his victory. She does not want Tim Greene to spoil her personal life too.

"I don't have to be the boss," she says. "Senior editor is good enough. I like editing books." It is true. She loves the partnership she has with writers. She loves unearthing emotions buried so deep in the conscious mind of the writers that though the evidence is there in the stories they tell, they are barely aware of the feelings that propelled them to create worlds, characters, plots. She prods and their stories open up again. Suddenly they are aware of patterns, motifs, tropes that had little personal significance to them before she led them to dig deeper. They begin again; they revise and revise. Yes, she says to Paul; she loves the work she does. It fulfills her.

"Then keep on doing it. Be the best editor at TeaHouse Press."

His hand is still on her wrist and she feels a tremor running through it. His fingers press deeper at her pulse. He must feel the quickening of her heartbeat too.

"Anna." He says her name with such tenderness, she wants to hold him. She places her other hand over his and squeezes it.

"This may be too soon, but we don't have much time. We are grown adults. We know what we want. I'll be fifty next month."

"I'm almost forty."

"Not too late to have children."

Her heart races.

"This isn't the place. This isn't where I wanted to ask you." He looks down on her hand covering his. "I had planned something nice. Dinner at a fancy place, dancing afterward."

"We don't need a fancy place or dancing afterward."

He looks up, his eyes meeting hers. "You'll make me the happiest man in the world if you say yes."

Yes, yes, yes. In the distance, an echo. Her father's voice. *Carpe diem.* She may have to wait; it may not be her turn, but it will be her children's turn, *their* children's turn. *They* won't have to wait. *Yes.*